D0906899

ILLINOIS PRAIRIE DPL

THE COURTSHIP OF PEGGY McCOY

THE COURTSHIP OF *PEGGY* McCOY

A Novel

by

Ray Sipherd

St. Martin's Press
NEW YORK

Design by Judy Dannecker

Library of Congress Cataloging-in-Publication Data

Sipherd, Ray.
The courtship of Peggy McCoy / Ray Sipherd.
p. cm.
"A Thomas Dunne book."
ISBN 0-312-04286-8
I. Title.
PS3569.I59C65 1990
813'.54—dc20 89-77680

First Edition
10 9 8 7 6 5 4 3 2 1

For
Anne Marie

Acknowledgments

With special gratitude to my friends Betty Hatfield and Louise Hardy of Georgetown, Maine. To Captain Charles L. Mull, U.S.N. (ret.), of Brunswick, Maine. To Jim McGregor and Paul Morin of the Bath Iron Works, Bath, Maine. To my mother, who encouraged the delight of words. To my father, who introduced me to the wonders of the sea. And to Polly, who was there at the beginning.

THE COURTSHIP OF PEGGY McCOY

1

FREE SPIRIT

The words, in bold black letters across the stern, were plainly visible as the sailboat approached the narrow channel out of Hasty Harbor. The boat cut smoothly through the blue-gray water, but even in the sanctuary of the cove there was a slight chop to the waves. The telltale of red ribbon that showed the wind direction fluttered outward from the rigging. Fifty yards ahead a conical red buoy bobbed, listing lazily with the incoming tide. The sailboat was of the Thistle class, seventeen feet long, white with dark blue trim. The mainsail curved forward in a wide arc that took full advantage of the steady northwest breeze. The jib lay crumpled on the foredeck, ready to be raised.

The boat's lone occupant, seated well down inside the open cockpit, was almost completely hidden. What could be seen was a bare tanned arm hooked over the tiller and an old worn sailor hat pulled down over a head of curly gray hair.

As she drew nearer the red buoy the sailboat tacked abruptly, the sail swinging over to the starboard side. For a short time the boat's course paralleled a series of tall wooden stakes set in a line ten yards apart to mark the channel. The bow of the sailboat pointed toward the slender opening between steep granite rocks rising to a height of thirty feet and topped by weathered firs. Tidal currents surging through the channel gradually began to pitch the boat from bow to stern as she moved forward. As if apprehensive of what lay ahead, the boat shuddered momentarily, and sailed on.

Among the hundreds of small coves, inlets, islands, and peninsulas that made up the midcoastal region of the state of Maine, there were special words—a few unprintable—for the passage that connected Hasty Harbor with the broad estuary of the Kerrenac River beyond. It was not so much the channel's narrowness, nor its fast-moving currents. Rather, it was the formation of huge ragged boulders at its mouth that reached into the river in the shape of a haphazard jetty. The rocks were called the Sawteeth. Unnaturally dark and continually washed and rewashed by the sea, they had a malevolent majesty about them that commanded awe as one approached. It was a sight that had appeared on thousands of Maine postcards captioned, usually, "The Stern and Rockbound Coast."

At twelve thirty on an afternoon in mid-July, *Free Spirit* sailed out of Hasty Harbor and began to pass the Sawteeth rocks. The skipper of the boat remained low, avoiding the spray that was thrown up against the bow. One hand operated the line leading the mainsail; the other hand gripped the tiller, deftly playing it against the wind and tide.

Then simultaneously two things happened: a downdraft whipped the sail in the opposite direction, and a rogue wave hit the far side of the Sawteeth, spilled over it, and slammed down on the boat. Suddenly adrift and helpless, the boat swept broadside toward the rocks.

The next moment, incredibly, the figure in the boat stood up and, within reach of the outermost rock, grabbed at it and with both hands gave a mighty shove. The sailboat shot by the Sawteeth, missing the rocks by inches, and drifted out into the open water. The figure sat down and regained control of the tiller and the sail. The mainsail caught the wind and billowed, and *Free Spirit* began reaching for the sea.

"Too close for comfort," Peggy McCoy said aloud. She took a slow deep breath and looked back at the rocks. Then she patted the boat's deck. "Good work, old girl. Another couple seconds and you and I would have become flotsam for the Gulf of Maine."

The woman played out the sail gradually and looked around. No other water traffic was within a mile of her and *Free Spirit* to witness their near collision with the rocks. Had there been any, the witnesses might have been surprised to see that *Free Spirit*'s sailor was, in fact, a trim woman in her sixties. They would have also seen that she was dressed in what she called her "summer finery": old sneakers without socks, a pair of khaki shorts, and a man's faded blue shirt with the sleeves cut off above the elbows.

Peggy McCoy moved forward and began to raise the jib. The wind filled it immediately and the boat sprang forward. Peggy returned to the tiller, checked the telltale again, and made a slight correction in her course.

She pushed the sailor hat down firmly on her head, tucking in a curl as she did. To those who knew her, the graying sailor hat was Peggy's trademark; she wore it every time she sailed. She'd had the hat for more than forty years, she once told a friend. It had been a gift from a young man, a Navy flier she had known during the Second World War. The face below the hat was round, with deep-set eyes, a turned-up nose, and a mouth that at times appeared perpetually pursed.

The jib started to flap noisily; the wind was shifting. Peggy noticed that it was also lessening. The caps of foam that topped the waves were fewer, and in the distance patches of smooth water rose and fell in undulating swells.

Peggy patted her shirt pocket and discovered she had forgotten her sunglasses. Shading her eyes with her hand, she studied the horizon. Ahead and shimmering in the summer sunlight was the Atlantic Ocean, or that part of it that she and other true Maine natives called the Gulf of Maine. Far to the east she saw the jagged line of trees and tidal marshes she had known since childhood. Nowhere-land, her father said it was, and as she still preferred to think of it. How often had he driven the family there in the old Ford coupe to picnic or to walk the rock-strewn shore. Now it was a state park named after some forgotten former governor. Campers, six-packs, and portable radios the size of small suitcases had replaced the world of silent green that she remembered with melancholy wistfulness.

Looking west, Peggy saw that she was passing Stiles Head, a massive outcropping of rock that had claimed more than a dozen ships over the years. Past Stiles Head the shoreline curved inward, out of Peggy's view. But she knew every foot of it by heart. Soon, surrounded by majestic pines, would emerge the twin turrets of Elysia-by-the-Sea, the venerable gray clapboard mansion built by a lumber baron in the twenties, which now served as a hotel in the summer months. Half a mile further would be a cluster of newly built leisure condominiums, each with a cantilevered deck that jutted arrogantly out over the water's edge. One good winter storm, thought Peggy, and those decks—and maybe the condos themselves—would be reduced to hunks of refuse drifting in the North Atlantic shipping lanes.

A mile beyond them, where the land rose briefly and a

coppice of scrub pine met the shore, Peggy knew what she would see—the small white saltbox with the tall flagpole in front of it. Every day, in almost any weather, two flags flew from that flagpole: the American flag, and below it, the blue and white flag of the U.S. Navy. The house was Peggy's. Past it there was no one, no houses, nothing but Mosquito Marsh and the mud flats, mongrel bushes, the decaying stumps of trees, a stubble of marsh grass, and finally, the lingering and barren stretch of sand that was called Lonely Point.

Peggy brought the sailboat about on a new tack, and as she did she scanned the water for other boats in the vicinity. Nearest to her was a lobster boat, inbound. Well beyond it she saw the high white superstructure of the Portland–Nova Scotia ferry outward bound. Also heading up the coast were two large sailboats. Rich summer people on their way to Camden or Boothbay Harbor, Peggy guessed.

The lobster boat continued toward her, with gulls wheeling overhead and dipping low into its wake. As the lobster boat drew closer to *Free Spirit,* it decreased its speed, and Peggy recognized the green hull of the *Mary G.* In the wheelhouse she could see the lean figure of Link Mallott in his ancient windbreaker, which still bore the emblem of the Boston Braves. On the open deck behind the wheelhouse Link's son and nephew were busy stacking lobster crates, the shiny darkish claws of the wet lobsters reaching out between the slats.

"Ahoy, Link!" called Peggy as the two boats came abreast.

Without altering his forward gaze, the lobsterman lifted one hand from the wheel in a faint and momentary gesture of acknowledgment.

"You're all personality! You know that, Link!" she shouted after the lobster boat as it resumed its speed.

Peggy swung the tiller over and the sail followed. On

this new tack her course would take her in the direction of Kidds Rock, the tiny steep-sided island of bare granite that lay four miles offshore. At its summit was the white lighthouse that served not only as a landfall for mariners, but also as a navigational dividing point between the Kerrenac River to the east of it and the Newell River to the west.

She was about to tack again when something caught her eye. Well out to the sea beyond Kidds Rock, on a course perpendicular to hers, she saw a large ship moving at great speed. Peggy felt sure it was a U.S. Navy ship, and judging by the wake, the vessel was probably traveling at close to thirty knots.

There were several miles of open water between the ship and *Free Spirit,* but the silhouette soon became apparent: slim lines, a narrow pointed bow, and a tall communications mast above the bridge. Undoubtedly a cruiser, Peggy thought, of the kind the Whitby Ship Works had been building for the navy recently. Peggy assumed that the ship was undergoing one of her sea trials, the series of performance tests conducted jointly by the shipbuilder and the navy before a ship was finally commissioned and sent into naval service.

Transfixed, Peggy watched the ship move through the water, waves exploding at her bow, the wake roiling up into a rooster tail of white foam behind the stern. The shipyard pilot or the navy men aboard are giving this ship all she's got, Peggy thought.

But Peggy knew that soon the ship would cut her speed, turn, and head inland toward Kidds Rock. From there she would continue running at ten knots until she reached the channel leading to the Newell River. Once in the channel she would decrease her speed still further. Then she would swing gracefully northward and begin the slow twelve-mile voyage up the twisting narrow river, passing several tiny villages and shoreline fishing shacks, until finally returning to the Whitby Ship Works, the huge shipbuilding complex in the town of Whitby, Maine.

By now the wind had shifted and calmed further to a modest onshore breeze. Peggy checked her wristwatch and saw that it was one o'clock. The watch was large and chunky with a black face and watchband. It looked oddly out of place on her thin wrist.

"Mess time, mates," Peggy said.

She reached down and found the handles of a plastic food bag near her feet. Unzipping the bag, she took out a sandwich wrapped in wax paper and a carton of fruit juice. She removed the wax paper and began to eat. "You make a terrific tuna sandwich," she went on.

"You bet I do," she answered herself.

Peggy opened the juice carton and drank, switching between it and the sandwich with her free hand while the other hand remained on the tiller. When she was done she crumpled the wax paper into a ball, carefully put it inside the empty juice carton, and returned them to the food bag. From the bag she now took out a jar of peanuts. She unscrewed the lid, tossed a handful of peanuts into her mouth, and placed the open jar upright in the bag.

The day had warmed considerably, was growing hot, in fact, without the usual sea haze filtering the light. Peggy stretched out her legs across the cockpit floor and turned her face to the sun. She tilted her head back and shut her eyes. This ritual was part of every summer sail. The sailboat rocked briefly, but her eyes remained closed. The wind touched her face fleetingly, and the sun felt warm and kind. Head back, eyes closed, the boat moving gently under her, she felt herself a spirit buoyed by the sea. But more than that, she was as something gossamer and airborne, carried effortlessly upward toward the sun itself.

* * *

First came the sound, the deep reverberations of the engines and the tumbling of water. Peggy opened her eyes. She wanted to shout out, but couldn't.

Less than half a mile from her, squarely in *Free Spirit*'s path, the navy ship was bearing down. For an instant Peggy remained frozen, watching as the ship came on, splitting the water, sending waves cascading past the large white number 37 on her bow.

Peggy leapt forward to strike down the jib, but in reaching for it she slipped and fell, her left knee hitting the cockpit deck. Without rising, she grabbed the boom with one hand and with the other swung the tiller out as far as it would go. For a moment the sailboat hung in the water motionless. Then she turned slowly sideways, parallel with the cruiser's heading. At the same time the cruiser abruptly altered course and immediately slowed.

Peggy took a breath. She looked down at the red streak across her palm where the line had bitten into it, and for the first time she was conscious of the painful throbbing in her knee. Raising her head again, she saw a new danger approaching her. The wake thrown up behind the cruiser's stern continued to spread outward in a rolling wall of water. *Free Spirit* had no way of escaping it.

Quickly, Peggy turned the boat and reset the mainsail, pointing the bow of the sailboat directly at the tumbling wake. Then, sitting down inside the cockpit of the boat, she shoved a cushion under her and put another at her back. She took the tiller with both hands and held on. Too late she remembered the life jacket she had brought, which lay out of reach beyond the centerboard. At her feet she saw the food bag with the open jar of peanuts sitting upright in it.

Peggy shut her eyes and waited.

A moment . . . two . . . and nothing. Suddenly, she felt *Free Spirit*'s bow thrust upward as the water rose. A second later the wave struck, crashing over the foredeck, bounding past the cockpit coaming, striking Peggy's head and chest and pinning her against the cockpit wall. As the afterwake now struck the boat, she felt the ice cold water douse her outstretched legs and heard some heavy object, probably the boat's anchor, slam against the inside of the hull as *Free Spirit* was propelled forward in the backwash.

Then there was silence. Calm.

Peggy opened her eyes and looked around. The jib was drenched, as was a good part of the mainsail. But the mast and rigging were intact. She released one hand from the tiller, worked her fingers, and ran them across her dripping face. She removed her sailor hat, which was full of water.

Slowly, she unbent her legs. Pain seized her injured knee. She raised herself, and as she moved, the water in the cockpit lapped at her sneakers and around the cushion she'd been sitting on. Beside the cushion was the food bag; its sides bulged with water. But still standing upright in it was the open peanut jar.

The mainsail began flapping noisily. At once, Peggy came about. As she did, she saw the navy ship once more, sailing arrogantly away, gentle waves now trailing in the cruiser's wake.

A sea swell lifted the sailboat. With effort Peggy stood up. She cupped both hands to her mouth to shout something, what she didn't know. Whatever words she might have flung after the retreating ship now caught in her throat.

Peggy sat down again. *Free Spirit* listed slightly, and the food bag fell against her foot. She reached down to move it off and saw the peanut jar, too, was full of water. Inside the jar loose peanuts floated aimlessly.

Peggy let go of the tiller and grabbed the jar. She turned, and with all her strength she threw it in the direction of the navy ship.

"Nuts to you!" she shouted.

The gesture and the words were hopelessly inadequate. But she repeated them. "Nuts to *you*!"

She turned back, came about at once, and began to sail up the river as quickly as her boat would carry her.

The four men stood on the deck of the cruiser saying nothing. They watched as the large ship was edged into its berth under the gentle prodding of the tugs. Three of the men, a lieutenant commander and two young ensigns, were in white summer uniforms. Each held his officer's cap under his arm.

The fourth man was considerably older, in his seventies, and taller than the rest. He was dressed in green slacks and a yellow sports shirt with crossed golf clubs above the breast pocket, in the same place that the young men displayed their service ribbons. But just as they did, and in contrast to his vivid shirt and slacks, the man wore black navy dress shoes that were polished to a high sheen.

The space between the cruiser and the dock drew closer and the older man leaned forward at the rail, his jaw set and his brow tight below a full head of white hair, as if he were docking the ship himself.

Behind him and out of view of the lieutenant commander, the two ensigns shared a look. One feigned a mock salute with crossed fingers; the other ensign smiled surreptitiously. He stopped as the older man turned back from the rail.

"What's her name again?" the man asked no one in particular.

The lieutenant commander stepped forward. "Who, sir?"

"This ship. I've forgotten her name."

"The *Corregidor*, sir."

"Too bad they don't name ships for women. Ships are

called 'she,' aren't they? Grace would have been a nice name. The U.S.S. *Grace*. Grace was my wife's name."

"Yes sir. But this ship is a guided missile cruiser, as you know." The lieutenant commander sounded very patient. "Nowadays they're named for great battles."

The older man grunted and moved again to the rail. There was a sudden bump, a brief whirr of the ship's propellers, and the rattle of chains as gangplanks were swung out.

When the forward gangplank was positioned and secured, the four men moved toward it, the three uniformed officers walking deferentially behind the older man. Without acknowledging them, he started briskly down the gangplank, ignoring the guide rope which the younger officers instinctively grasped for support as they made the steep decline. Once he reached the pier the man turned to watch as a hawser was thrown down past the white number 37 painted near the ship's bow and made fast to a bollard on the dock.

The three others joined him. As they walked on, the lieutenant commander edged forward in order to lead the party. But within a few steps the man in the green slacks had strode ahead again with crisp assurance, following the arrows that directed them toward the main gate. The three younger men once more fell in behind, and all of them continued through the labyrinth of passageways and vast gray metal structures that comprised the Whitby Ship Works.

Passing a hangar-size building, the older man abruptly stopped to peer in at the large sections of ships still to be assembled. He watched in awe as shipyard workers swarmed among the scaffolding, and welders' torches sprayed down pyrotechnic showers. Outside the great open door of another building, he paused briefly to say something to the other officers, but the cacophony of riveting and hammering from inside the building made hearing him impossible. At that moment a massive shadow passed across them. Together, the group turned and looked up. Swinging high above them was a four-hundred-foot red and white striped crane that towered over the shipyard, and over the town of Whitby itself, like a gigantic praying mantis. The older man seemed momentarily dumbfounded at the sight. Then he lowered his head, thrust out his chin, and moved on like a flagship leading a small convoy.

As the four men reached the main gate of the yard, a security guard raised the steel barrier arm, and a car bearing the navy emblem on its front doors drove in. It stopped and the driver, a young sailor, stepped out and opened a rear door. The four men approached the car, but short of it the older man halted, and turned to the lieutenant commander.

"It was a good run, Commander," he said with a firm handshake. "Thank you. Thank all the men."

"It was our pleasure. We were honored, sir."

The lieutenant commander saluted and the ensigns did also.

The older man saluted in return. "And thank you for letting me take the conn. My apologies for giving everyone a little problem out there."

"It was no real problem, sir," the lieutenant commander said blandly.

"I guess I don't quite have my sea legs back," the older man went on. "Still, if I'd had an officer of the bridge who performed the way I did today, I would have sent him back to basic navigation class." He chuckled mildly. The younger officers did likewise.

"It was no real problem, sir," the lieutenant commander repeated. "During the summer months we have to be watchful of a great number of private pleasure craft in the area of our sea trials."

"All's well that end's well, anyway. Nobody sank." The older man chuckled again.

"No, sir," the lieutenant commander said.

The older man gave a half-salute, which the other officers returned. He then stepped into the car and settled with a sigh into the back seat. The car made a quick U-turn and headed out the gate.

The distance between the small city of Whitby, Maine, and the village of Hasty Harbor is twenty miles by water, fifteen by land. Leaving Whitby, the overland traveler crosses the two-lane Bascombe Bridge spanning the Newell River and turns at once onto State Highway 23. From there the highway winds southward among a series of small interconnected islands that form a rough peninsula including the villages of Craigs Cove, Wilahasset, Dakins Ferry, Amanok, and Taggetts Neck. Along the highway and amid the timeless stands of firs and hemlocks are souvenir booths, often with folding chairs set by the roadside, for the display of everything from garish seascapes painted on black velvet to T-shirts boasting I'M A MAINE-IAC.

At a point well along the highway is an arrow, and below it, a faded green sign that states simply HASTY HARBOR (POP 423). The *o* in *harbor* shows the result of having been the target of repeated rifle shots; one of the local boys practicing his marksmanship, it is believed. The sign was put up in the early fifties, with the population figure for the village based on the 1950 census. No one has bothered to update it since, but the likelihood is that the figure has changed little in the years the sign has stood. The road leading from the highway is called River Road, a strip of patched and repatched asphalt that meanders through woods and marshes with no indication of a river anywhere nearby. Then, when one least expects it, over the last curving rise Hasty Harbor suddenly appears below.

At this spot is a large orange No Stopping sign in Day-Glo lettering, placed there after a number of traffic accidents caused by first-time tourists, who would abruptly halt their cars to gaze down at the postcard prettiness the scene presented or park and linger to take photographs.

The Maine Department of Transportation summer guide describes Hasty Harbor as "a small, picturesque harbor community typical of many along the midcoast region of the state." It says nothing about the clapboard houses, some with yet another coat of fresh white paint next to those with darkened unstained wooden shingles. Nor does it mention the tidy gardens of primroses and hydrangeas clustering at the ubiquitous picket fences that enclose each yard.

Beyond the village is the harbor itself, with boats of all sorts—cruisers, sailboats, lobster boats, and trawlers—dotting it. Totally protected except for the narrow opening to the Kerrenac River beyond, it has been considered a snug anchorage by coastal mariners for centuries. Ten years ago the harbor was dredged, and the channel deepened slightly. But Hasty Harbor continues to retain the meaning of the name the early Indians gave to it, The Place Away From Winds. The first French explorers called it La Petite Oeuf, the Little Egg, for the jagged line of rocks and trees that encircle it like the upturned half of a broken eggshell. When the English later claimed the territory they named it Hasty's Harbor after Jared Hasty, an English fur trader who established the first settlement there. Since then, the harbor and village have retained the name, losing only the apostrophe and final *s* in Hasty's to a forgetful sign painter, or to another local marksman years ago.

From the No Stopping sign River Road continues downward, ending at the water's edge. Here, at one side of a dusty turnaround is T. C. Dabney's general store, part of which also serves as a post office. Behind the store is a dilapidated building that was once a garage and a steel dumpster from which Smiley's Garbage Service twice a week picks up the trash. A few steps beyond the store is a large wooden pier belonging to the town, on which two buildings stand: a long low one that serves as the lobster pound, and a decaying salt-gray structure with its windows boarded shut and giving not the slightest hint as to its past or present use. At the peak of its roof a dozen seagulls perch, all facing windward, while across one weathered wall hangs a mosaic of sea-battered lobster floats.

Opposite the general store is a sign reading DODGE'S BOAT YARD and a dirt road. The road is short and narrow, and below it massive lichen-covered boulders meet the water. Near where the road reaches the boatyard pier, several cars are parked before a small white wooden building that is the boatyard office.

On this summer afternoon, Noah Dodge stood watching the activity. Tall, with a fringe beard and a faded flannel shirt, he was a familiar sight. Even those who didn't really know him always gave a nod or a word or two of greeting. Always, he returned it.

Between mid-May and mid-September, Dodge's Boat Yard was a busy place. There were the local lobstermen and fishermen and scallopers, who used the yard throughout the year. But this *was* Vacationland, if you believed Maine's license plates, and there were days when Noah wondered if America agreed. On every road, in every shop and restaurant were the out-of-state vacationers, and day-trippers up from Portland and Portsmouth and as far away as Boston. Added to their numbers were those who came down by the hundreds from the mountains and the woods of inland Maine itself: it was like a manic rush of lemmings to the sea.

For the other eight months of the year Noah managed reasonably well with Norris, his mechanic, who assisted him around the yard. But in the summer Noah had to hire several teenage boys to take care of routine maintenance as well as ferrying people to and from their boats moored at a distance from the dock. In the boatyard office his wife, Addie, handled the accounts and paperwork. Worse luck now that a bout of sciatica was keeping her temporarily housebound. But at least their daughter, Sarah, had returned from college and had volunteered to help him run the office for the next few weeks.

So Noah considered today an unexpected pleasure. The activity was light, and it gave him a rare opportunity to merely stand there in the sunshine and observe the goings-on. In particular, he was enjoying the sight of the two children on the floating dock below the pier. The boy, who was about eight, was demonstrating for his younger sister, about six, the subtleties of baiting a crab trap with a fresh fish head. Kneeling beside them was Noah's daughter, Sarah, talking to the children in her soft sure voice.

As the trap closed and the children cautiously played out the string that dropped it into the water, Sarah stood. It was then that Noah realized how much of a woman she had become in the last year. In her white shorts and T-shirt, she was as lean and lanky as any girl of her age. But that age was twenty-one now, as she continued to remind him, adding that she was quite capable of independence in whatever form it took.

Sarah wished the children luck and turned back in the direction of the ramp that led up to the pier. As she moved Noah watched her brush away the straight blond hair that fell around her shoulders. It had the look and color of pale silk, and her father wondered what unknown Viking sailor might have found his way into their ancestry to produce someone like her.

She came up the ramp, smiling. "I hope those two catch something in their trap. They're from Nebraska and they've never seen a crab before. In fact, this is the first time they've seen the ocean."

"Are you going to buy the crab from them if they catch one?" he asked her.

"Maybe. They're really sweet. Look how excited they are."

But Noah was now watching something else. "Strange," was all he said.

"What's strange?"

"Did you see Peg when she went out this morning?"

"Yes. Why?"

"Take a look." He pointed out into the harbor. Fifty yards from where they stood *Free Spirit* was coming at great speed.

"There she is now," Sarah said, and waved. "Hi, Peggy!"

"Something's wrong." Noah was sure of it.

"What could be wrong?"

"Don't know. But she's moving like the dickens, and at this distance she'd be waving back at us."

Without slowing, the sailboat headed directly for the floating dock, the mainsail and the jib still raised.

"Something *is* wrong," Sarah realized. She turned and raced down the ramp to the dock.

Twenty yards away, Peggy pulled the tiller in the opposite direction. Sails flapping, *Free Spirit* did a sudden about-face and came to rest against the dock with a loud thud. At the edge of the dock, Sarah was waiting.

"Peggy . . . ?"

"That's me," Peggy called. "Have one of the boys moor *Spirit* for me, will you, Sarah?" She let go of the tiller but remained seated.

The girl grabbed the side of the sailboat with one hand and held it away from the dock. With the other hand she took a kapok fender and shoved it between the sailboat and the dock.

"Forget the fender," Peggy said. "Might as well destroy my boat at dockside as out there." She stood, adjusted her sailor hat, picked up her food bag, and stepped out of the boat.

"Are you all right, Peg?"

"I'm tired, wet, and mad. That's just for starters."

"What happened?"

"First, I almost smashed up on the Sawteeth. Then some hot-shot navy type decided to play chicken near the lighthouse. Don't get me started. I'll talk to you tomorrow."

Peggy limped up the ramp. As she approached him, Noah reached down to help her.

"Peg—how are you?"

"Alive, at least."

"You're limping."

"No kidding."

"Come into the office and sit down. I'll fix you something."

"Good," Peggy said. "What can you give a person who today fought the Battle of Kidds Rock? On second thought, I just want to go home."

"Let me bring your car down to the pier," Sarah said. "I'll get your keys and things from the office."

"Thanks," Peggy murmured as the girl sprinted off.

"Peg, do you need a doctor?" Noah asked her.

"What I need is answers," Peggy told him. "I want to know who almost ran me down out there."

"What kind of boat was it?"

"It wasn't just a boat. It was a big damn *ship*. A navy cruiser from the ship works, probably."

"Did you get the number?"

"I'll never forget it. Number thirty-seven," Peggy said.

"Why don't you let Sarah drive you home?"

"No." Peggy shook her head. "I've still got one good leg. And when I get home I'm going to use it to start kicking a few butts."

Sarah drove Peggy's small blue Ford Pinto down the boatyard road and stopped just short of the pier. The older woman began limping toward it, carrying her wet sailor hat in one hand and her food bag in the other. Noah moved again to help her, but she shook the bag briefly, waving him away.

"I'm okay, I'm okay," she told him. "As you know, Commander McCoy can take care of herself."

"I know she can," said Noah as he walked beside her toward her car. "I know she can."

2

Until the telephone call it had been a fine day for Captain Robert Carnes. Arriving promptly at eight that morning at his office opposite the main gate of the shipyard, he had discovered a large manila envelope awaiting him. Inside it he found copies of the photographs that had been taken during his recent twenty-fifth class reunion at Annapolis. Looking through them, he had noted with a touch of pride that he still appeared as youthful and fit as he had at graduation, despite the few gray hairs that had crept into his crew cut. Putting the photographs aside, he had attended to his duties as navy supervisor of shipbuilding, Whitby Division. The first was to prepare his monthly report for his Pentagon superiors, advising them that of the sixteen ships the Whitby Ship Works was constructing for the navy, all were on budget and on schedule. At noon there'd been a splendid lunch of broiled fresh swordfish at a local restaurant with a former navy colleague who now owned a successful auto dealership in Massachusetts.

Then, just before the afternoon shift changed at the yard, Captain Carnes had leaned back in his chair and observed his lieutenant commander and two ensigns accompanying the admiral to the front gate. He had witnessed the mutual salutes and the pleasant banter, most probably about the day's sea trials, on which the admiral had been a guest observer. Finally, he had seen the admiral get into the navy car the captain had provided for him and be driven off. So far the old man's visit had been going very well. And he would be on his way again in two days' time.

It was late afternoon when the telephone intercom buzzed on the captain's desk. He picked up the receiver and responded with a brisk, "Carnes here."

"Excuse me, sir, but there's a lady on the phone who wants to talk to you," the captain's aide announced. "Except she doesn't sound much like a lady. Her name is Miss McCoy, sir. She says you know her."

"Everyone knows Miss McCoy. Thank you." Captain Carnes took a breath and patted his crew cut, as if he had to appear as presentable as possible even to speak on the telephone. The phone clicked, he took another breath and said casually, "How are you, Peggy?"

"I'll tell you how I am," the woman's voice said. "But first, you tell me: was it one of their men or one of yours?"

"Sorry, but you've lost me. Was who what?"

"Who was at the wheel of the ship that nearly ran me down this afternoon? There was a cruiser out there, probably on sea trials. I expected her to head in at Kidds Rock, as usual. But instead of slowing down and making for the Newell, she started up the Kerrenac at thirty knots. The ship was number thirty-seven, by the way."

The captain looked out his window in the direction of the shipyard dock area and had a sudden disquieting feeling, which he disallowed at once. Keeping his voice affable, he said, "Well, you're right about one thing. We did have a cruiser out there on sea trials today. What happened?"

"What happened was she almost ran me down when I was sailing. And I want to know who was at the helm. It couldn't have been the shipyard pilot; Bill Noonan knows his business. I'm betting it was one of your own drop-outs from navy navigation school."

From her seat at the table in her kitchen, Peggy glanced out the window at the two flags snapping briskly from the flagpole beside her house. "And when you tell me who it is," she added, "I'm going to hang him up there with my navy flag."

"First of all, are *you* all right?" Captain Carnes asked.

"Forgetting my knee, which I fell on trying to avoid a collision, I'm terrific. I'm also ready to declare war on the U.S. Navy. Another couple yards or so and me and my sailboat would be at the bottom of the Gulf of Maine by now." Peggy switched hands on the phone to take a swallow from the coffee mug in front of her.

At the same time, Captain Carnes looked out toward the shipyard docks again. The disquieting thought he had had earlier refused to go away.

"I'll check it out," he said, after a moment. "I mean, we can't have a navy man in a big ship running down a navy woman in a little one, now can we?" He laughed easily, or at least he hoped it would sound so. The reaction from the other end was total silence.

"Oh, while I think of it," he said, seeking to change subjects, "did you get my invitation to the launching?"

"Yes."

"It's tomorrow afternoon, you know."

"I know."

"Well," he pressed on, "I hadn't heard from you, and I really hope you'll be there. I have a seat saved for you in the reserved section. You've come to others, and I hope you'll come to this one."

There was another pause. Then Peggy said, "Robert, you're a nice young man. And in the two years you've been at the ship works, you've been very kind to send me invitations to your launchings, just because I'm an old blue."

"But you're a navy *officer*."

"*Ex*-officer."

"An ex-*commander*."

"Even so, I'm going to pass on this one," the woman said. "My knee's killing me, and my feelings toward the navy right now shouldn't be expressed over the phone. I'm sure whatever ship you launch will glide into the river without my help."

"The ship is a destroyer, in fact. And there are two reasons why you might want to attend," Captain Carnes said. "She'll be named the *Willoughby*. It's the first time a ship is being christened for a navy man who came from Maine. If I remember, he was born in Waldoboro, near where you grew up."

"There were only four boys I knew in Waldoboro, and all of them turned out to be farmers," Peggy said.

"Willoughby was a seaman who was killed during the battle of the Coral Sea. Didn't you do your first tour of duty as a navy nurse down that way?"

"Yes. So?"

"Well, I just thought it might bring back some memories."

"It does. What's the second reason?" she asked.

"The guest speaker at the launching is an ex–navy man who was in the same fleet command as Willoughby back then. Rear Admiral Charles Deering."

"Again—so?"

"He received some sort of medal from the White House last year. The citation called him 'the father of modern naval communications.' Or maybe you saw the television special on the 'new navy.' They said that what Rickover was to the development of the nuclear submarine, Deering was to sophisticated military communications. Especially for naval operations."

"What should I do? Whistle 'Anchors Aweigh'?"

"And, uh, there's one more reason I'd like you to be there," the captain added.

"Oh?"

"As you know, the military services in general are perceived as being male-oriented and male-dominated."

"They are. What's the big surprise?"

"Well, if people could see you at the launching, they might think differently. If you're in uniform, I mean."

"You want me to wear my old uniform?"

"Yes. The one you had when you were a Wave commander. You still have it, don't you?"

"I don't know. If I do, I haven't put it on in years."

"My thought is that some young women who are also visiting the shipyard might see you wearing it and decide to make the navy a career."

"You make me sound like a walking recruiting poster." Peggy drained her coffee mug and set it on the table. "Okay. I will attend your launching. And I'll wear my old Wave uniform, if I can find it. And if I can get into it."

"Thank you. I'd appreciate it," Captain Carnes said. And then added, "Very much."

"But I'm still going to file a complaint about that ship today."

"I understand."

"Good," Peggy answered, and hung up. She sat for several moments thinking over his request and staring at the empty coffee mug in front of her. Around the side of the mug was printed CAPTAIN'S PRIVATE PROPERTY, U.S.S. McCOY. The mug had been a recent gift to her from a local potter, who had made it up especially as a surprise.

Peggy raised herself from the table, favoring her knee, and moved to the kitchen sink. She rinsed the mug and set it in the dish rack, along with the single plate and juice glass that had been there since breakfast. From the kitchen window Peggy saw the broad mouth of the Kerrenac River, where she had sailed hours earlier. Visible far out in the water was a small sailboat about the size of hers, the solitary helmsman running free and confident before the wind. Looking seaward, she noticed that the shadow of Kidds Rock Light was now lengthening across the tiny island.

Islands, Peggy thought. Efate. Malekula. Epi.

Remote specks of rock and tangled vegetation. Years ago, after centuries of slumber, they had been stirred and wakened by the sounds of war. Yet when the sounds had faded, those islands had covered with a soft green shroud the dead who had been left behind, and hearing little except the beating of the surf against their shores, had sighed and pulled up the blanket of eternity to sleep once more.

And Toku. Tiny Toku Island. Of the men and women who had walked its coral beaches, smelled the scent of frangipani, or in the evenings stood beneath the cool comfort of the banyan trees, how many remembered Toku now? She did.

Peggy turned from the window and limped to the other side of the kitchen. She reached up and pulled the hanging chain that lowered the folding unit of narrow stairs leading to the attic. Slowly, she began to climb them.

After half an hour of searching and perspiring in the heat of the low-ceilinged attic, she found what she was looking for. It smelled musty, as did all the items in the trunk. The mothballs that had been placed around it to protect it had evaporated years ago. But it was still neatly folded, and the stripes on the sleeves remained a deep and solid blue against the white. She closed the trunk and locked it. Then, carefully carrying the uniform in both arms, she descended the attic steps. She replaced the stair unit in the kitchen ceiling and went into her bedroom.

Standing in front of the mirror that hung above her bedroom bureau, she unfolded the uniform and held it up in front of her. The brass buttons no longer had the luster she remembered, and the waist appeared so narrow Peggy wondered how she ever fit into it. But the rank insignia of a Wave commander looked almost new. Peggy guessed that if she brought the uniform up to the Whitby Cleaners first thing in the morning she could get it back by noon. The launching wasn't until four o'clock the next afternoon.

She decided she would try it on right now to make sure that it fit. Yet as she turned to lay the uniform across the bed before undressing, she saw the photograph. It was a small black-and-white snapshot set inside a thin gilt frame that rested to one side of her bedside table. The picture showed a young man and a young woman smiling and squinting slightly into the bright sun. Above them in the foreground the tip of a palm frond hung downward; behind them was a stretch of sand and water, and in the distant background was a high outcropping of blackish rock with lush tropical foliage clutching at its base. The young man in the photograph was tall and sandy-haired and dressed in the fatigues of a navy flier. One arm casually embraced the girl's slender waist. The girl was a good deal shorter than the young man. She was wearing a simple white dress and thin sandals. On her head, above her short dark curls, was a sailor's hat.

The expression on her face was one of complete happiness. Mixed with it also was a look of wonderment at how anyone who had known only the harsh granite hills of Maine could now be standing on the soft coral sand of a South Sea island and be this much in love.

Peggy picked up the uniform and held it in front of her again. To the photograph she said gently, "You never saw this uniform, Tom. Would you believe your little Pegs made it to commander? But you were never much for ranks or uniforms. Whatever I wore, you always said I was the prettiest girl on Toku. That was what you told me, Tom. Long ago."

The blue Pinto waited in the line of cars outside the main gate of the shipyard. From where she sat behind the wheel, Peggy watched the flow of people pressing around her and heading toward the gate. There were navy officers, sailors in their summer whites, and townspeople and tourists in a variety of outfits: suits and party dresses, jeans and T-shirts. There were also men and women who were obviously shipyard workers from the other shifts, who had come in their free time to watch the launching ceremony. In contrast to the coveralls and hard hats both sexes wore during their working hours, the men had changed to slacks and freshly laundered sports shirts, the women to bright summer dresses. As they moved past Peggy's car they talked and laughed among themselves, each with a look of proprietary, almost boastful pride that whatever their special task had been in building her, this was *their* ship that would be launched today.

The policeman waved Peggy through the main gate of the shipyard, and after circling the parking lot she found a space. She got out of her car, locked it, and straightened the skirt of her Wave uniform. People continued to stream past in the direction of the docks, and Peggy joined them. From the occasional curious looks directed her way, she realized that she was the only woman in the crowd who wore a military outfit. The thought made her momentarily uncomfortable, as if she had chosen to appear in public in some outlandish costume better suited to a masquerade.

"Yoo-hoo!" The shrill voice came from close behind her,

and she knew at once just whose it was. She also hoped the greeting was meant for someone else.

"Oh, yoo-hoo, Peggy! Peg-*geee*!"

With all the other noises surrounding them, Peggy was tempted to quicken her step and lose herself among the crowd, pretending that she hadn't heard. But her knee made a swift escape impossible, and after a few moments the woman appeared beside her, puffing.

"My dear, I *knew* it must be you," she gasped.

"Hello, Ernestine," said Peggy. She kept walking, but the woman managed to keep up.

The forward movement of the crowd slowed, then stopped, and Peggy found herself face to face with Mrs. Ernestine Doberman. Mrs. Doberman was the widow of the founder of the Whitby Seafood Cannery and was known as Jolly Ernie to her friends. But to Peggy and a few others, she would always be "the fishmonger's wife." Peggy noticed that the woman was perspiring from every visible skin surface and breathing like a boated fish. She was also staring in surprise and curiosity at Peggy's uniform.

"Don't you look *unique* in that attire," Mrs. Doberman announced.

Peggy looked at Mrs. Doberman and thought of saying the same thing. As Mrs. Doberman did frequently at local functions in the summertime, she was wearing a ridiculous frilly pink dress that was two sizes too small for her excessive girth.

"By the way," she said. "I'd like to talk to you about the Hasty Harbor Summer Festival. It's just two weeks away, you know, and I'm in charge of—"

They were interrupted by a loud cheer from a corner of the crowd, and everyone began to move again. Suddenly, a group of children carrying balloons pushed in between Peggy and Mrs. Doberman and Peggy seized the moment to escape.

"Sorry, Ernestine," Peggy shouted, and permitted herself to be swept off with the crowd. Making sure to keep within it, she moved past the gray wooden buildings that housed the shipyard's administrative offices and hiring center, and down a long avenue between assembly buildings, where workers on the present shift had put aside their rivet guns and welding torches to observe what they could of the impending ceremony.

As she emerged onto the broad tarmac of the dock area, Peggy saw the ship that was to be launched. She halted and looked up—and remembered with a chill that she'd been even closer to another ship the day before that had almost struck her and her sailboat. Yet this one sat immobile in the giant wood and steel cradle amidst the increasing activity surrounding her, a virgin vessel awaiting her annunciation. Peggy stood for several moments studying the ship. Lying at a forty-five-degree angle, the bow pitched in the air, she seemed more a part of the land than of the sea. In a short time that would change, and she would undergo the first of several rites of passage before becoming a member of the navy fleet. But at least for this initial rite she was colorfully adorned. Swathes of red-white-and-blue bunting trailed down her prow, and flags and pennants fluttered from her halyards and her mast. Near the base of the ship's bow a raised platform had been built, on which were a lectern and a dozen chairs.

The members of the crowd who, like Peggy, had received invitations to the ceremony were now filling the three hundred or so folding chairs that faced the platform and the ship. Shipyard workers and those without invitations gathered behind them around the wide dock area, standing where they found a space or climbing atop pieces of machinery to gain a view. At a point near the first few rows of chairs, which had been cordoned off by ropes, Peggy showed her invitation to a young man. Her name was checked against the clipboard that he held; she was presented with a program and moved on with the line of other invitees. There were still a few chairs in the front row, and although Peggy did not wish to be that close, she had no choice. She found a seat near the end of the row and sat down. Between her and the platform were the members of the Whitby Firemen's Band in their black and red dress uniforms, examining their instruments or adjusting music stands.

Peggy looked at her watch. The time was five minutes to four. Better get this show on the road, she thought to herself. She knew that any ship launched into the Newell River had to hit the water at slack tide, a period of just ten minutes. Otherwise there was the very real possibility that the strong currents and rapidly changing tides would catch her and carry her away before the waiting tugs could get their lines on her. Slack tide today began exactly at four thirty. Allowing half an hour for speeches and the christening itself, the ceremony had to begin soon.

At that moment, twelve people appeared, mounted the steps to the platform, and took seats. Of the nine men in the group, five were naval officers, including a navy chaplain and Captain Carnes. The others were of higher rank. The remaining four men were civilians; three executives of the Whitby Ship Works and a local congressman seeking higher office. Peggy guessed that the three women, two of whom were elderly, were related to the young sailor killed in the war for whom the ship was being named.

After several minutes the chaplain rose from his chair and approached the lectern. The crowd quieted, and some people among it bowed their heads.

"Let us recall the words of Psalm One Hundred Seven," said the chaplain. "'They that go down to the sea in ships, that do business in great waters . . .'" The launching of the United States Navy ship *Willoughby* was underway.

It was a routine that seldom varied, one that Peggy knew by heart from the other ceremonies she'd attended over the years. Following the invocation and a short prayer, there were the welcoming remarks of Arne Knudsen, the shipyard president. But, as he began his introduction of the other people on the platform, the microphone abruptly failed. Arne Knudsen stopped. While he stood in silence looking generally bewildered, a young man hurried up onto the platform and began disassembling and reassembling the microphone, disappearing now and then behind the lectern. The interruption took exactly two minutes by Peggy's watch. Arne's going to have to curb his usual expansive nature, she thought, or he'll lose a new billion-dollar destroyer to the outgoing tide.

The next speaker was a Commander Somebody-or-other from the office of the Chief of Naval Operations in Washington. With his smooth tan face and unctuous manner, Peggy guessed that he commanded nothing larger than a desk in the department's bureaucratic hierarchy.

"Now, it is with considerable pride," she heard him say, "that I present to you our distinguished guest this afternoon."

Peggy saw the white-haired older man in full dress uniform look toward the speaker at the lectern, and she assumed this was the admiral. She watched as he unfurled some papers he had in his hand and gave them a quick glance. Presumably, it was his speech. She wondered if something appropriate and totally forgettable had been written for him by a public relations hack in the Department of Defense.

"What's more," the commander was continuing, "as a naval officer in the South Pacific theater during World War Two, Admiral Deering fought in some of the same battles as the young man we honor here today, the young man whose name this ship will bear. It is with considerable pride that I present to you Rear Admiral Charles T. Deering."

As if a light had swept across him, the admiral stood up, nodded to the speaker, acknowledged the applause of the crowd and those seated on the platform, and strode quickly to the lectern.

"Give 'em hell, Admiral!" somebody shouted from the crowd. The admiral looked up in the direction of the shouter. And smiled.

"Young man, I compliment your spirit and your lung power. I wanted to say the same thing to *my* admiral before the battle of Leyte Gulf. I didn't—but we won the battle anyway. Thank you very much for your encouragement."

The crowd laughed and applauded again. As the admiral raised the microphone to accommodate his height and waited for the crowd to quiet, Peggy studied him. She realized that she was smiling—why, she wasn't sure. He was tall, well over six feet. In fact, he looked like some aging character actor cast in the role of a World War II admiral; the great mane of hair, the crisp white summer uniform, the colorful display of service ribbons from the battles he had fought, even the forthright jaw bespoke indomitable character.

The admiral waited for the noise of the crowd to fade before he began. Without sounding deferential, he paid brief respect to the young commander who had introduced him. He then noted by name, nodding to each one, the other people who were seated on the platform.

"Honored guests, former comrades in arms, ladies and gentlemen," he said. "On occasions such as this, you are expecting words from me that are solemn, patriotic, and profound. I will provide them to the best of my ability. But first, let me digress to comment briefly on this splendid ship we see before us now. She represents the best in modern military hardware and technology—and if I am to believe the press, that also includes seven-hundred-dollar hammers that are all shaft and no head."

The crowd roared, and Peggy knew at once that no Pentagon press officer had written *this* speech.

"This ship," the man continued, "is equipped with the most up-to-date computer guidance and weapons systems. She can communicate with any point on the globe directly by means of sophisticated satellites several hundred miles out in space. The fact is that in a few minutes the U.S.S. *Willoughby* will join the fleet of what the press also delights in calling 'the *new* navy.' Still, there are some of us, maybe even some of you here today, who remember the *old* navy. By the word 'old,' I mean the ships, the equipment, and the procedures. Definitely *not* the people. If some of us don't look exactly new, it's only because we've spent a little time in dry dock being overhauled."

More laughter from the audience, including Peggy's. Admiral Deering smiled broadly, grasping the sides of the lectern as he leaned forward.

"In the old navy we kept in touch by semaphore, not satellite. And if you wanted to let the navy brass know where you were, you sent a message in a bottle dropped at sea—a beer bottle if you were an enlisted man, a whiskey bottle if you were an officer, and a champagne bottle if you were an admiral."

The crowd was enjoying the speech thoroughly; the higher ranking officers on the platform looked nervous, but smiled wanly nonetheless.

Without intending to, Peggy glanced down at her watch again. It was now four fifteen. You better keep it moving, Admiral, she wished she could tell him. Time and tide wait for no man, especially in Maine, and with a full moon only a few days away.

"And yet," the admiral went on, "think just how much the old and the new navies have in common." The speaker raised his index finger high into the air. "In short . . ."

In short, Peggy realized she liked the man; she liked his vigor and his openness, his scorn of pompous speechifying, and his rough, wry humor.

"In short," the admiral repeated, "there are some things that have *not* changed as the present navy has come into its own. One is the devotion to duty of its men and women, their steadfastness to those principles that made the navy great, and their heroism in the defense of freedom everywhere.

"Looking out at all of you gathered here today, I see many who were not even born before the Second World War, or are too young to remember it. But I also see a few of you who fought that war, and who saw valor daily; those who in your own ways equalled it, whether you were an officer of the bridge or a navy nurse."

With a start, Peggy realized that the admiral was looking directly at her. She found herself nodding back and smiling, as if to reaffirm that, yes, she had been there, she saw, she knew.

Then, embarrassed others might have observed their moment of shared private understanding, Peggy bowed her head. No matter. All eyes were fixed on the admiral. Like that of a preacher warming to his subject and drawing energy from the attention and enthusiasm of the faithful, his voice boomed, then softened, and then boomed again. Had he pursued that calling, he could have also converted thousands to his cause, she thought.

Peggy did not need to be converted. She listened, breath held, as he recalled an incident when he was fighting in the battle of the Philippines and from it eased into a patriotic eulogy of the young sailor for whom the ship today was being named.

"Although I never had the honor of serving with Henry Willoughby," the admiral was saying, "I have known many like him, heroes all, to whom courage was inborn, and the defense of freedom natural as life itself. On the last day of

September, in the last year of the war, Henry Willoughby, of Waldoboro, Maine, sacrificed his young life so that all of you might live and breathe the air of freedom here today!"

He hit the papers on the lectern with his fist, set his jaw firmly, and swept his eyes across the crowd as the applause began to swell. The admiral raised both hands in the air, acknowledging it. Cheers and whistles followed, and to her surprise, Peggy found that she was cheering too.

Admiral Deering waited for the ovation to subside. Then he turned and extended his hand to a handsome gray-haired woman seated on the platform. Still holding her hand, he stepped to the microphone again and spoke. "Now it is with great pleasure that I present Mrs. Everett Hodges, sister of the seaman whose name this valiant vessel bears."

The woman nodded to the admiral. Captain Carnes rose, touched the woman's arm, and guided her to the rear of the platform, where the bow of the ship stood only a few feet away. A large bottle festooned with red-white-and-blue crepe paper hung down in front of it. Captain Carnes took hold of bottle and offered it to the woman, who grasped it in both hands.

In a strong voice with a distinct Maine accent, she called out, "I christen you the U.S.S. *Willoughby*!"

She swung the bottle with a sidearm thrust, smashing it squarely on the thick metal plate that had been welded to the ship's bow for the occasion.

What followed was immediate and overwhelming: simultaneously, the crowd roared, the whistles of the Whitby Ship Works shrieked, the horns and sirens of the other ships at dockside sounded at full volume, and the Whitby Firemen's Band struck up a rousing version of "Anchors Aweigh." Then, as banners streamed down from her halyard and her bow, the thirty-six-hundred-ton ship retreated slowly and gracefully from the platform as a renewed swell of cheers and applause added to the din.

It was a scene that Peggy had witnessed many times, but each time she felt a surge of pride and patriotic fervor rushing through her.

"Anchors aweigh, my boys, anchors aweigh . . ." She sang as loudly and applauded as enthusiastically as any person there.

The ship hit the river stern first, and great waves of spray and water exploded around the hull. At once, the waiting tugs moved in from all directions, taking her in tow.

"Farewell to college joys . . ."

On the platform many were shaking hands, and Captain Carnes and others were patting Arne Knudsen on the back.

Only one person stood facing away from the crowd, hands on his hips, watching as the tugs secured lines to the ship and began guiding her to her first berth. It was the admiral.

Was he recalling old commands of years ago? Peggy wondered as she looked at him. Or was he thinking wistfully that he would not command this ship, or any other ship, again? In short, to use his words, she wondered what sort of a man he was, this man with the unruly head of whitish hair, the jutting jaw, and the fervor and fire of an old evangelist.

"We sail at break of day . . ." the crowd sang.

Whatever he is, Peggy admitted to herself, no one had so stirred her curiosity and interest in a long, long time.

On all days of the year, including holidays, parking lot 6 at the south end of the shipyard complex contained an assortment of cars and motorcycles belonging to the shipyard staff and workers. Except on launch days. On those days when the launching of a ship was scheduled, the lot was cordoned off, and in the center of the empty asphalt rectangle a huge red-white-and-blue canopy was raised. Striped bunting decorated the supporting poles. Long tables were set up and covered with fresh white linen tablecloths. Trays of hot and cold hors d'oeuvres were placed on them, and the white-uniformed men and women of a Portland-based catering concern were at the ready to serve the guests invited to attend the postlaunching reception.

As the crowd in the dock area continued to disperse, most headed back to the other parking lots or to the main gate. But some, including those on the platform and in the special section nearest it, rose and walked together toward lot 6.

Peggy rose, too, when the ceremony was concluded, but she walked alone. Her mind was still fresh with the recollections and impressions of what she had just witnessed, and she wanted to savor them a little longer.

When she arrived at lot 6 she displayed her invitation and joined those already gathered under the canopy. A fair-size group had already arrived, and Peggy spotted some she knew among the mix of local citizens, shipyard executives, and navy personnel. In one group she saw Ferguson "Frenzied Fergy" Fitch, Whitby's discount appliance king, showing off his voluptuous new wife, redheaded CeeZee. The woman claimed that CeeZee was from the initials of her first and middle names, Cara Zöe, but gossip had it that Fergy had found her in a house of ill repute in Boston's Combat Zone and had married her right then and there. In another group was the congressman Peggy had seen on the platform at the launching ceremony earlier. At the moment he was earnestly addressing a gaggle of attentive men and women, accentuating his remarks on the dangers of substance abuse with the swizzle stick from his martini glass.

Standing at the hors d'oeuvres table, with a pig-in-a-blanket in each hand was Oren Bellweather, the local undertaker, looking as cadaverous as any of his lately deceased clients. He was dressed in a black suit, probably having just come from a funeral, and seemed greatly out of place among the white-uniformed navy men nearby. There was also a scattering of other Whitby notables—the newly elected president of the chamber of commerce, his bald pate gleaming in the late afternoon sun; the head of the local VFW chapter wearing his bemedaled overseas cap; and of course, the relentlessly social and still-panting Mrs. Doberman.

Near the far end of the bar tables, Peggy also saw a crowd of navy officers, with some local men and women in among them. There was a burst of laughter from the group; it shifted slightly, and for a brief moment Peggy caught sight of Admiral Deering himself standing in the center. She quickly made her way toward them, ordered a ginger ale, and stood at the edge of the circle of people. At first she could hear only snatches of the conversation the admiral was having with a short fat man in a seersucker suit.

The man was saying something about having been a naval officer himself once, and that he now owned a cabin cruiser with a wet bar and wall-to-wall carpeting in the head. The admiral said something in response, and the group laughed again. When the man standing in front of her turned to the bar for a refill, Peggy moved into the relinquished space.

"One thing I don't have on my boat," the man in seersucker was saying, "is a torpedo launcher. If I did I'd blow some of those summer sailors straight out of the water."

"Ah, yes. Why is it," the admiral asked, "that in the summer months would-be sailors attempt to navigate a boat, when most of them don't know their keel from their fantail?"

There were chortles from the group, and a few men raised their glasses in the air to murmurs of "Here, here."

The admiral gestured with his own drink and went on. "For instance, yesterday I had the privilege of being given the helm briefly of a new cruiser out on a sea trial. It made me proud to be a navy man, I'll tell you that. But wouldn't you know, as we were heading in our path was blocked by some little woman in a sailboat. Now I know what's meant by the term 'dames at sea.'"

More laughter followed, and the admiral beamed broadly. Peggy stared at the man and felt a sudden sharp pain course through her knee.

"God spare us from women sailors," a second man offered. Several women tut-tutted disapprovingly, but pleasantly.

"No offense to you ladies," the admiral said, "but as far as I could tell, the woman sailor we encountered yesterday was somebody's grandmother who had no idea how to sail or in what direction she was bound."

Peggy went numb. Here was a man she had admired, felt a kinship with less than an hour earlier, expounding at the moment like a pompous male chauvinist. Her next reaction was a flush of anger and embarrassment, as if she had been struck across the face.

A man in the group moved to the side, and Peggy suddenly found herself facing the admiral. Her mouth felt absolutely dry. Another person began speaking, but Peggy cut through, her own words sounding in her ears as if someone else were saying them.

"I would have thought, Admiral," she said, "that a large ship like a cruiser, with all its sophisticated systems, could have seen that little woman in the sailboat much sooner. Unless the cruiser was going too fast and in the wrong direction."

The admiral looked down at her, nonplussed for a brief moment. Then he saw Peggy's uniform and smiled. "I recognize the service ribbons of the South Pacific theater, Lieutenant."

"The rank is commander."

The admiral managed to take a small breath while continuing to smile. "Well, to address your question, Commander, the fact is, as I understand it, that area is reserved for naval operations, and that civilian craft are not—"

"The fact is," Peggy McCoy told him, "that's an ocean out there, and it's not reserved for anybody."

The man was silent, the group as well.

"The fact is," Peggy went on, "power craft, including navy cruisers, are supposed to give the right-of-way to sailboats. Or have you forgotten your rules of the road?"

Amid the hubbub of the crowd under the canopy, the silence of the small group seemed like a sinkhole. Finally, after several moments, the admiral recovered, waved his glass expansively, and thrust his smile down upon her again.

"Quite right, Commander. You're quite right. Forgive me if that woman in the sailboat was a friend of yours." He chuckled briefly to himself. "If the truth be known, when I was a young man I more than once gave way to a woman in a sailboat."

The men in the group laughed heartily, in chorus, as if to break the chill.

"The little woman in the sailboat is someone I know," Peggy said.

"I see. Well—"

"No, you don't see well. If you did you might have seen *me,* yesterday, before you nearly ran me down!"

This time it was the admiral who looked as if he had been struck. A man in the group coughed. The navy men looked at their polished shoes. Of the dozen or so people in the circle, no one spoke or moved.

Then suddenly, without at all having intended to, Peggy

snapped her right hand to her forehead in a sharp salute. "Good day, Admiral. And go to hell."

Instinctively, the admiral's own hand half lifted, returning the salute. But already the short gray-haired woman in the Wave commander's uniform had turned abruptly, pushed her way out of the circle, and disappeared into the crowd.

3

At dawn a low sea fog enshrouded Lonely Point. For some minutes Peggy lay in bed and listened to the lamentations of the foghorn from Kidds Rock Light. It was only by the time she had begun to fix her breakfast that the fog showed any sign of burning off. When she had finished breakfast, she poured herself a second mug of coffee and decided she would have it out on the small deck outside the living room.

She went to the glass doors that opened onto the deck and slid them aside. Generally her habit was to perch on the deck's wooden railing while she sipped her coffee, but although the swelling in her knee had lessened, she chose to sit in the old sling chair that was the single piece of furniture the deck possessed. The chair had a wrought iron frame that looked like a giant misshaped paper clip. Its canvas seat had once been yellow, but years of sun and rain had bleached it to a dull buff. Still, the frame was heavy enough not to blow around in stormy weather, and the seat was comfortable. And at her age, Peggy felt, familiarity and comfort counted a great deal more than fashion did.

The deck faced eastward, toward the water, and it always gave Peggy a sense of peace to sit outside on summer mornings. Maybe later she'd call Miriam, and they would . . .

Peggy caught herself. Dear Miriam. How difficult it was to realize that she was gone. Until that day three weeks ago, Miriam had never been sick a day in her life; all her friends and neighbors had remarked that at the woman's funeral. A widow almost Peggy's age, the two of them had been the best of friends for years. Now Miriam was gone. Dear Miriam.

In fact, Peggy admitted to herself, this had not been the best of years for friendships. A woman who had sometimes joined Miriam and Peggy on outings or for dinners had moved in April to some senior citizens establishment in Florida. In the beginning Peggy had received a weekly letter from her, but since June the letters had become a bit perfunctory and more infrequent.

Of course, if it was social contact Peggy sought, the Hasty Harbor ladies had their various activities—the bridge clubs, the church auxiliaries, the hospital volunteer program whose members delivered books to patients and did similar good works. But such organized endeavors, however charitable their intent, had never held much of an appeal for her.

Yes, thought Peggy, with the possible exception of young Sarah Dodge, good friends were decidedly in short supply this year.

Her reverie was broken by the beat of wings; she looked around to see a large gray and white herring gull descending onto the deck. It landed squarely on both feet, tucked back its wings, and stared up at Peggy, its beak open. Because of the bird's gross underbelly and short spindly legs, she had named him Captain Bligh.

"Well, I'm glad to see I still have my old feathered friend, at least," Peggy said. "Good morning, Bligh. Wait here. I'll get you some bread." She went to the kitchen, grabbed two slices of bread from the loaf on the countertop, and returned with them to the deck.

The seagull opened his beak wide again, watching her with his unblinking yellow eyes. As Peggy sat down in the sling chair, the bird quickly waddled toward her. She tore apart a slice of bread and offered a small piece. The gull seized it directly from her hand.

"So where have you been keeping yourself?" Peggy asked. "I haven't seen you in a week."

She tossed more pieces of bread onto the deck. "Don't tell me you've been hanging around with those gulls at the town dump again. They're a tough bunch at the dump. But no tougher than your relatives who chase the fishing boats. What I'm saying to you, Bligh, is that you shouldn't be influenced by any of them for the sake of company. Be your own bird. Independent, self-reliant, free to go where the wind carries you."

She tore into the second slice of bread and began to throw the pieces onto the deck one after another. The seagull leapt at them, gobbling them up. Finally, Peggy stood and held out her empty hands, palms up. "See? All the bread is gone. No more."

The gull looked up at her and burped as the outline of the last piece of bread moved down his crop.

"Sorry, Captain. But that's breakfast for today. Oh, by the way, this morning I'm going to start some repainting work around this house. The west wall first. Therefore, if you fly over it, be careful."

The seagull took several steps backward on the deck, appearing puzzled.

"One more thing," Peggy added. "Yesterday, I met a man. I liked him—until he got my feathers ruffled and I squawked at him. So, what is your advice? Forget him?"

Peggy thought, then nodded. "Yes, I guess I should. I will."

She waved her hands and started for the sliding doors. The seagull gave a farewell cry and lifted off from the deck. Peggy turned and watched the bird as he flew off above the trees.

"But I liked him," she repeated to herself. "I liked the man."

Captain Carnes was certain he was lost. An hour earlier he had left his office at the ship works. Twenty minutes ago he had turned off the main highway, following a faintly painted wooden arrow indicating that the Kare Free Kabins lay ahead. A second arrow and a third had put him on a narrow road that probably had been paved last by the WPA. After a circuitous two miles the road gave way to a graveled surface, and finally to a pair of tire tracks with a center ridge between them, which did its best to remove the entire undercarriage of the car.

Abruptly the tracks ended and Captain Carnes found himself staring through the windshield at a large sumac bush. He backed up cautiously, hearing branches scrape along fenders and doors, and wondered if he would have to pay personally for damage to navy property. At last he came to an intersecting set of tire tracks and saw, barely visible among the foliage, a fourth arrow pointing off into the woods.

He turned the car and followed this new set of tracks that soon emerged into a clearing studded with tall pines. Among the pines a dozen wooden cabins stood. In front of one cabin a man was fanning at the smoke that wafted from a metal barbecue grill; beside another cabin a small child was bouncing on a large inflated plastic pig. Captain Carnes parked off to the side of the clearing and got out of the car. As he walked past the cabins he noticed that each had a wooden plaque nailed above the door bearing the name of a fish. He checked the slip of paper in his pocket and continued on past Swordfish, Bass, Muskellunge and Sturgeon before he found the cabin whose identifying plaque read "Pike." He stepped up to the door, took a deep breath, and knocked quickly.

"Admiral? It's Captain Carnes," he called out, hoping not to disturb the man sleeping in the hammock at Perch cabin just beyond.

The door opened and the admiral looked out, his hair uncombed. "Carnes. Well, this *is* a surprise. Who's minding the store? Come in. Stand out there long enough and the mosquitoes will take all the blood you've got. Come in," he said again. "I'm just doing my breakfast dishes."

The old man disappeared from view and the captain entered the cabin. It was a good deal more pleasant than he would have expected. Although small, the main room had a rustic homeyness. There was a maplewood couch and armchair with floral chintz slipcovers and a knotty pine table that obviously served a variety of purposes. Two doors led off the room; one to a bathroom and the other to what Captain Carnes guessed must be a tiny bedroom. A lobster trap set on end served as a small table. In one corner of the main room was a fireplace. Diagonally opposite it was a kitchenette unit with stove, sink, and half-size refrigerator.

The admiral's appearance was not what Captain Carnes had expected either. The man stood at the sink wearing another golf shirt, turquoise this time, and an apron over a pair of red Bermuda shorts. He was barefoot.

"Have a seat, Captain. Be with you in a minute." The admiral scrubbed vigorously at a grease-encrusted skillet, waving it from time to time in Captain Carnes's direction as he spoke. "Mr. and Mrs. Hardisty, the owners of these cabins, gave me some fresh-caught whiting last night. And I mean *fresh.* I cooked up the whole batch for breakfast. Ever had fresh fish for breakfast, Captain?"

"No, sir."

"Try it."

"Yes sir." Captain Carnes looked around the room for some sign of packed luggage. There was none.

The admiral was now picking with his fingernails at the baked-on carbon on the skillet's sides. "So to what do I owe this unexpected visit?" he asked. "Don't tell me the ship we launched yesterday sank."

"No, sir. But as you know, you have a noon flight out of Portland. And rather than have one of our enlisted men take you to the airport, I thought I'd drive you there myself."

The admiral looked surprised. "You didn't get my message then? You must have left your office at the yard before I called. I'm staying."

"Sir?"

"A week or so, anyway." The admiral returned to the skillet, hacking with a fork at the black residue. "A place like this brings back some happy memories. That's why I'm glad you could book me in here and not at that fancy-pants motel your people planned to stick me in. My wife and I visited this same neck of the woods nearly forty years ago. I was stationed in Portsmouth then."

He looked away reflectively. "Dear Grace. It was the first time she'd spent more than a day this far north of the Mason-Dixon line. She was a Virginia girl."

"I see," said Captain Carnes.

"We had a cabin just like this. It was wonderful. Picking wildflowers, walking hand in hand along the beach. Grace loved it. So did I."

He turned off the water in the sink and set down the pan. "But I guess if you're with someone you really love, you love any place. Oh, and boating. We did lots of boating, Grace and I. Sailing mostly. Outboard motors were big noisy contraptions then. So as I said, since I was here participating in your launching, I thought I'd take a little time to relive those memories. As much as they can be relived, of course."

"Of course."

The admiral held up the skillet for inspection and shook his head. "Only thing that'll get this pan clean is barnacle remover. The hell with it. I'll buy the Hardistys a new one." He tossed the skillet in an open trash container near the sink and began drying his hands on his apron front.

"Sir," Captain Carnes began, "another purpose for my coming here personally was to apologize to you for the untoward incident yesterday."

"What incident?" Admiral Deering looked surprised. "Oh, you mean that woman? Forget it. I have." He chuckled. "Still, I'm not used to being chewed out by a junior officer."

"Well, Miss McCoy—"

"*Commander* McCoy. I learned that much about her yesterday."

"Yes. Commander McCoy. Again, I apologize on her behalf."

"Did she ask you to apologize?"

"No, sir."

"Good," the admiral said. "Because I was the one at fault. First, when I nearly ran her down at sea, and again at the reception when I tried to make a joke of it in front of her. She had a right to be upset. I was a jackass. Why, I don't know. Hubris, maybe. Plus embarrassment that I came close to striking her boat to begin with." He reached back and untied his apron.

"Peggy McCoy . . ." He pondered the name reflectively. "I'll say this for her. She has sass and substance. Spunk. And besides that, she's old navy. What else do you know about her?"

"She's in her sixties," Captain Carnes informed him. "She was born in an inland town not far from here. She became a navy nurse early in the war and was sent to the South Pacific."

"How did she get to be a commander?"

"She continued in the nursing service after the war ended. "

The admiral nodded. "I bet no sailors malingered in the sick bay if *she* had anything to say about it. Is she married?"

"No, sir."

"Was she ever?"

"Not that I know of."

"Well, that's neither here nor there." The admiral slapped his hands together as if punctuating the change of subject. "What time is it, Captain?"

The captain checked his watch. "Nine thirty."

"Good. They should be open now. Or will be by the time I get there. You're on your way back to the shipyard, I presume."

"Yes sir," Captain Carnes said. If I can find my way out of here, he thought.

"Then you wouldn't mind dropping me off at the car rental place in Whitby. Today I thought I'd drive around and get to know the area. Let me put my shoes on."

The admiral disappeared into the bedroom and emerged a short time later. He was dressed in the same turquoise shirt, but the Bermuda shorts had been replaced by white duck slacks, and he was wearing black shoes and socks. He started toward the front door of the cabin and then stopped.

"I just can't tell you how I'm looking forward to these days here, Carnes. I mean, other times of the year I could be home farting around a golf course with the rest of the old dinosaurs. But this should be something different. Special."

"Yes. I'm sure it will be, sir."

Captain Carnes opened the door for the admiral. But the older man continued to regard him.

"Does she live around here? Commander McCoy?"

"Yes sir. Down past Hasty Harbor."

"I'll say one thing for her. She's the real McCoy, all right." The admiral grunted and walked out the door.

The staccato of typewriter keys greeted Peggy as she approached the office of the boatyard early in the afternoon. She opened the screen door and saw Sarah hammering intently at a vintage Smith Corona.

"Hi, Peg," Sarah said, not looking up. She stopped typing and consulted a dictionary that was lying open on the desk beside the typewriter. She shook her head. "Sometimes I totally forget how to spell pelecypod. It's *y*, not *i*," the girl said. She turned back to the typewriter and resumed typing.

Peggy sat on the edge of the table opposite. "I know it shows my ignorance, but could you tell me just what a pelecypod is? In case I should run into one on a dark night."

Sarah looked up briefly. "Any of a class of bivalve mollusks that have a body bilaterally symmetrical, compressed, and enclosed within a mantle that builds up a connected shell."

"Frankly, you lost me after 'bivalve mollusks.' It doesn't sound like boatyard bills you're typing."

"They're notes for my senior thesis for next year. Since my major is marine biology, I've decided to write my thesis about clams."

"You're going to spend a whole year writing about *clams*?"

"Not all clams, really," Sarah told her. "Just those indigenous to the mid-Maine coast. There hasn't been a good study of them done in fifteen years."

"A pity."

"But this week I started going to the mud flats on the

other side of Lonely Point, at low tide. I'm conducting some experiments."

"It all sounds very scientific," Peggy said. "But I'm not sure I like the idea of you spending your free time in a clam bed. A pretty girl like you should be going out on dates, even at low tide."

Sarah shrugged. "Between helping in the office here and doing my experiments, I'm very busy. Besides, there's nobody around here I *want* to date. Most of the boys I went to high school with are working on their fathers' boats. Who likes going on a date surrounded by the smell of fish?"

"You've got a point," Peggy agreed. She stood up and glanced out the office window. "Anyway, I see they've got *Free Spirit* at the dock. I better go."

"How's your knee, by the way?" the girl asked her.

"Tender but okay. Good enough to climb a ladder. I've been saying to myself the last two years my house should have a fresh paint job. So I started it this morning."

"But that's work. You should get somebody to help you."

"Maybe. But the penny-pincher in me can't see giving all that money to a painter. And around here, if you want to get anything done—"

"You've got to do it yourself," Sarah finished the sentence with her.

Peggy laughed. "You must have heard that line before."

"Many times—from you," said Sarah. "By the way, Dad told me you were going to the launching at the ship works yesterday."

"I did."

"What was it like?"

"What's any launching like?" the older woman said. "The band played, speeches were made, a good bottle of champagne was sacrificed, and the ship slid into the Newell River just about on schedule."

"This morning's paper had a story about the admiral

who spoke. It said he fought in the South Pacific, just like you."

"He fought, and I took care of the fighters who survived the fighting."

"The newspaper said it was one of the best speeches they'd heard given at a launching in a long time."

"It was a good speech," Peggy admitted. "Very good. Let's leave it at that."

"What do you mean?"

"I mean I thought the speaker was terrific too. Until I talked to him in person."

"You *met* him? What's he like?"

"Tall. Handsome—or at his age, should I say distinguished-looking. We met at the reception afterward."

"And?"

"It turned out he was at the wheel of that navy ship that almost ran me down."

"He was?"

"And he treated it as if it was a joke. At the reception he had a grand time telling everyone about 'the little woman in the sailboat.'"

"What did you do?"

"I told him to go to hell."

"You *said* that?"

"My very words. And meant it." Peggy frowned. She started for the door but then stopped. "The newspaper was right. It was a terrific speech. See you when I get back."

Peggy turned again and headed out the door.

An hour later Sarah stood on the floating dock helping a fifteen-year-old girl attach a jib stay to the bow of the girl's Lightning class sailboat. When Sarah was done she turned back toward the pier; a tall elderly man in a turquoise shirt and white slacks was standing there, obviously in need of some assistance.

Sarah excused herself and went up the ramp to the pier. "May I help you?" she asked as she approached the man. "I'm Sarah Dodge."

"Miss Dodge, how do you do?" he said. "I was told this was a place where I could rent a sailboat."

"We rent them, yes. What kind of sailboat did you have in mind?"

"Something adequate. Twenty-five or thirty feet." He chuckled. "It needn't be a windjammer or a brigantine."

"How many in your party?" Sarah asked him.

"Just myself."

"When did you want to rent it?"

"Right now."

"Now? I don't think we have anything right now." She glanced down toward the far end of the floating dock. "Well, one did come back a little while ago. I can let you have it. But I don't think it's exactly what you had in mind."

"What sort of boat is it?"

"A Cape Cod Baby Knockabout."

"A what?" The man looked startled. "Just how long is this—Baby Knockabout?"

"Twelve feet."

"Good God. It sounds like it belongs in a child's wading pond."

"I'm sorry. But it's all we've got right now," she said somewhat doggedly.

The man shrugged. "In that case, beggars can't be choosers. All right. I'll try it."

"If you'll come with me to the office, I'll write out the form." Sarah turned and headed toward the office and the man followed. Once inside, she went to the desk, sat down, and inserted the rental form into the office typewriter.

"Name, please?"

"Charles Deering."

Sarah's fingers halted above the typewriter keys. "*Admiral* Deering?"

"Yes, ma'am."

"Well . . . I've heard a lot about you," Sarah said.

"Good things, I hope." He gave her an avuncular smile.

She gave him an uncertain one in return and rapidly began typing out the form. When it was completed, the admiral signed it and paid her the deposit. Then Sarah led him outside again and down to the floating dock.

Two young boys were kneeling on one side of the dock. Between them was a large open tackle box displaying a variety of brightly colored plugs and lures. Both boys had fishing poles to which they were attaching lures. Opposite them a small blue sailboat with yellow trim bobbed gently in the water.

Sarah went to the sailboat and checked its contents. "The oars and the life vest are still in it," she told the admiral. "All you have to do is raise the sail."

The admiral examined the tiny cockpit of the sailboat. "It looks like one of those boats I used to make out of a walnut shell and a toothpick when I was a boy."

"During the summer season the demand for rental boats is very high," Sarah said by way of an apology.

"I'm sure." He gave an understanding shrug. "Oh, well. It may not be the *Bonhomme Richard,* but I'll make the best of it." He pointed out across the harbor. "I presume there is a channel out there that leads somewhere."

"To the Kerrenac River," Sarah said. "And the Gulf of Maine. Just be careful of the rocks outside of the channel entrance. But the wind is light. You should be okay."

"Fine." He stepped into the boat and raised the sail.

"I'll help you cast off." She went forward to detach the mooring line from the dock.

"I shouldn't be long," he assured her. "I'll just go out into the river and do a bit of sight-seeing." He checked his watch. "It's two o'clock now. I should be back by four."

"Happy sailing," Sarah said. She gave the bow of the sailboat a gentle nudge out into the harbor.

"Thank you," he called to her, and waved. Then he settled down beside the tiller as the sail filled.

The breeze was light but steady, and it carried the little boat across the water more quickly than the admiral expected. Still, he felt confident. In spite of the size, the boat handled easily. Water traffic in the harbor was active, but he guessed that by angling a bit to starboard he could sail all the way to the harbor entrance on one tack.

Fifty yards ahead of him the admiral now saw a larger sailboat with a single sailor at the helm. As the larger boat approached, he realized that it was being sailed by a child. Well, a teenager. But a girl. If she can handle that boat by herself, he could certainly handle this one, he assured himself. It occurred to him that he hadn't checked the stern of his own boat to see if she had a name. He was afraid, in fact, it might be something diminutive and cute like *Bluebird* or *Bobalong*. Whatever name she bore it was probably a far cry from the last ship he had commanded during his active navy service—the U.S.S. *Defiant.*

The admiral's first tactical sailing challenge came as he drew nearer to the channel out of Hasty Harbor. From a distance it had looked reasonably navigable, but closer to it, he discovered with a surge of apprehension how narrow the opening actually was. Even so, he decided, he could probably sail through it without having to tack again. No other boats were in the channel at that moment or were about to enter it, as far as he could see.

He looked back briefly toward the harbor and took a long deep breath. He was pleased with himself at how quickly he'd picked up his sailing skills again. It was then he remembered he had forgotten to put on the orange life vest, which still lay at his feet. He probably should, he thought, but to do so now would mean trying to do it with one hand while managing the tiller and the sail at the same time with the other.

The sailboat glided past the row of vertical sticks projecting from the water that marked the channel entrance and thrust on toward the Kerrenac. The formidable size of the jagged rocks beyond the harbor entrance startled him the moment he saw them. But he sailed past them without incident. As he did, he felt the breeze begin to stiffen. He slowly eased the tiller over and played out the sail. The boat responded instantly; she bounded forward and her sail sought the wind.

Well out in the river now, he chose a downwind course that would give him time to get the feel of the sailboat in open water. It also provided him an opportunity to observe the rugged beauty of the Maine coastline. Directly ahead was a high promontory with a steep escarpment plunging down into the sea. Beyond it there emerged a large gray mansion with turrets at each end. It appeared to be some sort of hotel, and he wondered briefly if he should have chosen to stay there instead of at the Kare Free Kabins. But judging from the attire of the guests strolling the greensward fronting the hotel, the high point of their afternoon was probably a hot game of croquet.

He brought the sailboat about and was surprised to see a large yacht overtaking him. Near the ship's bow, lying supine in the sun, was a young woman wearing nothing but a pair of wraparound reflector sunglasses. On the afterdeck stood two young men in yachting caps, blue blazers, and white slacks. As the two boats came abreast, the young men saluted him with highball glasses. When the yacht was well beyond, he saw her name was *Daddy's Gusher,* out of Tulsa, Oklahoma. It amused the admiral to think of Tulsa as a seaport town. Most likely she belonged to some rich oilman, he guessed, proving that oil and water can mix under certain circumstances.

The admiral continued outbound for some minutes,

tacking back and forth with ease. Despite his earlier misgivings about the boat's size and seaworthiness, she handled well. Still, he discovered he was farther from the shoreline than he really wished to be, and he angled the sailboat back toward it. Along the sandy shore he saw a young couple making their way barefoot across some pieces of driftwood at the water's edge. For a brief moment, he remembered how he and his young wife had taken just such a walk so many years ago.

When the admiral looked seaward again he saw the object straight ahead, dark and glistening, barely visible above the water and waiting for his boat to strike.

"Rock!" he shouted.

He rammed the tiller over. The boat veered, the sail swung out, suddenly ballooning, and before he knew it, Admiral Deering was lifted up and flung out as the boat capsized.

He came up in the water sputtering and gasping; his arms flailed, he sought anything that he could grasp. He felt his hand hit something flat and he clung to it. When he looked he saw he was clutching the edge of the boat's centerboard. The upturned hull, to which it was attached, lay sideways on the surface of the water, as did the mast and sail.

His navy training almost led him to shout *Man overboard!* but he settled for a bellowed "Help!"

His view of the shoreline was now blocked by the hull, but he wondered if the young couple on the rocks had seen the accident and rushed for aid.

"Help me!" he called louder, than recalled dishearteningly that the only boats he'd seen in the vicinity were too far off to hear his cries. What followed was the realization that with the present wind he and his small boat were drifting slowly but inexorably out to sea.

"Help! Help! Can anybody hear me? *Help!*"

"Take it easy! I can hear you. Keep holding onto the centerboard!"

The voice came from behind him, from a distance of a hundred feet or so. He tried to turn around to face his rescuer, but he couldn't without letting go.

The voice continued, drawing closer, calling to him frequently. "I'm coming! . . . Just hang on. . . ."

He pushed up with both hands until he lay panting with the upper part of his chest on the centerboard itself. Suddenly, a large wave struck the boat, breaking his grip and plunging him again into the water.

"Help! Get help!" he shouted.

"I'm your help!" she shouted back. "You're near your rudder. Grab it and hold on! . . . That's it. Hold your rudder! Let your body float."

The man did as he was told, allowing his legs and torso to float upward to the surface while he held the rudder with both hands. Soon, out of the corner of his eye, he saw the hull of a white sailboat approaching him.

"Are you wearing your life vest?" the woman asked him.

"No," he admitted. "I intended to, but—" He was interrupted by the splash of a life vest hitting the water next to him.

"Take mine," the woman said. "But don't try to put it on now. Hold on to it and let go of the rudder. I'm going to try to right your boat."

Again he followed orders, releasing the rudder and pressing the life vest to his chest. A short time later the hull of his sailboat turned upright in the waves. The next moment his rescuer's sailboat appeared beside him, and he grabbed at the line that was flung down to him.

Peggy stood in the cockpit of *Free Spirit.* She looked at the man's face and at the wet mass of white hair that fell across his forehead. She said nothing.

At the same time, he raised his head and looked at her.

"How do you do, Commander?" he said. Under the circumstances, he realized it was a ridiculous remark.

"A lot better than you," Peggy answered. "Are you hurt?"

"No. I don't think so." He gagged, coughed, and spat out a mouthful of seawater.

"Do you think you can get into my boat?"

"I don't know. I'll try."

While Peggy remained standing near *Free Spirit*'s stern, the admiral maneuvered himself hand over hand along the side. He found a cleat, and using it as a handhold he struggled to get his body up and over the splash rail. Head down and arms reaching, he tumbled into the open cockpit of Peggy's boat.

He sat up quickly. "I'm in," he said. "Thank you for rescuing me. I mean, I'm glad you were out sailing today."

"I'm out sailing every day," Peggy said. She pointed toward *Free Spirit*'s bow. "We should get something stronger on your boat if I'm going to tow her back to Hasty Harbor. There's some line under the foredeck."

"I'll get it," the admiral said. He reached under the deck, found a coil of sturdy nylon line, and handed it to Peggy. Using the length of line she'd already attached to his sailboat, she pulled the boat alongside her own. She secured both boats with the stronger line. Boarding his boat briefly, she lowered the wet sail, draped it over the boom, and lashed it.

Peggy returned to her own boat. "Now, sit amidships on the starboard side," she told the admiral.

He wanted to answer, "Madam, I am not used to taking orders from a woman in the tone you're giving them." But instead he did as he was told, sitting on the starboard cockpit railing, opposite the sail.

Peggy sat again beside the tiller. She undid the line that held *Free Spirit*'s mainsail and played it out. The mainsail and the jib bowed forward, and the tiny convoy began to move.

"We've still got a west wind," Peggy said. "So I'll have to tack to get upriver. By the way, in sailing, to tack means to bring your sails over and start on a new heading. To change course."

"I know what the word means," the admiral said, somewhat defensively. "I know how to sail."

Peggy looked at him.

"What happened back there was an accident," he went on. "I turned to avoid a submerged rock and tipped over."

"There aren't any rocks in that part of the river," Peggy said matter-of-factly. "What you saw was probably some flotsam. Or a floating log."

"The fact is, in my younger days I did a fair amount of sailing. . . . But I guess I've forgotten a few things," he admitted.

He was grateful she said nothing in response. Instead, Peggy leaned out over the side and checked the sails. "Anyway, I think it's time we came about."

"You're the captain. Tell me what I can do."

"When I call 'Ready about,' crouch down in the cockpit, so the boom can swing across you. Then position yourself on the other side. Leave the sail handling to me."

"You can be sure of that."

"All right," Peggy said. "Ready about."

"Ready about," the admiral answered. He lowered himself onto the cockpit floor and kept his head down. Peggy pulled the tiller toward her, bowing her head as the boom swung across them. At once the mainsail and jib billowed out, and *Free Spirit* altered course. The admiral raised himself again, and sat on the opposite side of the cockpit, facing the sail.

From his new vantage, the admiral saw there was a good deal more activity on the water than there had been earlier, and he wondered what those people on the other boats were thinking when they looked at Peggy and himself. Did the two of them appear to be just another older couple on a Sunday cruise? Or with the empty sailboat behind them, was it obvious what had occurred? Were they chuckling that yet another "summer sailor" had mishandled his sailboat and was being ferried ignominiously back to port? The admiral put the questions from his mind.

He leaned back on the rail and felt the warmth of the sun on his face. But his clothing was still sodden, and the brisk wind made him shiver. When he moved his feet inside his shoes he could hear squishing.

"I've still got water in my shoes," he said to Peggy. "Do you mind if I take them off?"

"Be my guest."

He untied the laces and slipped off his shoes, emptying the water out of them over the side of the boat. He set them down on the cockpit floor to dry. But now his feet were cold in his wet socks.

"May I take off my socks too?" he asked her.

"Of course."

He stripped off both socks, and wrung them out, over the side of the boat. When he turned back he found Peggy staring at him. Suddenly she laughed.

"I'm sorry," she apologized. "But you're really a sight."

"I'm sure I am. At least I'm glad the local press took their pictures of me yesterday and not today." He paused. "Speaking of which," he went on, "I owe you an apology. I was wrong to say the things I did at the reception. And you were right to put me in my place."

Now it was she who paused. "Thank you," Peggy managed at last.

"I'm willing to forget the incident," he offered, "if you are."

"Fine with me."

They remained looking at each other in an awkward

silence. It was Peggy who finally spoke. "I think we're ready for another tack. Okay?"

"Ready about?" he asked.

"Ready about."

Again he lowered himself into the cockpit and bowed down his head as she began to bring the sailboat around. The breeze had stiffened further, and *Free Spirit,* even with her extra passenger and the little sailboat in tow, responded briskly.

"By the way," he said after he had raised himself again. "I noticed a small house near the shore a ways back. A white clapboard house. It had a navy flag."

"It's my house," Peggy answered.

"Yours? It's charming."

"Except it needs a paint job. I started today."

"How long will the painters take?"

"I'm doing it myself," she said.

"You *are*?"

"Why not?"

He hesitated momentarily. "No reason you shouldn't. It just seems like a big job."

"I can do it," Peggy told him. It was a simple statement of fact. She leaned out over the side of the sailboat and looked forward. "Listen, do you mind taking the helm? I want to fix the jib."

"Certainly." He moved into her place beside the tiller while she edged forward toward *Free Spirit*'s bow.

As she knelt down to wrestle with the jib, he had the opportunity to study her. It was the old sailor hat that caught his interest. He wondered if there was a story connected with the hat, and if he'd ever have a chance to find out what it was.

"Damn it!" She sat up abruptly. "Sorry, but that jib has been a problem all week."

She edged back along the deck and resumed her place beside the tiller, as he slid around her to the cockpit rail.

"What seems to be the matter?" he inquired.

"Too much slack. I think the turnbuckle on the jib stay needs replacing."

He leaned out also to inspect the jib and nodded to her. "Maybe. But when you're running with the wind, you could at least use a whisker pole and wing out the jib."

Peggy gave the admiral a brief, unanticipated smile. "I guess you do know something about sailboats, at that," she said.

"A bit," he answered. And returned the smile.

It was well past four o'clock when they finally approached the Sawteeth. Following more "ready abouts" than the admiral could count, Peggy arrived at a spot directly outside the entrance to the harbor channel.

"It may be a little tricky getting in," she told him. "The tide is in our favor, but the wind's against us. So I'm going to have to make some close-hauled tacks. Just stay low in the boat and keep your weight to windward."

"Aye-aye," he responded, and ducked down once more.

A short time later *Free Spirit* and the smaller boat were in the harbor and moving rapidly in the direction of the boatyard dock.

"Miss McCoy?" He decided he would ask the question after all.

She gave him an uncertain look.

"Your hat. The sailor hat. It looks like the genuine article. The kind the Navy issued in the war."

"It is," she said. "I got it from a friend."

"Someone in the navy?"

"Yes."

"Was he also in the South Pacific theater?"

Peggy nodded. "It's a long story."

He nodded in return and asked no more about it.

"We're going to be at dockside soon," she said after a

while. "I'll make a tack to starboard and take us in that way."

"Fine," said the admiral. Well practiced by now, he crouched down in the cockpit.

As they neared the floating dock, Peggy came around in a wide C. A minute later her sailboat and then the admiral's eased slowly up against the dock. While the admiral held onto a cleat, Peggy jumped out and secured *Free Spirit*'s forward mooring line.

"I can tie up my boat," he called to her as he too stepped onto the dock.

"Okay," she called back.

He retrieved his shoes and socks from *Free Spirit*'s cockpit and went back to his own boat. At the far end of the dock, beyond *Free Spirit*'s bow, he noticed that the tackle box and pair of fishing poles had been left unattended by the two boys who had been there when he cast off.

The admiral tied his boat to the cleat, then knelt down and joined Peggy as she removed the towline between the two boats.

"Thank you again," he said to her.

She looked surprised. "For what?"

"For rescuing me."

Peggy shrugged. "I couldn't let you drown."

"You know, I've decided to stay in Maine a while longer. Perhaps I could call you and we could get together."

Peggy stood up quickly. "I don't know."

He stood also. "Maybe we could go sailing again."

"I don't know," she repeated. It was apparent she was flustered by the invitation. "I guess if you're around the boatyard here, I'll see you anyway," she said, backing away from him. "Otherwise, I'm pretty busy. I—"

Too late, he saw the tackle box behind her. He tried to call out, but the heel of her left foot hit the box, her right foot struck the poles, and with a small gasp, arms outflung, she pitched backward off the dock.

He sprang forward just as Peggy's head and arms emerged from the water a short way from the dock.

"Help!" she shouted. "Throw me something!"

He grabbed the towline rope and tossed one end of it in her direction. Her hands reached for it but missed.

"The water's freezing! Help me!"

"Hold on!" he shouted down. "I'm coming!" And he plunged into the water after her.

4

"Carnes? Deering here."

Captain Carnes wasn't prepared for the abruptness of the greeting. He had arrived at his office early, and as yet there was no one to screen his calls. So when the office telephone rang at 7:45, he picked it up himself. At the sound of the booming clarion voice, the captain was unable to respond for several moments.

"Carnes—is that you?"

"Yes—yes, Admiral."

"Are you the only one topside at this hour?"

"Yes sir."

"I know it's a bit early, but I assumed you'd be there. I didn't even think. Who knows? I might have gotten one of those female enlisted persons." Then quickly, "Better scratch that remark. I got myself in dutch already for making certain comments about our navy women."

"I understand, sir." Captain Carnes had recovered sufficiently to ease back in his chair. "By the way, how are you enjoying your stay in Maine so far?"

"Very much. Except yesterday I nearly drowned."

"Sir?"

"Not really drowned, you understand. But I went into the drink. I took a small sailboat out of Hasty Harbor into the river and proceeded to capsize."

Images of the admiral splashing about helplessly swept through the captain's mind.

"And can you guess who rescued me?" the admiral asked. "None other than Commander McCoy."

"Peggy McCoy?" Captain Carnes sat upright in his chair.

"I had a very wet tail between my legs on the return trip, I'll tell you that. But then *she* fell into the water and I rescued *her*."

"I don't quite understand."

"Never mind. The point is, I've decided I'd like to take some sailing lessons."

"Under the circumstances, that sounds . . ." Carnes searched for the word. "Appropriate."

"I'm still a damn good sailor, mind you. But I could use a little brushing up. Is there anyone you can suggest who could give me a few private lessons?"

"Well, I know that the local Sea Scouts—"

"For God's sake, Carnes! I don't want lessons from a Boy Scout! Haven't you got somebody on your staff who knows how to sail?"

"I'm sure I have," Carnes said. "I'll check the roster." Just then his eye caught the batch of papers at the corner of his desk. On the top was a request for transfer from Ensign Joseph M. Marino to the U.S. Navy facility in San Diego, California. Good man, Marino, thought the captain. He recalled that Marino had once mentioned something about being head of the sailing team at the naval academy.

"Admiral," the captain said after a moment, "I think I have a young man who can help you."

"I told you, I don't need *help*. I just need to be reminded of the finer points of handling a sailboat. Who is he? Not some old boatswain's mate who's never sailed anything larger than an inner tube."

"No sir. This is a young man, an ensign here. His name is Marino."

"Marino . . ." The admiral seemed to be savoring the sound of it. "Means 'of the sea,' doesn't it? I can't go wrong with that. Send him over."

"Sir?"

"When can he give me my first lesson?"

"I don't know, I'll—"

"How's two o'clock this afternoon?"

"I'll check his schedule," Captain Carnes assured him, reaching for his assignment book. He flipped the pages, cradling the phone between his chin and shoulder. "He's not due for sea duty anytime soon," the captain went on. "I can let you have him."

"Good."

"Where shall he meet you?" Carnes asked. "At your cabin?"

"No. Let's say the boatyard. Dodge's. It's in Hasty Harbor."

"At two o'clock, you said."

"At two. I'll be there," the admiral confirmed. "Marino. 'Of the sea.' I like that. It's a good sign," the admiral added, and hung up.

Peggy made up her mind that she would drive to Whitby early in the day. By nine the temperature was in the seventies and climbing rapidly. There was also a southwest breeze that carried with it tropical humidity, something first-time visitors to Maine believed impossible in such a latitude. By nine fifteen she was on the road and driving north to Whitby, giving little notice to the line of cars and campers headed outbound toward the beaches to escape the heat.

As she drove, Peggy tried not to think about what had happened yesterday. After being pulled out of the water by the admiral, she'd mumbled her embarrassed thanks and hurried home. The truth was that in the days since her encounter with the navy ship, her life had lost the careful order that she prized. She acknowledged to herself she was confused—about the admiral, about what sort of man he really was, about his casual suggestion that they meet again. But mostly, Peggy was confused about herself. Even if his invitation was sincere, and others followed, did she want to put in jeopardy the total structure of her life as a single woman, which she had so carefully created and protected?

Peggy didn't know. So rather than confront the question, she decided she would go to town. Arriving at the major highway, she turned onto it and drove the short distance to the narrow bridge spanning the Newell River. Looking to her left, she saw the sprawling complex of the Whitby Ship Works on the far side of the river. Because it was a weekday and between shifts at the ship works, traffic on the bridge was light. To the right, upriver of the bridge, was the business section of the town of Whitby. Along the riverside there was a small marina serving pleasure craft and a scattering of recently remodeled shops and restaurants, to which tourists flocked. There was also a minuscule theme park, Olde Tyme Whitby, which some residents referred to as a Down East Disneyland. Across the bridge now Peggy saw the central thoroughfare of Whitby. Known as Main Street for several centuries, this year it had been renamed Maine Street by a tourist-conscious board of aldermen. Peggy turned onto Maine Street and found a parking space almost at once. But instead of getting out, she sat in her car for several minutes looking at the stores that were just now opening for the day's shoppers. At the corner nearest her was the Whitby Chandlery, "Provisioners to the Seafarer Since

1848." Beyond it was Crofut's Drug Store, and beyond that Proctor's Five and Ten. But there were new stores, too: a bakery called Patty's Cakes and Baker Man, owned by a pair of former flower children. Beside it was Melissa's Pottery, and beyond that the shop Peggy most enjoyed visiting, Auld Lang Syne, a charming little place crammed full of bric-a-brac and old lace and run by three enterprising young women whose combined ages didn't even total Peggy's own.

The drugstore was her first stop. Lester Crofut was the fourth generation of Crofuts to maintain the business in the same crumbling brick building. Once a week he could be seen polishing the brass trim of the large red and green show globes that hung in the front window. A conversationalist he was not. In fact, his speech was so laconic that he made the typical Maine native sound like a compulsive blabbermouth. At Crofut's, Peggy bought several items from the sundries sections, exchanged a few words—very few—with Lester Crofut, and went out.

On the street again, she saw that all the parking spaces had been filled. Whitby had recently celebrated its three hundredth anniversary, and it still chose to think of itself as a rustic little town immune to the vicissitudes of time. Thus when gridlock struck on a particular Friday afternoon in August several years ago, Whitby and its police department were woefully unprepared. They still were. In the course of this day, Peggy knew, the vehicles of tourists and vacationers would jam the streets, and those few who found a place to park would fill the sidewalks and the shops. Like Peggy, many of the locals tried to do their in-town shopping early and be outbound by eleven at the latest.

Two blocks down the street a sign blinked the time and temperature from the corner of the First National Bank. The time was ten sixteen; the temperature, 84°. The repeated flashing of the figure made Peggy feel that much warmer. Across the street, the Mr. Igloo Ice Cream Shop was already doing a brisk business. She crossed the street and bought an ice cream soda from the open storefront window. To her surprise, the bench outside the store remained unoccupied, so Peggy took it.

As she sat sipping the ice cream soda, she watched the passers-by. Their number was increasing, and they were a disparate assortment: families with young children, local laborers and naval officers, tourists wearing outfits that would probably get them arrested at home, and Whitby businessmen in suits and neckties, arms folded, deep in conversation.

It was then she saw the young woman and the young man. The girl was in her early twenties; a nurse, probably a trainee at the Whitby hospital, wearing her nurse's uniform. The young man was a few years older, sandy-haired, wearing tan chinos and a white short-sleeved summer shirt. They had been walking hand in hand when suddenly they stopped abruptly in the middle of the sidewalk, oblivious to everyone around them, embraced, and shared a deep impassioned kiss. The act was so unexpected and incongruous in the surroundings that Peggy gave a little gasp. After a long moment the young couple parted. They took each other's hands again and continued on along the street.

Perhaps it was their age, the girl's nurse's uniform, the boy's sandy hair. The comparison with her and Tom was inescapable. She and Tom—they had also been very much in love, of course. But times were different then, and lovers wouldn't have considered such a public display of their affections. She and Tom . . . Suppose there'd been no war; suppose instead that she had been in nurse's training here. Suppose Tom had been a local boy. Suppose . . .

But there had been a war. And only she had lived to see it end. Still, suppose . . . But that was many years ago, she told herself again. Today, I am sitting here alone, a woman in my sixties, drinking a vanilla soda and watching my life and the world pass me by.

There was the grinding scrape of brakes. A jitney bus pulled up to the curb in front of her. Peggy checked the time on the bank clock: ten thirty. Every morning at that hour the bus brought elderly men and women from the Whitby Senior Center to the stores in town. Some wag had once called it the Gray-haired Greyhound. An hour later it would return to the same spot, reclaim its passengers with whatever purchases they might have made, and drive back to the senior center. As Peggy watched, the dozen occupants began to file slowly off the bus. Some of the women were in long flowered summer dresses, and many wore large hats. A few of the men, some of them the husbands of the women, sported ties and jackets, even in the heat.

Peggy's attention was particularly caught by a couple well into their eighties moving slowly past her. The man walked with a cane, but otherwise looked "spry," a term Peggy loathed as a description of the elderly. It was the woman whose disability was evident. Short and round, with a cherubic face, she wore dark glasses and a wide-brimmed hat that shielded her eyes. She walked with her head down, and after every four or five steps, she would stop and raise a hand to further shade her eyes. Each time the woman stopped, the man would stop as well. Each time he would take her arm, squeeze it, and gently whisper something in her ear. Then they would set off again for four or five more steps.

Again, suppose. Suppose Tom and I had married, as we promised one another we would. Suppose Tom had lived. Suppose after the war we had come here to Whitby to live our lives together, raising children, sleeping side by side in the big four-poster bed we talked about, flying kites along the beach in summer, waking together in winter to a snowfall, the firs bedecked in white; a thousand seasons passing one into the next, until one day we too were in our eighties. Might we also walk those four or five steps just as they do now, eyes failing, limbs unsteady? But together. Just suppose . . .

The jitney was about to close its doors when Peggy saw another woman. She was small, perhaps in her mid-seventies, and she wore a dress of yellow taffeta. She had been among the passengers aboard the bus, but unlike them she had not moved on along the street. Instead she remained standing just beyond the open bus doors, eyes darting left and right, her breathing quick and shallow, as if paralyzed at having been abandoned in some hostile alien environment.

"Go shopping, Mrs. Peel," the driver called out from inside the bus.

In what seemed a burst of panic, suddenly the woman turned and tried to clamber back aboard the bus. The driver quickly shut the doors halfway, preventing her from getting up the steps.

"No, Mrs. Peel. *No,*" the driver scolded her. "Go *shopping,* Mrs. Peel. I'll be back to pick you up in an hour."

Dutifully the woman stepped back from the bus doors, raising her hands skyward like a suppliant. The doors shuddered closed, the vehicle ground forward into traffic, and drove off.

Arms still upraised, the woman watched the bus until it turned a corner out of sight. When it had finally disappeared, she lowered her arms slowly and uttered a soft moan. A few heads turned toward her, then away. People passing on the sidewalk arced around her with an expression not so much of pity as disdain.

With measured steps, the woman moved across the sidewalk to the window of a jeweler's, where she pressed her hands and face against the glass. Turning once more, she began her slow hegira of the stores along the street. At this one or that—The Toy Chest, Conetti's Deli, Markham's Clothes—the woman stopped and stared in through the open doors and then moved on again.

"Mad. Absolutely bonkers," said a young blond girl on a bicycle to her bearded companion.

"What do you expect?" said the bearded young man beside her, pedaling into the lead. "She's old."

Old.

Until that moment, the word *old* had not been a part of Peggy's lexicon. Yet the specter of that woman, alone, perhaps a victim of dementia or senility, chilled Peggy. More than that, it terrified her totally.

Peggy gulped down the last of her soda, hurried to her car, and drove out of Whitby as swiftly as she could.

At precisely two P.M., the black sedan bearing U.S. Navy insignias on its front doors drove down the narrow road and stopped near the office of Dodge's Boat Yard. At first the admiral was not aware of it. He had arrived several minutes earlier and was standing on the far end of the pier studying the water traffic. He noticed Miss McCoy's sailboat, a tarpaulin covering the cockpit; obviously the boat had not been used today.

It was only when the admiral started back along the pier that he saw the navy car. Knowing Carnes was something of a snob, the admiral assumed the officer Carnes had assigned to help him would probably be some young patrician-looking ROTC lieutenant out of Yale, who, when his service stint was over, would be on his way to Wall Street and The New York Yacht Club. Then he remembered Captain Carnes telling him the fellow's last name was Marino. Italian. Well, the Italians were pretty good sailors, some of them. Although how Columbus thought he could get east by sailing west made the admiral wonder if old Chris hadn't laid in too much vino on the *Santa Maria.*

Thus the admiral was not prepared for the officer who finally stepped out of the navy car. He was young, all right, and Italian. But he was also about five feet five—didn't the service have a height requirement?—with an aureole of black curly hair and a face as round and ruddy as the Neopolitan sun.

For a moment the admiral wondered whether this was a different young man, here on some other business altogether. But when the admiral saw the look of recognition as the officer waved in his direction, he knew this was the one Carnes had sent. The ensign, dressed in his summer white trousers and shirt, carried his cap under his arm. As he approached the admiral he stopped and saluted.

"Admiral Deering? I'm Ensign Marino, sir. Joseph Marino."

The admiral returned the salute and the two men shook hands. "Ensign Marino. I'm pleased to meet you."

"Captain Carnes suggested I might be of some assistance to you, sir."

"Yes, well, I sailed sailboats some years ago," he assured the ensign. "But I'd like to brush up a bit now."

"Yes sir."

"Not that I need a lot of help, you understand. Just pointers mostly."

"Yes sir."

"But since the captain sent you to me, I assume you're a fairly good sailor yourself. More than just boats in the bathtub as a boy, that is."

Joe smiled pleasantly. "Yes sir. I was captain of the sailing team at the academy."

"Where?" The older man looked down at him.

"The United States Naval Academy."

"You're an Annapolis man?"

"Yes sir." Joe smiled again, ignoring the look of uncertainty that lingered on the admiral's face. "Just as you are, sir. You're still remembered there with fondness."

Admiral Deering appraised the young man for some moments. Then he smiled in return. "Remembered the way Old Ironsides is, I'll bet."

"I heard you were called 'Daring Deering' then. But I never learned the reason why."

He noticed Joe's inquiring look and shrugged. "Never mind. I'll tell you the story sometime. But right now, let's limber up our sea legs and get out there on the water."

"Fine. I'll—" But the admiral had already turned and was walking toward the ramp down to the floating dock. "Should I rent us a boat?" Joe called, starting after him.

"No," the admiral said over his shoulder. "I've already done that. Got the boat I rented yesterday."

Joe approached the ramp—and came to a sudden halt. He looked down. On the far side of the floating dock a Melody class sailboat was raising her jib and beginning to cast off. But it was not the sailboat that Joe was watching.

Standing on the dock and waving to the Melody was a tall blond girl with the most captivating back view he could remember in a long, long time. Her hair hung halfway to her waist and the pink T-shirt she was wearing above cut-off jeans clung to her back with perspiration. Her bare tanned legs were long, slender, and exquisitely shaped.

Joe admitted to himself that abstinence was getting to him. He had sworn off the Whitby town girls who hung around the ship works after an embarrassing incident in which one girl had shredded the upholstery of the backseat of his car. But this girl was something else.

She turned to give a last wave to the departing sailboat. Joe saw her profile and decided this girl was better than good, she was fantastic. Like the Melody, she had great lines fore and aft. As yet, she was probably untried in heavy weather, but the potential for speed was definitely there. And my oh my, the way she trimmed her sails.

At that moment the admiral approached her, and she turned again to face him. Joe started down the ramp, covering it in three broad strides, and crossed the dock to join them.

The admiral gestured as Joe came up. "Miss Dodge, this is Ensign Marino from the navy unit at the ship works."

Sarah looked at Joe. She gave a neutral nod, but neither spoke. She was a full two inches taller than he was, but Joe was used to that and it didn't bother him. He smiled and returned the nod.

"Pleased to meet you, ma'am," he said.

"And this is Miss Dodge," the admiral went on. "She was very helpful to me yesterday when I rented my sailboat."

"Oh?" Joe asked pleasantly. "What kind of boat was it?"

The question was addressed to Sarah, but the admiral pointed to the small blue sailboat tied up at the dock nearby. "It's that one."

Joe looked down at the boat and frowned. "Talk about bathtub boats," he said.

"It's a Cape Cod Baby Knockabout," Sarah told him. "Lots of our beginners use them."

"But the admiral isn't a beginner," Joe said, looking at the man. "I'm sure he can handle something bigger and a little more sophisticated. Am I right, sir?"

"Yes. Well, yes, of course." The admiral cleared his throat.

"I'll see what else we have." Now it was Sarah who frowned. She turned abruptly and walked toward the ramp.

"I hope that's all right with you, sir," Joe asked. "That is, that we get another boat."

"Yes, fine." The older man was quick to nod.

"I mean, you could capsize in a little boat like that."

"Exactly. A bigger boat is better. Safer. It's a good idea." The admiral was beginning to think that Captain Carnes had made the right decision sending this young fellow.

Sarah appeared at the top of the ramp and called down to them, "There's a Lightning available." She looked directly at Joe, asking with a touch of sarcasm, "Will that be acceptable to you—Ensign Marino?"

Joe smiled up at her ingenuously. "Yeah. Sure. A Lightning is fine. Thank you very much—Miss Dodge."

"One of the boys will bring it around," she announced. Joe was about to thank her again, but she had already turned her back and started off.

A few minutes later, a blue nineteen-foot Lightning class sailboat was delivered to the floating dock by a teenage boy. While the boy secured it to the dock, Joe looked over the boat, pulling at this line and that and testing the action on the tiller.

"Is she seaworthy?" the admiral asked, watching him.

"Shipshape," Joe declared. "But first, let me get my orders straight. I'm told you're not a novice sailor. Around sailboats, I mean."

"I know my boom vang from my cringle," the admiral assured him.

"Okay. You're not a novice. How about a cruise?"

"Let's go." The admiral began to step from the dock onto the stern of the boat.

"Stop!" Joe called to him.

"I beg your pardon?" Sheepishly, the admiral stepped back onto the dock.

"Rule one of lesson one," Joe said. "Always board a small boat near the center." Joe knelt near the stern of the sailboat and tapped the flat deck area with his hand. "This area is meant for sitting on when you're at the helm. The nearer the center you put your weight, the more stable the boat will be."

"You're right. I'm sorry." The admiral was visibly chagrinned. "I guess I wasn't thinking." Cautiously, he stepped into the center of the sailboat.

"Good," said Joe. "Now have a seat beside the tiller, and I'll settle in amidships."

As the admiral moved to the stern, Joe climbed aboard and sat down on the starboard side, bracing his legs against the centerboard trunk. Once seated, he reached under the foredeck and brought out two life vests, one of which he offered to the admiral.

"Better put this on," Joe said. "Can you imagine what the navy would do to me if I lost one of their admirals at sea? I'd be in the brig for a hundred years."

The older man shook his head. "For losing a retired admiral it's only fifty years."

They donned the life vests, and the teenage boy who had been standing by helped them cast off. Joe checked the telltale for the direction of the wind.

"Southwest," the young man said. "We'll practice some maneuvers after we get out into the river. So let's take a port tack toward that shed." Joe pointed to an abandoned fishing shed on the far side of the harbor.

The admiral obviously disagreed. "If we're going to the river, then I'd say a starboard tack—"

"Sir," Joe interrupted him, one hand raised. "Sir, you requested someone to provide you with some 'brushup' sailing lessons. I have been given that assignment, as you know. You also know there can be only one captain of a ship. I don't outrank you, but right now, I *am* your instructor." Joe felt awkward suddenly, addressing the much older man as if he were a plebe.

Joe hesitated, then went on. "So I'd like your heading to be a port tack in the direction of that shed. We're going to tack a dozen times before we leave the harbor."

"Yes sir." The admiral's answer was immediate, spontaneous and natural. And it surprised them both. They stared at one another for an instant; in the next, they laughed.

"Port tack as you ordered—*sir,*" the older man added, snapping off a crisp salute. He swung the tiller over, the boat came about in answer, and the sail filled.

It was the window trim that took the time. Throughout the afternoon Peggy had maintained a steady pace, spreading the white paint across the long wide clapboard siding of the west wall of her house. But it was when she started on the trim around the bedroom windows that her efforts slowed. Still, she was pleased she'd accomplished as much as she had. The day had remained hot, and several times she'd wished that she had spent it on the water. But after the incident of yesterday, she was embarrassed to put in an appearance at the boatyard. Maybe she would sail tomorrow, if it didn't rain.

She stepped down off the ladder and examined all that she had done. Near the peak of the roof, above the windows, Peggy saw a spot she'd missed. It would have to wait. Already, clouds were building, and the rain, in fact, would probably arrive tonight.

Peggy set the paint can on the ground and lifted the ladder away from the house, laying it flat across the lawn. She replaced the lid on the paint can, washed the brush under the garden hose, and put both the can and the brush in the storage cabinet beneath the deck. Coming back up to the lawn, she noticed spots of white paint mottling her hands, and she used the garden hose again to wash them off. But her success was limited, and she admitted to herself that only the scrub brush at the kitchen sink would do the job.

She went up the steps to the front door, started across the living room, and was halfway to the kitchen when she stopped. What startled her had been the ticking of the brass ship's clock above the chest. It was louder than she had ever heard before. The clock chimed four bells—six o'clock—and went on ticking. She took a deep breath, and another. Although the front door was wide open, and the windows, Peggy felt as if she were about to suffocate; the living room oppressed her like a tomb.

Peggy hurried to the kitchen sink and scrubbed vigorously at the paint spots on her hands. After drying them, she reached up and took a half empty bottle of white wine out of the cupboard above the sink. It was rare that she had wine before her dinner, but she frankly felt that it might help to calm her nerves. She poured a glass and tasted it. The wine was sour; the wine bottle had sat open for too long. Peggy poured it all down the sink.

Looking out the kitchen window, she saw for the first time the wall of fog several miles out to sea, fusing seamlessly with the gray water. There was nothing left to do, Peggy thought, but have an early dinner, get a book, and go to bed.

She turned to the refrigerator, opened the freezer compartment, and took out a packaged frozen dinner. The contents were some sort of beef concoction in a glutinous brown sauce, flash-frozen in a plastic boil-a-bag. When cooked, it would resemble something more medical than edible.

Peggy tossed the box back into the freezer, went to the telephone, and dialed.

After a few rings, Sarah came on the line. "Hello, Dodge's Boat Yard."

"Sarah, I'm glad you're still there. It's me, Peggy." She pulled up the kitchen stool and sat down.

"Hi, Peg. What's up?" the girl asked.

"Listen, how about having dinner tonight? Here at my house. I'd say we go up to Solly's or somewhere, but the knee I fell on is giving me a little trouble. What do you say?"

"Peg—"

"It's spur of the moment, I know. But I've got some spaghetti I can do up, and I'll fix a salad. I thought—"

"I can't tonight," Sarah interrupted.

"If it's the mud flats and your clams, then at least stop on your way back. How's that?"

"Peg, is something wrong?"

The question surprised Peggy. "Wrong? Why should anything be wrong? I just get bored sometimes with eating dinners by myself and talking back to TV anchormen."

"I just wondered."

"Nothing's wrong," the older woman said.

"I'm really sorry, Peg. But tonight I have to go to Portland."

"Portland? Don't tell me you've got a date."

"It's not that."

"Thank God," Peggy sighed. "I was afraid one of the Fister boys finally shaved and asked you out."

"Actually, there's a marine biologist from Woods Hole who I'm going to hear. He's speaking at the university extension."

"Is he an expert on clams too?"

"Kelp," Sarah said. "He spent a year in the Sargasso Sea."

"Sounds like a million laughs."

"Really, Peggy, I am sorry about tonight. Maybe I can stop by tomorrow night, if you're home."

"*If* I'm home. Nights I'm always home. I don't even have a good kelp man to keep me company."

"I better go. I'll talk to you tomorrow, Peg."

"Whenever," Peggy said.

"But thanks for the invitation, anyway."

"You bet."

Peggy heard the phone click.

In the living room, the wall clock chimed again and went on ticking.

* * *

That afternoon, on a momentary impulse, the admiral had bought himself a small club steak at the general store in Hasty Harbor. Now it smoked and sizzled in the frying pan. To one side of the sink, a lettuce and tomato salad was heaped in a red plastic bowl. He added oil and a touch of vinegar and threw on a dash of pepper. He checked the oven timer. Another few minutes and the baked potato would be done.

As he waited, he looked out the window facing him and saw that fog had begun to obscure the more distant cabins and the tall pines surrounding them. Before he'd left the boatyard late that afternoon, he'd heard there would be rain tonight. The admiral hoped not; he had enjoyed his first sail with the young officer Carnes had sent. Marino of the Sea. The young fellow had turned out to be a skillful sailor. The admiral even admitted Joe had taught him several things about sail handling today that he'd never known. Besides, he liked the ensign's sharp intelligence and offhand manner. Yes, he hoped the two of them could sail in the morning as they'd planned.

The oven timer rang. The admiral speared the club steak with a fork, watched briefly as the crimson juices oozed out, and put it on a plate. He opened the oven door with a towel and grabbed the baked potato, which he put beside the steak. Then he carried the plate and the salad bowl to the small table in the living room and set them down.

On the table next to the stained rattan place mat stood a bottle of red wine, also from the store in Hasty Harbor. It would hardly win a sommelier's medallion, he was sure, but it was the only wine they had. He had bought it when he bought the steak, after deciding to make tonight's dinner a festive event, even if he was the lone celebrant. The wine bottle had a screw cap, which diminished its distinction further, but the admiral twisted off the cap and poured the wine into a small jelly glass, the closest thing to a wineglass he could find.

He raised the glass and began, "Here's to . . ." and could not think of anything to toast. In fact, looking at the upraised glass, he felt absurd. He lowered the glass and took a sip. The wine was better than he had anticipated, and he sipped again.

Suddenly, memories came flooding back of the last anniversary, their forty-fifth, that he and Grace had shared. She had insisted on preparing the dinner herself and had set the table with their finest china plates and silver service, plus two Baccarat crystal goblets remaining from the set they had received from Grace's uncle on their wedding day. The wine that night had been a red as well; an exquisite cabernet for which he'd paid an outrageous price. It had been just the two of them, and with the candles lit he had proposed a toast "to the most wonderful woman in my life; the one who *is* my life."

Well, her life had reached its end four years ago, four years ago last May, to be exact. And since then, he had gone on alone, all the days and nights that followed. How many mornings had he wakened with the knowledge that the pillow next to his was empty and unmarked? How many more meals, like this one, would he eat alone? At least at home in Maryland he could divert his mind by watching television, or skimming the newspaper while he ate, or feeding table scraps to his pet bulldog Halsey. But the cabin was without a television set, he had no newspaper, and Halsey was spending his own vacation in a kennel on the Chesapeake.

Enough of memories, the admiral thought. The steak was probably getting cold. When he bit into it, he discovered he was right. He ate his dinner quickly, drank a second glass of wine, and carried the empty plate and utensils to the kitchenette.

As he washed them, he looked out the window again at

the other cabins. In front of one a boy about three years old was hopping from foot to foot, seemingly delighted with his solitary game. The child was a towhead, his blond hair bouncing on his forehead as he hopped. How much the boy looked like Chip at that age, the old man thought.

The admiral returned to the table, poured himself another glass of wine, and sat down on the couch. He looked at the open front door of the cabin. Darkness had come quickly with the fog. Beyond the door, beyond the screen, he could see almost nothing now.

Here I am, a man in his seventies, he thought. Is that what I await, to face the dark alone? And yet tonight there didn't seem to be much more that life promised him. For more than four years he had been a widower. When Grace had died that bright spring morning, his grief, at first, had been ameliorated by relief, relief for her sake that her wasting illness and her pain no longer drained the spirit from her. But there had been relief also for himself. His servitude on her behalf was finally done. No longer did he have to cook her meals, no longer did he have to bathe her on the days between the hired nurse's visits, no longer did he have to constantly display a dogged optimism in her company, when they both knew the truth with hopeless certainty.

In the days soon after she had died, he'd found comfort in solitude. He had felt a void in his life, of course. But he knew he could not fill it with the solicitous attentions of well-meaning friends. Neither could he abide it when some of those friends would trot out so-called "eligible ladies" for his inspection—widows, spinsters, and divorcées—as if they were brood mares at a horse auction. He would have none of it, although he knew he had offended more than one acquaintance by his refusal to be "sociable" at their behest. At the same time, he admitted, he had rediscovered a streak of independence he had not known since his teens. He could sleep late for the first time in many years, though he rarely did, see just those few friends he wished to see, and travel wherever and whenever the mood struck him, despite Halsey's anxious whining when the dog was dropped off at the kennel door. The admiral's modest reputation as "The Father of Modern Naval Communications" brought him just enough celebrity to keep his ego stirred.

Still, it was at times like this when the solitariness with which he led his life seemed threadbare, even pitiable. Was "solitude" actually a euphemism for loneliness? Was his freedom not much more than shallow self-indulgence?

Some people could deal with their loneliness, he decided. Like that McCoy woman. But, of course, she'd never married. Marriage changed things. She had never loved and lost in the same way as he had. Oh, maybe there had been a few romances in her life, especially in the South Pacific during wartime, where men probably outnumbered women five hundred to one. But that was not the same as being married almost fifty years.

The admiral stood up, drained the jelly glass, and shook his head. What the devil was he thinking about *her* for anyway? He'd suggested that they see one another again. But that was yesterday. And the invitation had been totally spontaneous, out of gratitude that she had rescued him.

Well, yes, she'd sparked his interest for a while, it was true. But maybe it was really just his curiosity that kept her on his mind. Or was it glands, even at his age?

He went to the sink, carrying the wine bottle and the glass. He looked at them, thought about a refill, then thought otherwise. He put the bottle in the cupboard, washed the jelly glass, and left it in the dish rack.

All right, he would probably see her at the boatyard sometime. Maybe they could have a lobster roll and a soda on the Hasty Harbor pier. That would be fine. But as for dinner, that was something else. The next time he saw her he'd be cautious, circumspect. In a week he would be gone

from here. To get her hopes up—and his own—would be unfair.

And yet . . . and yet she had affected him as no other woman in his life had done since Grace.

In a flash he realized it: that was the word he associated with her—*life*. Sass and substance, he had called it. Spunk.

As he went back into the living room, his eye fell on the dog-earred phone book and the telephone on the upended lobster trap that served as an end table. He opened the book and thumbed through the pages. McClanahan, McCormack, McCosherty, McCourt . . .

The ringing of the bedside telephone cut steadily into Peggy's sleep. When she was finally awake enough to comprehend the sound, she reached for the phone and in so doing knocked over the alarm clock, which fell onto the floor.

Peggy found the receiver, put it to her ear, and mumbled a hello.

"Commander McCoy?" said the male voice at the other end.

"Who is this?"

"Charles Deering."

"Who?"

"Charles Deering. Did I wake you?"

"Do you know what time it is?" She looked for
and remembered she had knocked it onto the

"It's nine o'clock. And I *did* wake you. I ap

Peggy lay back on her pillow and said n
surprise, she found that she was less angr
she should be.

"Hello? Are you still there?" he inq

"What do you want?" she asked fi

"Well, it occurred to me I really d
for rescuing me."

"What?"

“Yesterday, at sea.”

“Oh, that. You’re welcome. But you also rescued me. Listen, I’d like to go back to sleep, if you don’t mind. I spent most of the afternoon painting my house.”

“What color?”

“Huh?”

“What color are you painting it?” he asked. “White again?”

“Yes. Why?”

“If you’d like help, I’ll get some paint in Whitby and come down.”

“I thought you were here on vacation.”

“I am,” he assured her. “But I thought I could do something for you. For the help you gave me yesterday.”

Peggy was about to tell him he could help her most by hanging up the phone. But she did not. For a reason that she didn’t understand, she was glad their conversation had continued.

“That’s okay,” she told him. “I’m doing it myself. But thanks anyway.”

“Dinner then?”

“What?”

“I would very much enjoy taking you to dinner. There’s a place in Whitby I’ve heard recommended. Galahad’s.”

“I’ve been there a few times.”

“I gather it’s a favorite of the navy personnel at the shipyard. So I trust they could probably handle a couple of ld salts like us. Tomorrow night? What do you say?”

“No.” Peggy said at once. “I can’t.”

“Day after tomorrow, then.”

aybe she was sleepier than she had realized, but for tever reason, after pausing a moment, Peggy an- ed yes.

d I hear you correctly?” he asked. “Yes?”

.”

"That's splendid!" His voice was ebullient. "Shall we say, I'll pick you up at seven."

"Fine."

"Lonely Point Road. Is that right?"

"Yes," she said again.

"I'll see you then. Good night."

"Good night," she said. She hung up the phone. But she did not let go of the receiver. And in the darkness of her room, she repeated, "Yes."

5

The rain began at midnight and continued on throughout the day, a cool, soaking rain with gusty winds that gave a feeling more of late September than July. The beaches were deserted, except for those few runners who appeared to relish such conditions. The town of Whitby, on the other hand, was crowded with adult vacationers, who could do little else that day but shop. The Whitby Cinema was also packed at every showing of a film called *Devil Board,* a teenage horror movie featuring a skateboard that possessed demonic powers.

Denied an opportunity to sail as he'd hoped to do, the admiral amused himself by keeping a small fire going in the cabin's fireplace and finishing a paperback detective novel he'd brought with him on the flight to Maine.

As for Peggy, she stocked up with a week's supply of groceries from the supermarket outside Whitby. In the afternoon she cleaned and dusted her house thoroughly and wrote a letter to her woman friend in Florida. Toward dinnertime she thought of calling Sarah and reissuing the invitation of last night. But with the bad weather she was certain Sarah had decided against visiting the mud flats and her clams. So Peggy ate alone.

Before dawn the next day, the rain ended, promising a dry and brighter morning and a brisk breeze from the north. The admiral and Joe had rescheduled their sail for nine thirty. But the young man arrived at Dodge's Boat Yard half an hour early. During the night Joe had suddenly remembered he had neglected to replace the tarpaulin cover on the sailboat's cockpit, and the boat would certainly need bailing out.

Joe parked the navy car to one side of the boatyard road and got out. He had gone halfway across the pier when it occurred to him: Sarah just might be in the office now, he thought. He went over to the office door and opened it.

He called out, "Hello? Anybody home?"

Joe heard movement from the back, then footsteps. He removed his officer's cap and waited, smiling.

"Morning," Noah Dodge said as he appeared. He came forward and moved in behind the office desk. "Something I can do?"

"Yes sir. I'm Ensign Marino. From the navy unit at the ship works."

Noah nodded. "You're the one I heard about." The man removed a pair of half-glasses from the pocket of his shirt, put them on, and studied Joe for several moments, saying nothing. He took off the glasses, folded them, and stuck them back in his pocket. "You're the one who's giving sailing lessons to the admiral," he said. "My daughter told me."

"Yes sir, that's right."

"I'll get one of the boys to bring the boat around. Which one is it?"

"A blue Lightning." Joe took out a piece of paper and consulted it. "M-E, six three four eight. It's the one without the canvas tarp," he added sheepishly. "I guess I'll have to do some bailing."

"I guess so," Noah said.

Noah started for the door; Joe followed. "By the way," Joe said, "the admiral and I really appreciated your daughter's help yesterday."

"I'll tell her."

"For that matter, I can tell her myself. Is she around?"

"Nope."

"I see," Joe answered. He said nothing more.

Noah studied Joe again. "I'll see about your boat," he told Joe, and went out the door.

At nine thirty Joe finally finished emptying the sailboat of the accumulated rainwater. He put the plastic bailing bucket on the dock and stood up to ease his back.

"Too bad you didn't have a bilge pump," the admiral called to him from the pier. Joe looked up. The admiral was dressed in a seafarer's yellow slicker and a sou'wester hat that reminded Joe of pictures of the Gloucester fisherman.

"It was my own fault," Joe said. "I forgot to put the tarp on when we left the other day."

"Just remember, for sailors rain is only seawater in another form." The admiral strode down the ramp to the floating dock. "Besides, what would my instructor have done if I'd skipped a lesson because of a little water in the bilge?"

"Probably have you court-martialed." Joe smiled. "Or at least, threaten you with disciplinary action."

"Wouldn't be the first time," the admiral said. "Of course, that was when I was a plebe at the academy. Another fellow and myself were dressed down for dressing up the statue of Admiral Farragut in a pink tutu."

"I'll bet old Davy looked good in pink."

"I thought so. But my superiors thought otherwise."

The admiral clapped his palms together. "So. What are we practicing today? I feel in a splendid mood."

"I thought we'd concentrate on some short tacking work right here in the harbor. Then maybe we'll go out into the river."

"Fine. Let me get out of this costume. I wore it just in case it rained again. But I trust that it won't."

Joe began to raise the sail while the admiral removed the slicker and hat and returned them to his car.

"Tell me," he said when he rejoined Joe, "do you know a restaurant in Whitby by the name of Galahad's?"

"Sure. I've been there a few times."

"With a girl?" the admiral asked.

Joe looked surprised. "Yes, as a matter of fact."

"Is it romantic? Candles and checkered tablecloths? That sort of thing?"

"Candles, yes, checkered tablecloths, no. If the weather is nice, there's a little garden room in back. There are tables in the bar, too, and the bartender is a *zaftig* blonde named Cheryl. Great bazooms. It's worth ordering martinis just to watch her shake 'em. The martinis, that is."

"But it's still the kind of place you can take a lady?" asked the admiral.

Joe nodded. "Not a lot of tourists go there," he said. "Mostly navy men and some of the better locals. I'd recommend it."

"Good. That's where I plan to take my date." The admiral beamed.

"You have a date?"

"Does the idea strike you as impossible?"

"Not at all." Joe hesitated. "I didn't think—I mean, you've only been here a few days. And I thought you'd stayed on in Maine to sort of just relax."

"I did," the admiral said. "But relaxation can take different forms. Don't worry. The lady in question is not one of the town girls. I'll leave them to you."

"You certainly work fast," Joe said. "And I'm glad to hear it's not one of the town bimbos either."

The admiral laughed. "This woman is hardly what you'd call a bimbo."

"When is your date?"

"Tonight."

"Man, you *do* work fast." There was admiration in Joe's voice. "Maybe someday you can take her sailing and impress her with your seamanship."

"I have a feeling that my seamanship is the *last* thing that would impress her," the admiral said, and laughed again.

It was just after noon when the Lightning made a sharp tack to starboard, slowed, and gently glided in against the fenders of the floating dock. The admiral released his grip on the tiller and allowed the sail to go slack.

"Neat," Joe told him. "Neat and clean." He leapt out of the sailboat and began securing a line to a mooring cleat.

"Thank you," said the admiral. "I thought I did fairly well myself."

"You should. You were good out there. It was a good lesson."

"Better than you would have thought for an old man?" the admiral asked Joe, an eyebrow raised.

"Age has nothing to do with it. People in their seventies still circumnavigate the globe."

"I'll pass on that particular adventure, thanks." The admiral started to remove his life vest. "On the other hand, maybe I should think about joining the navy."

"What? And see the world?" Joe stood and removed his own life vest. "The fact is, the navy's not all it's cracked up to be. The pay's not great, the food is so-so, and as for seeing the world, look how far it's got me. Hasty Harbor, Maine."

The admiral looked around. "You're right. Hasty Harbor is not your most exotic port of call."

"But there is something I would like you to do," Joe told him. "Keep a log."

"A ship's log?"

"Sort of. Make an entry every day after you've had a lesson, while it's still fresh in your mind. Get a notebook or a writing pad, and after every sail put down the date, the weather and the sea conditions, and what the subject of the lesson was. Then write down the things that you did well, and what areas you think you need to work on. The log is for your benefit. I won't ask to see it."

"Sounds like a good idea. I'll start this afternoon." The admiral stepped out of the boat gingerly and began securing the stern line to a piling. When that was done, he looked down at the boat for several minutes.

"I just realized something," he said finally. "This boat doesn't have a name."

"So? It's got a number."

"No, no; it's not the same. A ship without a name is like a person without a name. A name gives a ship personality and character."

"Then let's find one. We'll hold a christening ceremony." Joe seemed amused at the idea.

"Just what I was thinking."

"What?"

"I'm serious. Wait here." The admiral crossed the dock and started up the ramp. He spotted Sarah on the pier and called to her. "Miss Dodge, may I speak with you a minute?"

Sarah turned in his direction, as did the half dozen other people on the pier.

"Miss Dodge, I'd like to give my boat—that is, *your* boat—a name. I'd like to hold a little christening. Is that all right?"

The girl looked at him uncertainly. "I guess so."

"Then come down to the dock and be a witness, will you? It'll make it more official."

"Sure."

The admiral nodded his gratitude and started down the ramp, with Sarah following. The people on the pier moved closer to the edge, their curiosity aroused.

Admiral Deering approached the sailboat and took up a position opposite the bow. He beckoned to Joe and Sarah. "You two. Step up, please." Dutifully the two moved nearer to each other and to him.

The admiral lifted his hands. "Ladies and gentlemen, I'll make this short and sweet. Just as every child is provided with a name at baptism, so should every ship be given one, to sanctify her and protect her as she ventures forth across the sea of life."

Out of the corner of his eye, Joe caught a glimpse of the people on the pier above. They stood with heads bowed as if in prayer.

"Therefore," the admiral went on, "I christen this ship—"

"Wait a second!" a voice on the pier called down. "Aren't you gonna break a bottle of champagne over the bow?" The other spectators glared over at the speaker, a young man in denim shorts and sunglasses.

"Can you provide us with some champagne to use for the occasion?" the admiral shot back.

The young man looked embarrassed, and shook his head. "I got a six-pack of Miller in the car," he offered meekly.

The admiral snorted. "Beer? This ship deserves more respect than that."

"I've got a wine cooler," a young woman on the pier volunteered.

The admiral considered it. "Yes. Wine will be acceptable," he said.

The young woman opened the picnic hamper she was carrying and took out a small green bottle, which she tossed down to the admiral.

He caught it. He turned to Sarah and extended the bottle to her. "Miss Dodge, will you do the honors?"

"Me?" Sarah looked nonplussed.

"Please. And don't worry," he assured her. "Just open the top and pour the contents on the bow. We don't want to destroy the boatyard property by smashing up your boats."

Sarah stepped forward and poured the liquid from the bottle over the foredeck of the boat.

As she did, the admiral intoned, "I christen this ship the—let's see, the *Invincible*. And may fair winds forever fill her sails."

Applause from the spectators was enthusiastic and immediate. The admiral raised his hands above his head again, acknowledging his audience. Looking at him, Joe thought, If this guy had gone into politics or the priesthood, he'd be president or Pope by now.

"Thank you. Thanks to you all," the admiral went on. "And thank you, Miss Dodge," he said to Sarah. "Is this your first christening?"

"Yes. Yes sir." Sarah blushed.

"Then it will give you practice for future christenings, of the beautiful children you will have." He gave her a paternal pat, and Sarah went on blushing.

The people on the pier had begun to drift off. The admiral turned to Joe and Sarah. "Nice little ceremony, don't you think?"

"It was wonderful," Sarah said.

"Until tomorrow then," he said to Joe. "What time would you like to make our lesson?"

"How's ten o'clock?

"I'd prefer eleven." The admiral winked. "Remember, I have a hot date tonight."

"Eleven it is." Joe agreed.

The admiral looked down at the sailboat once more.

"*Invincible,*" he repeated to himself. "I like that name." With that, he turned and started up the ramp.

"He's a great guy," Joe said to Sarah as the admiral disappeared across the pier.

"And a real gentleman," she added. Sarah started toward the ramp with Joe behind her.

"He told me he's really enjoying his stay in Maine," Joe said.

"Good. I'm glad."

"Besides, he's learning that there's more to Maine than trees and rocks."

"Oh?" Sarah said. She kept on walking.

"I mean, he's got a date tonight. You heard him."

"Then she's a very lucky woman." Sarah continued toward the office.

Joe strode to keep up with her. "Listen, sailors are great people. Especially on dates. But you should find out for yourself."

Sarah stopped and looked at him evenly. "What's that supposed to mean?"

"That we should go out tonight. Us. You and me."

"You get right to the point, don't you, Ensign?"

"Yep. *Carpe diem,*" Joe said. "It's an old Italian saying."

"Sorry," Sarah told him. "But tonight I'm writing about clams."

"I beg your pardon?"

"I'm studying clams for my senior thesis in marine biology. There's a clam bed down past Lonely Point where I'm doing some research."

"You mean you dig them up?" he asked her.

"Sometimes."

"Hey, I dig clams too. Especially deep-fried, with tartar sauce." He saw at once that the joke had fallen flat. "I only meant—"

"Excuse me, Ensign. But today's a busy day. Bye." Sarah turned again and walked away.

Joe watched her disappear into the boatyard office and thought, She's a tight one, she is. Very tight. No wonder she likes clams.

He headed slowly to the navy car and got into it. Clams, he repeated to himself, as he drove up the boatyard road. They're hunks of rock pretending to be animals. Who wants to study *clams*?

He paused before the stop sign at the turnaround and looked across at Dabney's Store. So this is the place Sarah Dodge calls home, he thought, the center of her universe—Hasty Harbor, Maine; population, four hundred and something; stimulation, zilch. Granted, in the summer the village had a quaint provincial charm. But what sort of life could it offer anyone like Sarah if she stayed there? To continue working in her father's boatyard? To pursue a Ph.D. in clams? What did she want to *do* with her life, anyway?

Joe admitted he didn't know the answers to those questions. But at that moment he decided that if he accomplished nothing else that summer, he would make it his business to find out.

Peggy had sailed early in the afternoon; that left her several hours to continue with her painting of the house. By five o'clock she had completed a major portion of the south-facing wall. When she was done she went to the kitchen and poured herself a large glass of iced tea from the pitcher she had made that morning. She had just taken a sip when she heard a tapping on the glass doors of the deck.

She listened. There was a loud squawk, followed by more tapping.

"Take it easy, Bligh!" she called out. "Don't break your beak on my door!" Peggy opened the refrigerator, found a loaf of bread in a plastic bag, and headed for the deck. At the sight of her the gull let out a piercing shriek and flapped his wings.

She slid the doors open and stepped onto the deck. Captain Bligh backed up several steps to give her room. Peggy reached into the bag and took out a slice. She knelt down to tear the slice into smaller pieces when the gull lunged forward, snatched it with its beak, and swallowed the slice whole.

Peggy stood up. "What a greedy bird you are! If you knew the price of bread these days, you'd take your time before you ate it all."

The seagull gagged briefly and opened his beak, ready for another slice at once. Peggy held it out of the gull's reach as she began to tear it up.

"Listen, Bligh. I have some news for you. Tonight, I have a date."

The gull stared at her.

"But maybe you'll only understand it better in bird terms," she added. "I'll explain." She tossed out a small piece of bread, which the gull caught in midair.

"A date is when two birds who aren't mated get together for a little fun. Usually, the male bird, all preened, flies over to the female bird's perch. Maybe he even gives her a quick peck with his beak, if she allows it. Then they fly off to some birdfeeder in the neighborhood to eat seeds and to chatter. Of course, all the time the lady bird keeps wondering if what the male bird really has in mind is to get her into some soft, feathery nest somewhere and do what birds as well as bees are famous for."

Peggy continued to tear up the slice of bread. "Don't worry, though. That's not going to happen tonight. For old birds like the admiral and me, our tail feathers molted long ago."

She threw a handful of bread pieces out across the deck; the seagull skipped among them, devouring one after another.

Peggy leaned against the railing of the deck and closed the bag of bread. "So what do you think of that? Of me having a date."

The gull gazed up at her, gave a muted squawk, and deposited a sizable amount of guano on the deck.

Peggy paused. "I knew I could count on you to say just the right thing." She clapped her hands and waved both arms; the gull jumped, wheeled, and took flight.

"And don't come back until you learn some manners!" she shouted after him. But the bird had already disappeared beyond the trees.

Peggy returned to the kitchen. She was about to put some more ice in her tea, when something caught her eye.

Pulling into her driveway was a lengthy yellow Cadillac. Peggy sighed. Only one person on the peninsula had a car like that. As she watched, the door on the driver's side opened slowly. Lower legs the size of Prestologs emerged, and after some effort so did the rest of Mrs. Ernestine Doberman. Besides being the widow of the cannery owner, she was Hasty Harbor's richest citizen and the doyenne of town society. Despite her size, however, she considered herself a blithe spirit who sought, in her words, to "reach out and embrace the world." But to those thus embraced, her grip was more like a half nelson. Her fatuous manner irked Peggy no end, and once trapped by her there was almost no way to escape.

As the woman stood adjusting her foundation garments, Peggy thought of fleeing to her bedroom and pretending that she wasn't home. But she was sure that Mrs. Doberman would enter the house anyway and go from room to room in search of her.

Finally, Mrs. Doberman walked up the path and up the front steps to the house. She paused to catch her breath, then leaned in at the screen and warbled "Yoo-hoo!" in a singsong voice. Getting no response, she opened the screen door, planted one foot over the threshold, and again called out "Yoo-hoo!"

"I'm here, Ernestine," Peggy said, coming into the living room. "And would you please shut the screen? You're letting in the bugs."

"You *are* here!" Mrs. Doberman enthused. She was wearing a lavender sundress that hugged her figure like a sausage casing. She came into the room, leaving the screen door open.

"You know, it's been *so* long since I've been inside your little house," the woman said, studying every corner.

"I know," said Peggy. She went and closed the screen.

"It's charming, really. May I sit?" Before Peggy could reply, Mrs. Doberman had sunk onto the sofa.

"I'll get us some iced tea," Peggy said, and hurried to the kitchen. When she returned, Mrs. Doberman was continuing to scrutinize the details of the room.

"So quaint," the woman said. "And that little toy boat there." She pointed to a model of a World War II aircraft carrier that sat on the windowsill.

"It's called a ship. It was sunk during the battle of the Leyte Gulf." She handed a glass of iced tea to Mrs. Doberman.

"How quaint. But you know what this room could use, if I may say so, Peggy, are some flowers. Flowers do add such a touch."

"You're right," Peggy said. "I'll remember to steal some the next time I go past the cemetery."

Mrs. Doberman regarded her. She smiled uncertainly. "Oh, Peggy. Always the tease."

"That's me. What brings you down to Lonely Point, Ernestine?"

Mrs. Doberman held up a hand. "I shall be brief."

Impossible, thought Peggy. And she sat down in a chair on the far side of the room.

"As you know," Mrs. Doberman began. She stopped,

rapidly drank half the contents of her glass, and began again. "As you know, our annual summer festival will be occurring soon."

Peggy nodded. The Hasty Harbor Summer Festival was little more than a glorified clambake intended to lure dedicated locals and unsuspecting tourists, subject them to homemade dishes perpetrated by the ladies of the town, and in general, to bring fleeting attention to a community that would otherwise remain forgotten and forgettable.

"Of course, I'm on the planning board again," said Mrs. Doberman.

"Of course."

"And the order of events will be the same this year. The grand parade and auction in the morning; in the afternoon, the sailing race, followed by the presentation of the Hasty Harbor Cup. As always, in the evening on the beach, there will be the covered dish supper and the clambake. And after dark, the pièce de nonrésistance—that which no one can resist—the fireworks."

"Who's in the race this year? The usual boys?" Peggy asked. The "boys" who competed in the ragtag sailing competition were always men from the peninsula who had blind faith in their own seamanship, but who sailed as if they were in fact blind—or blind drunk. Peggy remembered last year's race as a free-for-all that looked less like the America's Cup and more like pictures of the evacuation of Dunkirk.

"My guess is that Mr. Rexford and the Commodore will be among them," Mrs. Doberman said. "But I understand the race committee will soon release the names. Be that as it may, I myself am in charge of the committee for the gathering of *objets* for the auction. Giving is its own reward, the poet said, and this year nearly everyone has given something."

"Such as?" Peggy asked her.

"Daisy Williams has contributed a needlework tea cozy,

Cletis Fern is giving us a clam rake, and Miles Robinhill is offering free snowmobile lessons."

"In July?"

"And I have come to ask you if there's something you yourself can donate to the auction." The woman smiled. "*Will* donate." She finished her iced tea.

"I'm not sure," Peggy said. "Maybe I still have that matching pair of porcelain chamber pots my grandmother and grandfather used. They should make great *objets*."

Mrs. Doberman blinked, then nodded, once again uncertain. "Whatever you contribute will be most appreciated, dear."

Peggy stood. "I'll see what I can find, Ernestine."

"Yes. Well . . ." Mrs. Doberman slowly pushed her way up out of the sofa. "I'll stop by in a few days—Friday morning, if I may—to pick up whatever you decide upon."

Peggy took the iced tea glass from her hand. "You know, the more I think about those chamber pots, the more I'd like to see that they get a happy home."

"I understand." Mrs. Doberman backed toward the door. "Well—till then. Bye-bye, dear." She wiggled her fingertips at Peggy and opened the screen door.

"Bye, Ernestine," said Peggy, wiggling her fingers in return. "And close the screen on your way out. Dear. You're letting in the bugs."

Driving to Whitby after his sailing lesson, the admiral had stopped at a bookstore and purchased two manuals on sailing. Ignoring a book entitled *The Beginning Sailor*, he had chosen instead *The Complete Book of Sail Handling*, and a smaller volume, *Master of the Winds*, which he thought had a romantic sound to it. He had also picked up a tide table for midcoastal Maine at a stationery store, as well as a spiral notebook and a ballpoint pen. Leaving Whitby, he had paused for lunch at a roadhouse called The Cranky

Anchor, parking next to an RV full of screaming children, and once inside ordering a lobster roll and a ginger ale.

Back in his cabin, he sat down on the couch and read the first chapter of the book on sail handling. It was five o'clock when he realized he had not yet done as Joe had asked him and begun his log.

So he went to the table, opened the spiral notebook, and took up the ballpoint pen. On the first page of the notebook he wrote

The Log of the Sailboat "Invincible"
By her Captain
C. T. Deering

He turned the page and continued.

> Wednesday, July 20. Fine weather to be on the sea, after rain yesterday. Steady N. wind, approx. 12–15 knots. Practiced tacking in harbor, then on the river for a bit, and really had a feel for it. Approach to dock upon return was "neat and clean" according to Ensign Marino. Nice young man Ensign Marino. Or Joe, as he wants me to call him. Afterward, as we were leaving, he wished me "a ball" tonight.

The admiral paused. Then he wrote,

> As for tonight . . . ? ? ?

Early evening sunlight slanted through the trees as the admiral turned off the main highway onto the peninsula road. Dressed now in a blue blazer and white linen slacks, he was reminded of some of the outlandish outfits he had worn on dates during his college years. But that was more than fifty years ago; thank heavens fashions had changed a good deal since that time.

The digital clock on the car's dashboard read six twenty-eight. Having checked the road map before leaving Kare Free Kabins, he guessed he was too early for their seven o'clock date. By the time he reached Lonely Point Road, he was certain of it. Finally, a mile or so short of where he believed he would find Peggy's house, he saw a wide place in the road. To the left was a tangle of scrub pines; to the right, a sandy beach enclosed by bullrushes at both ends. He pulled over on the beach side and stopped.

Another car was parked nearby, but it was empty. The admiral stepped out onto the hard-parked sand. He stood a moment and surveyed the scene. He realized there was a tension growing in him in anticipation of tonight, and he took a deep breath to relieve it. As he began to walk again, he noticed movement in a cluster of bullrushes at the far end of the beach. Then he caught sight of two pairs of tan young legs, and a moment later the bra of a girl's bathing suit came flying upward. It spun briefly in the air, then fell, catching in the top of one of the bullrushes, where it hung like some brightly colored banner announcing the activity below.

The admiral stopped and stared at the bullrushes. Soon they began to shake and sway as if an animal were foraging among them. The admiral turned away and walked quickly back toward his car. The presence of the young couple, and their obviously unself-conscious passion, made him feel old suddenly. Perhaps it was their first date, too, and this was how they chose to get acquainted—copulating in the reeds.

He and Peggy, on the other hand, born in another time and to a different set of standards, would probably spend their own first date in nostalgic conversation. While that young couple were absorbed in matters of the moment, he and Miss McCoy would live tonight as if it were twenty, forty, even fifty years ago. At their age, the past was what they had the most of. At their age, they knew that pleasures of the present, if they came at all, were transitory; the future was increasingly finite, the shadows stretched and deepened with each passing year.

The admiral got into the car, swung onto the road, and continued until he saw the small white house with the two flags flying from the flagpole in front of it.

Peggy was standing at the door as he arrived, wearing a blue dress that made her look younger and more feminine than he had somehow expected. In her hands she clutched a small white purse.

"Seven o'clock on the button," she called to him as he opened the door of the car.

"Or if we're being nautical about it, six bells on the twilight watch." He stuffed his hands into the pockets of his slacks and started up the walk.

She remained fixed in the same spot, just outside the door.

He nodded. "Hello."

Peggy nodded back. "Hello."

For a moment, they stood face to face, neither of them quite sure what to say next.

"Well . . . it turned out to be a nice day," Peggy said. "After the rain."

"And a perfect summer evening, yes sirree."

There was another silence, broken only by the admiral's unconscious jingling of coins in his pocket.

Peggy asked him, "Would you like a drink?"

"If you would."

She shrugged. "I'm not much of a drinker. But I think I have some sherry. Is sherry okay with you?"

"Fine," he said agreeably. "Just fine." If there was one drink he hated it was sherry.

They went inside to the living room and Peggy went on into the kitchen. The admiral remained standing near the door and looked around the room. It had the neatness of crew quarters, he thought. There was a small sofa covered with a plaid slipcover, several armchairs, a sideboard, and a heavy mahogany table, probably a family piece, pushed up against the wall. Then his eye caught the brass clock on the wall. It was a ship's clock, set to chime the eight bells of the watch. Only a real sailor would have a clock like that. He noticed other nautical memorabilia. On the windowsill near the clock was a wooden model of a World War II ship. There were a few pictures on the wall, most of them seascapes. But there was also a framed piece of petit point that spelled out Peggy's name in yachting flags, and a little metal plaque engraved ABOARD THIS SHIP THE CAPTAIN'S WORD IS LAW. But what interested him most was a short prayer embroidered as if by a child or a beginner at the craft.

He was reading it as Peggy returned from the kitchen empty-handed. "Sorry," she admitted. "But I'm out of sherry, after all. I had some wine but it went bad."

"Then what do you say we have something at the restaurant? Our reservation is for eight. I'm sure if we arrive a little early they'll accept us."

For the first time since his arrival, Peggy smiled. "I'm sure they will. Tonight's the night they set aside for senior citizens."

The drive to Whitby took them half an hour and was accomplished mostly in silence. When they arrived the admiral found a parking space directly opposite the restaurant, which he considered a good omen. He said so to Peggy. She looked at him with an expression that seemed to answer, we'll see.

The enclosed garden of Galahad's was crowded, but the maître d' led them to a table in the corner, apart from the other diners. Moments later, a young waiter with flowing white-blond hair and one gold earring in his left ear appeared at their table. He lit the stubby candle planted in the Perrier bottle and was off again before the admiral could speak.

The admiral frowned briefly. "How about a drink?" he asked Peggy. "Sherry for you?"

"No. I'll have white wine." Peggy unfolded her napkin and spread it in her lap.

"Would you mind if I had a bourbon?" the admiral inquired.

"Not at all."

"You know, living down among the somewhat southern gentry, bourbon is the drink of choice. Bourbon and branch. Branch means branch water, you see. In the south a branch is what they call a stream."

"I see."

"Well, what do they call a stream up here in Maine?"

"They call it a stream."

"That figures." The admiral shifted in his chair. "Tell it like it is. Good old Yankee plain speaking, eh?"

Peggy looked at him and he said nothing more. It had been bad enough that the trip from Peggy's house to Whitby had occurred with very little conversation taking place between them, but his occasional attempts at joviality, he thought, were almost worse. Fortunately the waiter reappeared with menus and a pad. He noted their drink orders and slipped away again. Simultaneously, Peggy and the admiral took out their eyeglasses, picked up their menus, and began to study them.

Finally, he asked her, "Anything you recommend?"

"I hear the fish is good."

He thought of asking her what *kind* of fish but decided that would just confirm the obvious: that their conversation was going absolutely nowhere, that their date had been doomed even from the start.

The waiter returned. He set down Peggy's wine and placed the admiral's cocktail before him. The admiral picked up his glass and held it out toward her. "What say we have a toast."

"Fine." Peggy raised her wineglass.

"Let's see. There's an old navy toast that goes something like, to friends, ships, and—" He stopped abruptly. "On the other hand," he muttered, "that may not be the appropriate toast for this occasion."

What surprised him was that Peggy smiled for the second time that night. "I know that toast." She lifted her wineglass again. "To friends, ships, and women; may all of them be fast."

He smiled back. "It is a somewhat more imaginative toast than 'cheers.'"

"You're okay, you know," she said. "If I didn't say much on the ride here, I guess I was just nervous. I still feel a little bit like a schoolgirl on her first date."

"Frankly, so was I. Nervous, I mean," the admiral admitted. He eased back in his chair. "But let me tell you about first dates. I was in seventh grade when I fell in love with the girl who sat at the desk in front of me. More than anything, I wanted to go out with her. Well, finally I asked her out. And she accepted."

"What's wrong with that?"

"The girl's name was Stella Stettinius. The whole time we were on that date, I stuttered. Just try saying Stella Stettinius *without* stuttering."

Peggy gave a small laugh. Then she was serious once more. "I'll also admit it's taken me a while to decide."

"About what?" he asked her.

"You."

"Me?"

She sipped her wine. "I just haven't been sure . . . what I thought. To begin with, you nearly ran me down at sea." He started to speak, but she held up a hand. "Then after the launching, when we met, you made that remark."

"I told you I was sorry."

"I know," she nodded. "But I wasn't sure you meant it. I'm not all that used to trusting people. I've lived most of my life by myself and for myself. And that's how I've wanted it."

"Well—"

"Let me finish. What I mean is that I'm sometimes ready to think the worst about people. Or at least to suspect their motives. Such as when you asked me to join you for dinner."

"And what were my motives?" he inquired.

"I wasn't sure about that either. First I thought you were just lonely. Second, that you wanted another old navy swab to reminisce with. And third—"

"May I tell you tonight's specials?" cooed the waiter. He stood poised at tableside, pad and pencil ready. "There's monkfish jardiniere—"

"We're not ready," the admiral snapped back.

The waiter gave a breathy "Oops" and backed away. The admiral turned again to Peggy. "And what was my third motive?"

"For right now, let's stick with the second," Peggy told him. "Navy reminiscences. Why did you want to join the navy in the first place?"

"I was encouraged by the example of Themistocles."

"Who?"

"Themistocles. He was the Greek naval hero of the battle of Salamis in the Persian Wars. That's what my middle initial T stands for. It was my father's idea."

"Funny, you don't look Greek."

"Actually, English and Scotch-Irish, on my mother's side. And I was born about as far from the sea as you can get. Grand River, Iowa. My father was a schoolteacher there. But how he loved literature and the classics. As a boy I can recall him reading aloud to me the exploits of men like Lord Nelson, Oliver Hazard Perry, John Paul Jones. I became so fascinated by the *idea* of the sea that when I graduated from high school he asked our local congressman to write a letter to Annapolis on my behalf. And to everybody's great surprise, I was accepted."

"So how was it you got into communications?"

"Since I can remember, I loved to fool around with

telegraph keys. Then it was crystal sets, those early radios. But my first assignment in the navy was as a signal officer. It sometimes meant standing out on deck in the damnedest weather, whipping those semaphore flags back and forth. Nobody else wanted the job. I suppose all my years of walking to and from a country schoolhouse against those prairie winds made me impervious to gales. Anyway, I started out with semaphore and ended up with satellites. Naval communications have come a long way in my time."

"Moral of story," Peggy said. "Keep your flags flying and there's no telling where you'll end up."

The admiral laughed and took a deep swallow of his drink. "In fact, I still remember every letter of the semaphore alphabet. I'll show you. Give me your napkin and I'll spell out your name."

As he took up his own napkin, Peggy handed him hers. He unfolded both napkins and held them open, one in each hand. "Now imagine these are semaphore flags." He thrust out his right hand with the napkin hanging from it so that it was horizontal with his shoulder. He lifted his left hand into the air above his head. A few patrons in the restaurant looked around.

"That's the letter P." With sharp rapid motions he began snapping the napkins up and down, above and below, spelling out her name, "E . . . G . . . G . . . Y!"

With a flourish he executed the last letter, flinging his left arm outward, and at the same time sending his drink and the Perrier bottle with the candle flying to the floor in a great crash. Every diner in the room turned at the sound. The maître d' appeared. The white-blond waiter rushed toward them with a towel. A busboy followed with a brush and dustpan and began sweeping up the broken glass.

In the midst of the commotion the admiral sat saying nothing, ignoring the activity around them. After several moments, he slowly folded Peggy's napkin on the tabletop and handed it back to her. Only the busboy remained, sweeping the floor beneath the table. Most of the people in the room had returned to their dinners.

"If you don't mind," the admiral said, "I won't spell your last name."

"Maybe we should order," Peggy said.

He grunted his assent.

They picked up their menus and scanned them again. Peggy closed hers and set it down. The admiral looked over. "Have you decided?"

"The sole sounds good."

"I'm tempted by the lobster." He also closed his menu and put it on the table. "Yes. The lobster. But I guess that will mark me a tourist, won't it? Do the sons and daughters of Maine ever order lobsters in a restaurant?"

Peggy shook her head. "Not much in the summer. Right now the price is double, and the lobsters that they get are mostly shedders."

"Shedders?" he asked.

"Young lobsters that have shed their shells. I prefer the big old boys with their hard shells and crafty ways. They haven't lived that long for nothing."

"I'll remember that."

The waiter wafted casually in their direction, the admiral signaled him, and the young man lingered long enough for Peggy and the admiral to give him their orders. The waiter drifted off among the tables once again, and the admiral looked around the dining room.

"I see what you mean about summer tourists. I was told this place didn't get a lot of them, but as I look around the room, I don't see anybody who looks like a native."

"What about me?" Peggy asked.

"You're right," he admitted. "I guess when I came up here I expected everybody to be wearing yellow oilers and carrying a clam rake or a lobster trap."

"I'm glad I don't fit your image."

"So am I." He paused. "But what about you? You haven't told me anything about yourself."

"There isn't much to tell." She shrugged. "I was born in Gaffney, Maine, about forty miles north of here. No brothers, no sisters; only a pet dog named Woof when I was small. My father ran the local hardware store. I went to the state college near Augusta without any idea of what I wanted to do or be. Except married maybe. In those days if you got married the future took care of itself, one way or another. After college I worked for my father for a year. Then I thought I might become a nurse. My mother had been ill my last two years of college, and I did a lot of taking care of her. I'd had a year of nurse's training when the war broke out. So when my mother died, I enlisted in the Navy Nurse Corps."

"And you were sent to the South Pacific."

Peggy nodded. "They needed nurses, and I couldn't wait to see another part of the world. Oh, I was a regular Nellie Forbush in those days. You know, the nurse in *South Pacific*?"

"Except you didn't marry a French planter."

"No . . . I didn't marry anyone." There was a brief silence. "When the war was over I came back to the States and worked in several navy hospitals. Navy nurses were part of the Waves then."

"Women Accepted for Volunteer Emergency Service."

"Yes," said Peggy. "But sometimes we joked that the acronym was really meant to stand for, 'We Are Virgins, Eager Sailors.' At any rate, I made it up to head nurse at a navy hospital near Boston. That's where I got my commander's stripes. I retired from the navy in 'sixty-eight and moved back to Gaffney to live with my father. He died two years later, and the year after that I moved here." She shrugged. "Pretty boring story, isn't it?"

"Not at all."

"You're just being polite. It's not the sort of life story Hollywood makes into a movie. Unlike yours. I bet they had John Wayne cast to play you in some patriotic navy epic."

"Hardly likely," the admiral said, although it flattered him a bit that Peggy thought so. "Except for seeing service in the South Pacific," he went on, "my career has been a series of navy bases, with a few years spent at the Pentagon."

"Was that when you became the father of modern naval communications?" Peggy asked.

"Oh, that. No, that was later. After I retired. It came at a time when the media was fascinated by what I like to call the paternity thing. Rickover became 'the father of the nuclear submarine,' and I sired modern naval communications. I think they even found somebody they called 'the father of the flushless head.'"

Peggy laughed. It was obvious that she, too, had relaxed considerably. He noticed that her wineglass was nearly empty.

"Another wine?" he asked.

"No. No, thank you." She raised both hands. "The one was just enough."

A moment later their dinners arrived. The waiter set them down and made an elaborate ritual of tying the paper lobster bib around the admiral's neck. The admiral took the shell cracker that was provided and began attacking a front claw of the lobster.

"How's your sole?" he asked Peggy as she sampled her fish.

"Good. Your lobster looks good too."

He nodded, still struggling to break the claw. "I'll let you know if this monster ever decides to crack. The old boy's definitely been around awhile." The shell finally gave way, and the admiral began picking at the meat inside.

Peggy stopped eating and looked up. "I've changed my mind," she said.

He stopped in midbite. "About what?"

"I'll have a second glass of wine."

"Splendid. I'll join you." He summoned the waiter, ordered the drinks, and he and Peggy resumed eating.

The garden room of Galahad's continued to flow with people arriving and departing. But the older couple at the corner table did not seem to notice, so caught up were they in their own conversation. As the remaining daylight faded to a deep lapis hue, the admiral and Peggy talked on. They talked easily about inconsequentialities, such as the size and sting of Maine mosquitoes compared with their bloodthirsty cousins in the South Pacific. They reminisced about their navy days during the war years. They recalled names—Halsey, Kinkaid—and places—Mindoro, Samar, and the Coral Sea. The candle in their Perrier bottle sputtered and went out, but neither noticed until the waiter interrupted to replace it.

At last, the admiral pushed aside his plate, the lobster's carapace stripped clean. He patted his midsection. "I could almost handle another one of those," he sighed.

"You did very well," Peggy assured him. "For a tourist."

"I take that as a compliment, coming from someone such as you." He went on, "But I have a technique, you see. First, I work on the front claws, then the tail, and leave what I call the fuselage for last. But the tomalley—ah, that is the ambrosia!" He put his thumb and forefinger to his lips and kissed them with delight. "Now how about some coffee or dessert?" He began untying his lobster bib.

"Just coffee," Peggy said. "Decaffeinated. We older folks need our sleep. Besides, tomorrow sounds like a perfect sailing day. I'd like to get an early start."

"Of course." He ordered two decaffeinated coffees and asked the waiter for the check.

By the time they left the restaurant it was dark. But

many of the shops along the street were still open, hoping to attract the tourists who ambled casually along or rested on the sidewalk benches, taking in the summer night. As they drove through Whitby the admiral discovered there was more traffic on the streets than he expected. But taking a shortcut Peggy showed him he was soon onto the Newell River Bridge and heading toward the road to the peninsula.

Crossing the bridge, both he and Peggy glanced off to the right. Downriver, illuminated by innumerable lights, was the Whitby Ship Works. The admiral realized that he had never seen it after dark. Cruisers and destroyers in various stages of completion were berthed along the river's edge, glowing under floodlights strung on cables stretched from bow to stern. It looked as if a summer garden party was about to take place on the decks below. The giant crane itself was bathed in brilliant light, outlined by aircraft warning signals that blinked red along its sides and top.

Peggy pointed to the scene. "I come across this bridge four, maybe five times a week. And every time I look down at the sight of all those ships I get a—what should I call it? A special feeling."

"I understand," the admiral responded. He said nothing more. But he did understand. Completely. Only someone who loved the navy as he did could look at those ships and feel such an overwhelming sense of awe and pride.

They continued down the peninsula road in silence for some miles. But now it was a different sort of silence than it had been earlier on the drive out. At one point the admiral started to switch on the car radio, then abruptly turned it off again. "Automatic reaction," he said to Peggy, when he saw her looking at him. "I guess I listen to the radio a lot. Too much, probably. There have been times when it was the only company I had."

"Listen to it if you want."

"I don't want. I have very pleasant company right here, right now." He added, "Besides, this radio only gets one station, and all it plays is rock and roll. In fact, it's been years since I've heard a good melody. Why don't they write songs like 'Stardust' and 'Sweet Lorraine'?"

"One of my favorites is 'Long Ago and Far Away,'" Peggy said. "It was popular during the war. I haven't heard that in years, though."

He nodded. "I remember. It was nineteen forty-four. Let's see . . ." He thought for several moments, then sang in a rough but rich baritone, "*Long ago and far away* . . ."

Peggy picked it up. "*I dreamed a dream one day* . . ."

"*And now that dream is here beside me* . . . ," they sang together.

They looked at each other somewhat embarrassed and sang no more of the song.

At last they approached Peggy's house. The admiral pulled into the driveway and turned off the engine.

"Thank you for tonight," Peggy said, and reached for the door handle.

"May I see you again?" he asked her. "May I call you tomorrow?"

The question caught her totally off guard. "I guess so. Why not?"

"Why not, indeed!" He slapped the steering wheel with his hand. "I will!"

Peggy opened the car door.

"Another question," the admiral said quickly. "In the restaurant, you mentioned three motives I might have had for asking you to go out with me tonight. One, that I was lonely; two, that I wanted to share navy stories with a fellow sailor. But you didn't tell me what you thought my third motive might have been. You said you weren't sure."

"I'm still not."

"Can you tell me what you thought it was, at least? My third motive."

Peggy took a breath. "I hoped it was because you liked me."

"I do. I . . ." He wanted to continue, but had absolutely no idea what to say.

It didn't matter. The next moment she was out of his car and hurrying up the front steps to her house.

6

The navy car appeared down River Road, slowed, turned, and continued on the narrow strip that led to Dodge's Boat Yard. When it was out of sight the two men sitting on the wooden bench in front of T. C. Dabney's store exchanged a look. One man bit into an orange he had spent the last ten minutes peeling. He spat a seed in a trajectory that carried it far into the turnaround.

The other man pointed in the direction that the navy car had taken. "What's the navy doing at the boatyard at this hour of the morning?" Jimmy Smiley wondered.

"Beats me," Able Fenstermacher said.

Jimmy Smiley and Able Fenstermacher were men in their late fifties. Both wore flannel shirts and Levi's, although Able's were a recent acquisition from a surprise summer sale down at L.L. Bean. Able was a retired road crew foreman, now on a pension from the state. He was also the fish and game warden of the town. He had a short gray beard that he trimmed weekly with a fish knife. Able's appearance was what tourists brochures liked to describe as "the archetypal Yankee." In fact, tourists now and then asked him to pose for snapshots, and Able genially obliged.

Jimmy Smiley, on the other hand, was seldom asked to pose for anything, perhaps because of his unconscious habit of continually digging wax out of his ears. Together, Jimmy and his two sons ran Smiley's Garbage Service, crisscrossing the peninsula in an open garbage truck, which, depending on the wind, announced its presence in advance of its arrival.

"You told Cabot about our committee meeting?" Jimmy asked him.

Able nodded. "That I did."

"Then where's he at?"

"Beats me," Able said again. "Except today I think we can dispense with the committee folderol and go get breakfast. The picking and the choosing's done. We got our racers for the Hasty Harbor Cup."

"And not a day too soon," said Jimmy. "I never knew how tough meetings and committee work could be."

At that moment, a battered green Dodge Dart drove up and parked beside the store. The driver, a large round man also in his fifties, got out and waved to the two men on the bench.

"Hi, Cabot," Jimmy Smiley called to him.

"Hi, Cabot," Able said.

The man, who was wearing high rubber waders of bright yellow, waddled toward them. His name was Cabot Lodge. Although he made his living as a scalloper, he was, he assured anyone who asked, very distantly related to the Boston Lodges; a fact that unquestionably would have startled the more distinguished bearers of that name. Cabot Lodge, too, wore a flannel shirt, but it was the waders that gave him his celebrity. No one could recall seeing Cabot wearing any other leg wear *except* his waders. Local gossip had it that he ate in them, slept in them, and even made love in them; the last being all the more remarkable since he had sired seven daughters in ten years.

"Either of you see the U.S. Navy car go down the road?" asked Cabot.

"Yep," said Able.

Jimmy nodded. "Yep."

Cabot sat down on the bench. "Do you suppose they're gonna turn Hasty Harbor into a navy base? A base here sure would be okay with me. I wouldn't mind one of my daughters marrying a navy man."

"Figures," Able said. "Your daughters have been poked by every sailor at the ship works. Putting the boys within walking distance is a good idea."

Jimmy Smiley hooted, Cabot set his jaw, and Able spat an orange seed.

Together the three men comprised the race committee for this year's Hasty Harbor Summer Festival. A festival rule required that each member of the race committee had to have a boat, and each in his own way qualified. Cabot Lodge had his scallop boat *Persephone*, which he and almost everyone in Hasty Harbor called the "Percy-phone." As fish and game warden, Able Fenstermacher had a rowboat with a five-horsepower Elgin outboard on the stern. Of the three men, Jimmy Smiley had the least nautical experience. His boat was actually a small flat-bottomed barge that Jimmy used surreptitiously on summer nights to dump his trash at sea.

"You may laugh," said Cabot. "But him who laughs the last, laughs loudest."

"Come on, Cabot. No offense," said Able. "Let's go have breakfast."

"When you hear the news I got, you're not going to *want* breakfast," Cabot told them. "The Rexford fella's out."

"What do you mean?" Jimmy asked.

"I mean out of our race. Remember, it was you and Able who voted for a two-man race this year."

"We did." Able nodded. "Last year's cup race was a laughingstock. We're lucky no one drowned."

Cabot looked him in the eye. "So you picked Rexford and the Commodore to be your only racers. And now you just got one. The Commodore."

"So what happened to Rexford?" Able asked.

"I always told you Rexford drinks too much," Cabot went on.

"Rexford's a good sailor, and his family's had a place here forty years," said Jimmy. "What he does on land is his own business. Besides, his *Silverfish* is a good boat."

"*Was* a good boat," Cabot told them. "Last night Rexford tied one on and tried to sail under a South Yarmouth bridge at night."

"So?" Able pressed him.

"Right now Rexford's boat has got a busted mast and a hole where the deck was. And the man himself has got a compound fracture of the arm."

"So who do we get to replace Rexford?" Jimmy wondered.

"Beats me," Able Fenstermacher said. He sighed and leaned back against the bench. "At least, we got the Commodore," he said.

The Commodore, as he was known to everyone on the peninsula, was Commodore Hugh Fitzroy Pugh, a man of ample wealth and size, who had owned a summer house in Taggetts Neck for more than half a century. He had been a noted gentleman sailor in his younger days, and although his age remained a mystery, it was rumored that he had crewed for Sir Thomas Lipton in a trans-Atlantic sailing race in 1923. His beautiful old sailboat, *Wing Song*, in which he took considerable pride, had a lapstraked mahogany hull, original canvas sails, and brass fittings, which the Commodore himself kept polished.

"In fact, thank God we got the Commodore," Able said, "or we'd be in the deep."

"Thank God," echoed Cabot.

"Thank God," Jimmy Smiley repeated.

"What is this? A prayer meeting?" The voice came from the doorway of T. C. Dabney's store. The three men turned. At the door stood the owner himself, a lean man in his sixties with a large nose and ferret eyes.

Able spoke up. "Seems we lost Rexford for our sailing race next week. We were just saying that at least we got the Commodore."

"Guess you didn't hear the news, then," Dabney said. "He went last night. A heart attack while in the act of love, they say."

"What a man," said Able. Everyone agreed.

"Maybe we can get someone else to sail *Wing Song,*" Jimmy ventured.

"'Fraid not," Dabney said. "The story is he'll use *Wing Song* as his coffin. They're going to wrap the Commodore in his best mainsail and lay him in the cockpit of his boat. Then they'll tow her out to sea, open the bilge cocks, and let the master and his boat go down together."

"Rest in peace," said Able, frowning. "But a waste of a good ship."

Dabney turned and went back inside his store. For a long while none of the men spoke.

"I don't feel much like breakfast," Jimmy said at last.

"Me neither," Able readily agreed.

"So what do we do now?" asked Jimmy.

"Beats me," Able said.

The three men remained sitting on the bench. They thought. They did not look at one another. In the silence that again consumed them, Cabot Lodge toyed with a buckle on the left leg of his waders, Jimmy Smiley searched for ear wax, and Able Fenstermacher spat another orange seed.

* * *

It was seven thirty in the morning when Joe arrived at the boatyard. That day's sailing lesson was not scheduled until eight, but he had gotten an early start, and the traffic through Whitby had been light. He also hoped he might find Sarah.

He did. As he walked across the pier toward the floating dock, he gave a sidelong glance in the direction of the office. The door was open, and he could see Sarah moving about inside.

Joe halted at the ramp and looked down. The *Invincible* was moored beside the floating dock. One of the teenage helpers at the yard had probably brought her to dockside earlier, Joe guessed. But it gave him an idea. Crossing to the office, he knocked briefly on the door, then opened it.

"Hi," he called out.

Sarah turned from the table where she had been standing. "Hi. Can I do something for you?"

"I just wanted to thank you for readying *Invincible*."

Sarah shrugged. "The boys must have done it. They get here at seven."

"Well, thank them for me, then."

"I will."

"You're here on the early side yourself," Joe said.

"It's a good time to get my other work done."

"Other work?" he asked, stepping into the office. "Oh, you mean the thesis that you're writing. What's it called? 'The Life Story of the Clam from Birth to Bouillabaisse'?"

"You might find the subject funny," Sarah told him, "but I don't."

"Sorry. And you're right. It was a flip remark. To be honest with you, I don't know much at all about clams. Maybe you could fill me in."

Sarah looked at him with her level gaze, unsure if he was serious or not. Finally she stepped back and pointed to a

Plexiglas cutting board that reminded Joe of high school biology class. On the board were two clams, both open. One was in its shell, the other had been deshelled and dismembered, its parts lying side by side on the board. At that hour of the morning, Joe thought, it was not a particularly appetizing sight.

Sarah held up a dissecting knife and pointed to the shell with the clam still inside it.

"Clams," she informed him, "should not be confused with other marine bivalves such as brachiopods."

"I'll keep that in mind," Joe said.

She touched the knife tip to the point of the shell where the two halves had been joined. "This part of the shell is called the umbo. Just inside it is the chondrophore. Today, I'm trying to learn more about the chondrophore."

"Fascinating."

She indicated the globular body of the clam itself. "This section consists of the visceral mass, a so-called foot for digging in the sand, and a pair of tubes or siphons; one to bring food, oxygen, and water in, and the other to pump water and waste matter out."

Joe peered down at the slimy whitish blob. "And what makes the clam open and close its shell?"

"The adductor muscles on each side of the body." She touched them with the knife tip. "Here, and here. Other details of the soft anatomy are used to define orders within a class. But malacologists differ in their views on this."

"And how do—uh, malacologists—tell Mr. Clam from Ms. Clam?" Joe asked. "If that's not too bold a question."

"Clams are asexual," Sarah answered.

"You mean they don't have any fun together in the mud? Too bad."

Sarah's pale blue eyes were impassive. But above the collar of her T-shirt Joe saw her neck redden slightly.

He decided this was not the time to explore the sex life of a clam. "Anyway," he said, "thanks for the short lecture on our hard-shelled friends. You taught me more in five minutes than I ever knew before. But in order to continue my education, I'd like to visit one of your clam beds with you someday. Could I?"

"I'm sure you'd find it very boring," Sarah said.

"Oh, I'm sure I wouldn't. I could help you dig them up. And carry them. A bucket of those things must be pretty heavy."

"I really don't think that'll be necessary. But thank you, Ensign." She glanced past him out the open door. "The admiral is here," she told him.

Joe turned and saw the admiral striding briskly in the direction of the ramp. He turned back to Sarah again. "By the way, one question and I'll go. Do clams have feelings? The way people do?"

"I don't know," the girl said. "But I'd guess so. Rudimentary ones."

"Then maybe something does go on between 'em down there in the mud at that." Joe smiled. "See you." He gave a quick wave and went out the door, catching up with the admiral at the top of the ramp.

"Good morning, Joe," the admiral said cheerily. "A fine day for sailing, wouldn't you agree?"

"Yes sir." Joe followed him down to the floating dock.

"And what's our lesson going to be today?"

"I thought maybe some jib work. In the river."

"Splendid," the admiral said ebulliently. "Today I am prepared to take on the mighty Kerrenac."

"We've got a good wind from the west."

"'It's a warm wind, the west wind,'" the admiral quoted. "The poet is John Masefield, in case you didn't know." He stopped at the edge of the floating dock and spread his arms expansively. "'I must down to the seas again; to the lonely sea and the sky.'"

"I know that one," Joe said. "That's Masefield, too. The first line of *Sea Fever*."

"My father used to recite it from memory when I was a boy," the admiral said. "That, and 'I will go back to the great sweet mother; Mother and lover of men, the Sea.' Swinburne. No wonder I wanted to join the navy as a youth."

"You're certainly in a good mood."

The admiral beamed. "And do you know why? Because I spent the evening with a most interesting woman."

"Really?" Somehow, the statement startled Joe. He still found it hard to think of anybody the admiral's age having "dates," and certainly not getting turned on the way the admiral obviously was. She must have been some number, Joe thought. Probably a Whitby divorceé, in her fifties—forties even—who had the hots for navy blue.

The admiral had already set about raising the sail, thrusting in the battens as he did.

For the next hour and a half they sailed up and down and back and forth across the river, tacking again and again, the admiral resetting the jib what seemed to him innumerable times. In a few instances he set it incorrectly, after which the sail would flap noisily in the wind. When that happened he would look at Joe, who looked back at him as if to say, "You're the captain of this ship. Do something about it." And each time the admiral stood, went forward, and adjusted the jib until the flapping stopped. Returning aft, he'd look at Joe again. Each time Joe nodded approval and immediately ordered a new tack, which would require still another setting of the jib.

Once, as their boat was on a broad cross-river heading, the admiral looked back and thought he saw Peggy's boat moving rapidly downriver at a distance. He raised a hand to shade his eyes and watched the progress of the small white craft.

Yes, it *was* her. He was certain of it.

Suddenly, he heard the sound of flapping sails again,

and this time Joe was shouting, "Yo! You're in stays. Head her up!"

Embarrassed, the admiral realized his boat was drifting aimlessly. He quickly came about and took control of it once again.

"Sorry," he mumbled to Joe as he resumed headway. "I just lost my concentration for a moment."

Joe made a wry face. "That's what the lookout on the *Titanic* said after he was pulled into the lifeboat."

The lesson continued without incident, and several times Joe nodded in acknowledgment of the admiral's increasing proficiency at sail handling.

When they returned to the boatyard dock, Joe leapt out at once and began to tie the bowline to a cleat. The admiral undid his life vest and looked at Joe, saying nothing. Joe went toward the stern of the boat to tie up the aft line.

"Well?" asked the admiral at last.

Joe looked surprised. "Well, what?"

"How was I?"

Joe shrugged. "Not bad," he said. He knelt and began to wrap the line around a cleat. The admiral stared at him. He wanted to respond, to say something, to demand elaboration. But he didn't.

Joe looked up again. "You were good. Very good, in fact."

"Thank you," the admiral said quietly. He tried not to reveal just how pleased he was to hear those words.

For Peggy the conditions had been almost perfect—a brisk steady breeze from the west and a moderate outgoing tide. The sun was bright, but filtered just enough by haze to make it seem benevolent. Peggy was surprised there weren't more sailors on the water enjoying the day.

She did remember seeing a blue Lightning class sailboat several hundred yards away, crossing the river in a series of short tacks. Probably a student, Peggy had thought. But whoever had been at the helm was sailing well.

So was she. And for three hours her attention was directed to the nautical requirements of the moment. So it was not until she reentered Hasty Harbor shortly before noon that she thought about the admiral again.

The admiral. Rear admiral, actually, but she still recalled that to a navy nurse anybody with the rank of admiral was considered just a step away from God.

"Rear Admiral Charles T. Deering, U.S. Navy," she said aloud, and smiled to herself.

From the time he'd brought her home last night until midnight, when sleep finally overtook her, she had lain awake replaying every moment of the evening in her mind. During dinner they had joked about behaving like teenagers on a date. But that was how Peggy felt.

Still, she decided, she would keep it to herself. Telling anybody, even Sarah, would have made her feel like that same schoolgirl, overdramatizing the details in confidential tones. Instead, when she'd returned to the boatyard she simply waved to Sarah in the office as she walked across the pier and headed toward her car.

Peggy drove quickly up the boatyard road and halted at the stop sign. Remembering that she needed to get a few groceries, she drove straight across the turnaround to Dabney's Store. As she got out of her car, she saw the three men sitting on the bench in front.

"Ahoy, Commander," Able Fenstermacher said. The others also greeted her.

"Ahoy yourselves," Peggy said. "Why is it every time I see you three you're sitting on this bench?"

"Oh, we do work," Cabot Lodge protested.

"We work hard," Jimmy Smiley said.

"Maybe that's why they made us into a committee," Able added. "Fact is, right now we're holding a committee meeting."

"A committee meeting?" Peggy asked.

Able nodded. "We're the race committee for this year's summer festival."

"By order of the Hasty Harbor First Selectman," Jimmy said.

"*You* three are the race committee?" Peggy stared at them. The men beamed.

"Lots of other folks have asked us the same question," Cabot told her.

"Well, what's the committee committed itself to while you've been sitting on this bench?" she asked.

"First off, we've decided this year it's going to be a two-man race," said Able.

"Except we're having a little trouble finding the two men," added Jimmy.

"We had 'em," Cabot told her. "But we lost 'em."

"But some new names have been suggested to us," Able went on. "One's a fellow named Leif Ericstein."

"Leif Ericstein?" asked Peggy. She wondered if he was a descendant of a little-known Jewish Viking explorer.

"He's an out-of-stater," Jimmy added. "Bought a big place up near Dakins Ferry. Rich, we heard. But more important-wise, he sails."

"Have you spoken with him?" Peggy asked.

"Well, no, not yet," admitted Cabot. "But after we explain to him the prestige that goes with the winning of the Hasty Harbor Cup, how can he turn us down?"

"A once in a lifetime chance," said Peggy. "What other name have you got?"

There was a silence. The three men looked at one another. "It's Elwood Slagg," Able finally said.

"You're kidding." Peggy laughed. "The man's in prison."

"Was," corrected Able. "He paid his debt to society as of last Monday night."

"Slagg's nothing but a forty-year-old juvenile delinquent," Peggy said. "He stole other people's sailboats and sold them to a Boston syndicate."

"Which proves that he can sail," Cabot answered. "Anyhow we're going to talk to both of them this afternoon."

"Should be an interesting race," Peggy offered. "Good luck." She stepped over their outstretched feet and went into the store.

Able leaned back on the bench. He put his hands behind his head and intertwined his fingers till the knuckles cracked.

"Frankly," Able said, "whatever two men we *do* choose, that woman could probably whip either one of 'em, hands down."

"That she could," said Jimmy.

Cabot added, "That she could."

The three men on the bench fell silent once again. It was almost a full minute before Able looked at Jimmy. "Are you thinking what I'm thinking?" he asked him.

"I'm definitely thinking it," said Jimmy. He turned his head and looked at Cabot.

Cabot nodded. "That makes three of us who are thinking what we're thinking."

All three men simultaneously turned their heads again, and looked in through the open door of Dabney's Store.

In the store, Peggy purchased several items she'd forgotten to pick up at the supermarket several days ago. In spite of the convenience, she disliked shopping there. The goods were outrageously priced, especially in summer when vacationers filled it. What passed for lettuce had the look and texture of limp seaweed. Many times Peggy had promised herself that between the first of June and Labor Day she would not set foot inside the store. Always, it was a promise she broke after the second week.

But since the Hasty Harbor post office was located in the store, at least it gave her the opportunity to get the mail from her postal box. The post office consisted of a section of boxes similar to hers. Beyond it was a wooden kiosk-like structure not much bigger than a telephone booth. It had a grille window and a counter, behind which T. C. Dabney doubled as postmaster when he wasn't busy in the store. It was generally known that Dabney also used the post office as a front for an illegal betting operation, taking bets on everything from Boston Red Sox games to the on-time performance of the Portland–Nova Scotia ferry.

Peggy got the mail from her box and leafed through it quickly. Among the usual assortment of bills and shopping circulars was a letter urging her to join some association of retired Waves. There was also an official-looking notice that the annual rental fee on her postal box was due. She went to the post office window and waited for the one patron ahead of her to conclude his business.

"Morning, Peg," T. C. Dabney said through the grille. "You want to pay your box fee, ayuh?"

"Ayuh," Peggy said. She could always tell it was summer when T.C. slipped into his put-on Maine accent. Usually he saved it only for the tourists, but now and then he would forget and use it with the locals too. She thought of asking him for directions to Bah Hahba but did not.

"That'll be thirty-nine dollars," Dabney said.

Peggy took the money from her purse and slid it under the grille. "Tell me, T.C., what's everybody betting on this week?" she asked.

He paused in his counting of the money and gave her a look of absolute incomprehension. "As you know, I am a deacon of the church and a man of upright morality. Betting is an activity I disdain."

"What do you call it, then?" she wondered.

"Uh . . . let's just say the folks of Hasty Harbor often

have—feelings about certain things, one way or another."

"And what do their feelings concern this week?" Peggy asked him.

"Mrs. Coggeshall, the sexton's wife."

"She's just about to have a baby."

"That's the one," he said. "Some folks feel it'll be a boy; some a girl."

"What are the odds?"

Dabney cleared his throat and pushed some change across the counter toward her. "Three to two in favor of a boy," he answered in a low voice. Then he added, "But maybe you'd like to express your feelings, too."

"Sorry, T.C.," Peggy said. "But I've got my own bookie in Portland. And he's as immoral as they come."

She gathered up her change and left the store.

It was early afternoon when the admiral opened his logbook. He thought for a moment and then wrote:

> Thursday, July 21. Another good day to be on the sea. W. wind, at 15 knots. Set sail at low slack tide in the late a.m. We practiced jib work in the river. It was a real workout for the old legs, I'll confess it, going back and forth from bow to stern. But Joe said I did well. And I agree. Except I goofed once. I wasn't paying attention and I got us in stays. It was because I saw her sailing downriver and I lost my concentration. Speaking of her, I've thought about her most of the day. Last night I told her I would call her today, and I wonder if she's waiting for my call. What I have in mind, in fact, is even better than a phone call. And if I'm going to do it, I'd better put my plan in action soon. The weather forecast for tonight doesn't sound good. But maybe it'll hold off until later in the evening. Will it work, the thing I have in mind? Who knows? But as another old admiral once said, "Damn the torpedoes—full speed ahead!!"

The telephone had not rung when Peggy stopped to eat her lunch. It hadn't rung when she went to retrieve the paint and paintbrush from the storage cabinet beneath the deck. The day had become hot and hazy. Thunderstorms had been predicted for that evening, but most likely, Peggy guessed, she would have the afternoon to paint her house before the weather changed.

She started to set the ladder against the wall where she had finished yesterday, but another thought occurred to her. She would paint at ground level on the side of the house nearest the door. Just in case the telephone should ring.

The paint spread easily across the clapboards and Peggy's mind wandered. As they often did, such thoughts included memories of Tom. His birthday was not far off. Had he lived, he would have been seventy years old. His sandy hair would probably be white, with possibly the small suggestion of a bald spot at the back. But he would have maintained his trim, almost boyish physique, and his angular face would have attractive lines. And still those hazel eyes would dance. They were what had drawn her to him first, those loving eyes.

She thrust the brush into the can of paint and in bold strokes wrote TOM across the board she was about to paint. She looked at it for several moments, the fresh white paint drying rapidly against the weathered dullness of the wall. Then she painted over it. The song she and the admiral had begun to sing on the drive home last night came back to her; those times with Tom were long ago and far away.

After Tom, there had been no one in her life to take his place, at least, no one she cared about enough to fill the emptiness Tom's death had left. She'd been in her twenties then, and attractive in a perky sort of way, and heaven knew there had been plenty of young servicemen to choose among. But they were boys, really; lonely, far from home, being marched relentlessly toward manhood by the war.

After the war ended there had been a romance with an unmarried navy doctor at the hospital where both of them were stationed. She hadn't thought she was ready to love another man again, but in fact she loved him, deeply and with passion—until she read of his engagement to another nurse, a friend of hers. The hurt and anger that she felt at first were almost more than she could bear. Now she looked back on that time with a sort of wistful sadness. Since then she gradually accepted the belief that Mr. Right was not to be. In her fifties, and increasingly as the years went on, she had embraced solitude. Her own "cozy singularity," as she preferred to call it, she wore like a protective armor, which though heavy at times fit her better every year, shielding her from the disappointments life could inflict.

Then uninvited, accidentally, and unexpectedly, the admiral had come into her life. He had broken through the armor that protected her. The moment she had seen him at the launching ceremony, she felt something stirring within her, something she believed had died long ago.

The song again played in her head; words coming back in fragments now:

Long the skies were overcast,
But now the clouds have passed
You're here at last . . .

And more still:

Just one look and then I knew,
That all I longed for long ago was you . . .

The more she thought about the man, the more she wanted to be with him, to know all about his life, to share her own. How he felt about her, Peggy wasn't sure. But from his behavior last night . . .

Peggy smiled to herself. And went on with her painting.

When Peggy checked her watch again it was almost four

o'clock. The new paint had dried already in the midsummer sun. Although clouds had begun to billow in the west, the afternoon continued to be bright. Of course, *that* was the reason that he hadn't called, she told herself. The day was so pleasant, he'd gone on some sort of an outing. He would call when he returned.

Peggy put the lid back on the paint can, hosed off the brush, and carried the can and paintbrush to the storage cabinet. She rinsed off her hands under the garden hose and headed toward the house. In the kitchen, she poured herself a tall glass of iced tea. Leaning back against the countertop, she found that she was staring at the telephone again.

Ring, damn it, she thought.

But it did not.

By six o'clock, thunderheads had gathered in such numbers that the sun was frequently obscured. Peggy had just switched on the television set in the living room to watch the news from Augusta when the lights flickered. The sky had darkened rapidly. There were rumblings of thunder in the distance, and the wind had increased, blowing fitfully in sudden gusts. Flashes of lightning were random, but more frequent. Peggy abandoned the newscast and went from room to room, closing windows. As she did, a snapping noise caught her ear, and she remembered that the two flags on the flagpole were still flying.

She ran outside and untied the halyard as the first large drops of rain began to fall. By the time she had detached the second flag, her hair and much of her shirt were wet. She took the flags and bolted toward the house as lightning struck somewhere in the nearby woods and thunder shook the ground. She slammed the front door shut. The living room was even darker than before, illuminated only by the still-chattering face of the television news reporter on the screen.

Peggy moved around the room turning on lights. From her experience with summer storms, she guessed that given the intensity of this one, loss of her electric power was just about a certainty. Better have my dinner soon, she thought. She went into the kitchen and looked in the refrigerator. She could take a chance and throw a frozen pizza in the toaster oven and hope that the power remained on for the time the pizza took to bake. There was also a package of spaghetti in the cabinet, but again, it would take time to get the water boiling on the electric stove. Or she could quickly fix a sandwich with some cold cuts she had found.

Rain was falling furiously now, flung against the windows by the wind. No question; tonight's dinner would be a sandwich. Peggy took out the bread, lettuce, and mayonnaise. From the meat tray she removed the foil-wrapped cold cuts. She was in the process of unwrapping them when the lights flickered and went out. Peggy swore softly to herself and got a flashlight from the kitchen drawer. She found candles and took two into the living room, where she put them in holders and lit them. Then she returned to the kitchen, lit another candle, and started making the sandwich.

It was then she heard the sound.

At first she thought it was the wind. But as she listened, she knew that it was someone knocking. She picked up the flashlight and listened again.

The knocking came from the front door, she was certain. And it made her shudder.

Louder knocking. It was followed by a muffled male voice calling, "Anybody home?"

She edged into the living room, keeping to the shadows. Peggy heard the screen door open. In the candlelight she saw the knob of the front door begin to turn. She caught her breath.

Above the wind the voice said again, "Hello! Is anybody here?"

She shined the flashlight at the door. "Who is it?"

"Me!"

"Who?"

"It's Charles! Charles Deering! May I come in?"

Peggy flew to the door and opened it. Outside, still holding the screen door, stood the admiral. His sports shirt and madras shorts were completely soaked.

She stared at him. "For God's sake, what are you doing out there in the rain?"

"Getting wetter—if that's possible. May I come in?"

She flung open the door and he stepped in at once, dripping water onto the rug. "Get me a towel and I'll explain," he said apologetically. He ran a hand across his hair, which was plastered to his head.

Peggy went to the linen closet in the bathroom, grabbed a large bath towel, and brought it to him.

"Thank you. Thank you very much." He began to dry his face and hair. "I'm glad you're home, believe me." He patted at the water that ran down his neck. "Otherwise I might have had to spend the night under your deck."

He unbuttoned several buttons of his shirt and dried his chest. "You wouldn't have an extra pair of pants I could put on, would you? Forget that. Silly question. You and I are hardly the same size."

Throughout it all, Peggy continued to stare at him. She said, finally, "I have an old pair of my father's."

"Do you really?"

"They're in my closet. You can try them on in the bathroom." Peggy handed him a candle and pointed to the bathroom. Carrying the candle, he went toward it dutifully, water squeaking in his loafers as he walked.

Using her flashlight, Peggy found the box of her father's clothes in a corner of her bedroom closet and returned with the trousers and a shirt. She knocked on the bathroom door, and when the admiral opened it a crack, she placed the clothes in his outstretched hand.

"I brought you one of his shirts, too," she said. "I found these things in the attic last week. I was going to give them to the Salvation Army."

"Tonight, they're salvation to me, I'll tell you," he called. From within the bathroom she heard the sound of a wet article of clothing being deposited into the tub.

"Would you like a drink?" she asked him through the door.

"Wonderful. How does the line go? Out of these wet clothes and into a dry martini. Except I think I'll take a bourbon or a Scotch. Oh, that's right—last night you were out of wine." She could hear the disappointment in his voice.

"I bought some bourbon today," she told him. "And also some wine."

"Splendid," he called back. "Bourbon on the rocks with water, if I may," he added. She heard another wet garment being dropped into the tub.

"Bourbon with branch?" she asked.

"You remembered. Good for you!"

Peggy went into the kitchen and got out the bottle of bourbon. She had bought it that day with him in mind, along with a bottle of good expensive domestic wine. She put ice cubes in a glass and poured the rest with bourbon. In the light cast by the single candle she had burning in the kitchen, the glass had an inviting amber glow. Peggy put it to her lips and sampled it. The taste was sharp but tingling. Why spoil it with water? She debated whether to pour one for herself but decided against it.

She started back into the living room carrying his drink—and stopped. The admiral stood dressed in her father's shirt and trousers. Both were several sizes too small; the trousers ending inches above his ankles, the cuffs of the shirt sleeves well above his wrists.

The admiral raised his hand that held the candle. "I know, I know. I look ridiculous. But at least these clothes are dry. May I sit down?"

"Certainly," she told him. Peggy handed him his drink and sat down in an armchair. He moved to the sofa opposite and sat as well. As he did there was the loud sound of fabric tearing.

Peggy saw the embarrassment that crossed his face. He gestured in futility. "These pants are *many* sizes too small, I'm afraid. I hope the Salvation Army accepts trousers with split seams. So," he went on, "I said I would explain my unorthodox arrival. Simply put, I wanted to surprise you."

"You did."

"No, I mean, I told you last night that I'd call. But then today I thought, why not just show up at your door. Without keeping my weather eye well peeled, I sailed down here in my sailboat. Unforgivable for an old navy man like me." He paused, picked up his bourbon, and took a sip. "Dear lady!" he gasped, putting down the glass at once. "If you poured medicine when you were a navy nurse the way you pour drinks, you would have taken care of the wounded in no time at all—either they'd be cured or dead." He sniffed the glass and shook his head. "I'll bet on cured."

"Charles," Peggy said. "I like that."

He looked puzzled. "You like what?"

"Calling you by your name. Tonight, when you arrived, you said, 'It's Charles.' It's much easier than calling you Admiral."

He seemed pleased. "I'd be delighted if you would," he said. "But please, not Charlie. And especially, not Chuck."

A lightning bolt struck suddenly at what was probably the flagpole, and the accompanying bang of thunder shook the house. The ice in the admiral's glass rattled.

He glanced up at the ceiling as if he almost expected it

to fall and kill them both. "Any port in a storm. But especially this one." He added, "Thank you for providing it."

"You're welcome. Where's your boat?"

"Pulled up on the beach about a quarter mile down. Along with what is probably by now a very soggy picnic hamper and a ukelele."

"A *ukelele*?"

"I rented it. I'll admit, I don't look or sound like Rudy Vallee. But, well, I thought tonight I might surprise you with a picnic on the beach. And then take you for a moonlight sail."

"While you serenaded me with golden oldies?"

"Corny, isn't it?"

Peggy smiled. "Yes."

"I'm a corny sort of man, sometimes."

She didn't answer him. The room grew brilliant briefly from another flash of lightning and then was dark again, lit only by the candles that threw dancing shadows on the walls.

"I think you're a very nice man," Peggy told him. She went and sat down on the sofa next to him.

"Thank you," he said. After a moment, he said again, "Thank you." He put down his glass, held out his hand, and placed it over hers. "I think you're quite a woman too."

She looked at him silently, the candlelight illuminating her face. He lifted his hand and touched his fingers to her cheek. "A wonderful woman," he said.

At that, the lights went on.

He pulled his hand away abruptly. "Lights! I don't believe it! How could they restore power in the middle of a storm?"

But in the blaze of lamplight, Peggy had retreated to the far end of the sofa; any hope of an incipient romance was stolen from him by the quick work of the Maine Electric crews.

Peggy stood up and motioned vaguely in the direction of the kitchen. "How about some dinner, while we still have the electricity?"

"How can we be sure the power won't go out again?"

"We can't," said Peggy flatly.

"Dinner, yes. Then let's have dinner," he agreed.

"Is spaghetti okay?"

"Sounds good to me."

"Good." She turned and headed toward the kitchen. He followed, carrying his drink.

As he watched, she filled a pot with water and set it on the stove to heat. "I'm all out of tomato sauce," she said. "Can you make do with grated cheese?"

"Fine. But let me help. We often made dinner a team effort, Grace and I, when . . ." he hesitated. "Grace was my wife. She died four years ago."

"I see," said Peggy. That was all. She reached up to the cabinet to get the package of spaghetti. She tore the end off the box and began taking out a handful of strands. "But you're not married now," she went on, as if awaiting confirmation of the fact.

"Heavens, no. As far as my marriageable potential, I am probably considered hors de combat by most women."

"I doubt that."

"Then at least, an old military man who has forgotten the rules of engagement."

She half-turned and gave him an amused look. "Sounds to me as if you're actually in the reserves. Ready to see action once again if called upon."

"Perhaps," he said, nodding. "But thus far there has been no such call to arms."

She looked up at the open cabinet. "I see I do have a can of clam sauce. How would that be?"

"Fine. Why don't I make some salad for us, while you're doing that?"

"It's a deal," Peggy said. From the refrigerator she took out a head of lettuce, a tomato, and a cucumber, and put them on the countertop in front of him. "Knives are in the drawer to your left, salad bowls are above." The admiral began fixing the salad.

Peggy waited for the water in the pot to boil. Rain still pelted at the windows; several times the lights flickered but they remained lit. As the spaghetti was cooking, Peggy set two places at the small table in the living room. She went back to the kitchen to drain the spaghetti. She took the wine from the refrigerator, handed it to the admiral, and found the corkscrew for him. He thrust the corkscrew into the bottle and began twisting vigorously as Peggy served the spaghetti and the clam sauce.

"Okay," Peggy said at last. "I guess we're ready."

He followed her into the living room. Each took a seat at the table facing one another. He poured the wine, they touched wineglasses briefly, said, "Cheers," and began to eat.

"Good pasta," he said after a few bites. He took a drink from his wineglass. "And the wine too. But I forgot to read the label. What kind is it?"

Peggy shrugged. "A local product. Château de Kennebunkport."

He laughed. "And what vintage?"

"Probably April of this year."

He took another sip and raised his glass to her again. "You know, I like your sense of humor."

"Thanks."

"Grace always—" He stopped at once, and his face clouded. "I'm sorry. Even after four years, I still talk about her as if she were alive."

She looked at him impassively for several moments.

Then she said, "For you, she probably still is, in many ways."

"I guess," he murmured, and resumed eating.

"Would you like to talk about her?" she asked. "Can you?"

"Yes, to both questions," he said, finally. "For a long time I couldn't. Talk about her, that is. Now I can."

"How long were you married?"

"Forty-five years."

"That's a long time."

He nodded and picked at a loose strand of spaghetti that was edging off his plate.

"What year?"

"'Forty-one," he told her. "December sixth, nineteen forty-one, to be exact. How's that for irony? A day of joy, followed by the Day of Infamy. I was a young lieutenant stationed at the Norfolk base. That's where I met her. She was FFV—from one of those 'first families of Virginia.' Postdeb, and all that. Fine-boned, upswept hair, a classic profile. I was her blind date for some society cotillion. Not that she was snobbish, not at all. Quite the opposite. We met in June, and six months later we were married. Our honeymoon in the Great Smoky Mountains lasted just two days. By that time, the U.S. was at war, and a week later I was on a cruiser bound for the Panama Canal."

He anticipated her next question. "We had one son, Charles junior. Called him Chip. A chip off the old block."

"Where is—"

"He died during the Vietnam war."

"I'm sorry."

He took a swallow of his wine. "So these days I'm just another retired salt, who makes port in Maryland, south of Annapolis on the Chesapeake Bay. A good deal of the time I play golf or poker with a few other ex-navy types, and now and then I'm asked to be guest speaker at a launching ceremony. End of story."

There was a flash of lightning, a thunderclap, and once again, the lights went out.

"But with dramatic punctuation," Peggy told him in the darkness.

He grunted. "Maybe. Or it's God's way of telling me I talk too much."

Peggy relit the candles, and they resumed their dinner. They talked generally about the storm that was now passing, tomorrow's weather, and Peggy's love of sailing. She told him she had begun sailing in her teens but had not picked it up again until she moved back to Maine twenty years ago. Now it was her sole passion, her compulsion, Peggy said. From May through October, every day the weather and the sea were good, she sailed. And she was the best sailor around Hasty Harbor, Peggy added modestly but with assurance. Better than any man.

When they had finished dinner, Peggy asked, "How about dessert? There's sherbet."

"No dessert for me, thanks." The admiral patted his midsection. "Doctor's orders. Don't misunderstand. For a man my age, my health is excellent. Except maybe for the usual complaints. It makes me very uninteresting company to lots of my contemporaries. Get a few of them together going on about their gout and cataracts and operations to take out this or put in that, and they sound like an AMA convention."

"I'll skip dessert too," Peggy said. "So what shall we do now? After I do dishes, I mean."

"Beg your pardon?"

"I mean, we can't watch television with the power out, and I don't play cards. So I think the thing you and I should do is go to bed." She looked at him across the table. "What do you say?"

He looked back at her, saying nothing.

"But dishes first," she said. She got up from the table, took the plates, and went into the kitchen.

He sat. Good heavens, he thought, did she mean exactly what she said, the way she said it? It may not have been romantic, but it *was* direct. If anything this woman was direct. Still, for her to make such a suggestion at this early stage in their relationship . . . Well, nowadays young people, even girls, were encouraged to be candid in such matters. Why not older people too?

The more he sat and sipped his wine, the more he thought, the more it made sense to him. She is lonely, has been lonely many years. And in out of a raging storm he comes. Not exactly a prince charming, he admitted to himself, but not bad either. For his age, he had vigor. He also had a certain craggy handsomeness, he knew. And the candlelight, the wine, the sanctuary of this house amid the storm, all must have combined to fill her with romantic urges she felt necessary to express.

He poured the remainder of the wine into his glass and drained it. Sailing was her single passion, she had told him earlier tonight. As for tomorrow . . . He wondered.

He picked up the empty wineglasses and went to the kitchen. She was at the sink, washing the plates under the glow of the candle. He stepped behind her and put one wineglass on the countertop to her left, the other to her right, so that his arms almost encircled her. "Yes," he said softly. "I think getting into bed would be a wonderful idea."

"Okay," Peggy said over her shoulder. She moved to the side and dumped the leftover spaghetti in the garbage can below the sink. "There's extra sheets and blankets in the hall closet," she announced. "You can make up the sofa for yourself. I'll finish here."

He was suddenly confused. "The . . . sofa?"

She grabbed a wineglass and began to scrub it.

"The sofa. Of course," he said. He backed out of the kitchen, and using a candle that dripped wax on his hand he located the linen closet in the hall. As he finished making up the sofa in the living room with sheets and a blanket, Peggy came out of the kitchen, carrying a candle.

"Ready to bunk down?" she asked him.

He thought of asking her to make hospital corners for him. Instead, he nodded. "Ready."

Peggy watched him as he pulled back the top sheet. She came to him and stood before him.

"Good night," she said.

He looked down at her. "Good night. And thanks for dinner. And . . . the bunk."

"I'm glad that you were here tonight," she said.

"So am I." He wasn't sure what else to say.

She paused. "And I know what you thought I meant before."

"I'm sorry if I—"

"Don't be. Today, I thought about it too. I even hoped . . . But it's just been . . . a very long time. Since I was close to anyone."

"May I ask you a question before you go?" He pointed to the windowsill nearby that held the model ship. "That replica. The aircraft carrier. Is that the *Princeton*?"

Peggy looked surprised. "How did you know?"

"I recognized her lines."

"She sank, you know."

"I know. October twenty-fourth, nineteen forty-four."

Peggy set down her candle and picked up the tiny ship. With a finger, she gently wiped away some dust that had accumulated on the deck.

"Did you know someone aboard?" he asked.

She nodded, continuing to look at the ship. "His name was Tom. He was a pilot. We were going to be married two months later. Christmas. . . . But that day the *Princeton* was with a task force in the Leyte Gulf. A Japanese plane broke through the overcast and dropped a bomb directly on the flight deck. There were explosions. Hundreds of her crew got off, but Tom stayed to help the wounded, I was told. I know they sent a medal to his mother. . . ." Peggy put the little ship back on the windowsill.

After some moments she went on. "Some other ships did try to help. Destroyers and cruisers. The *Gatling* and the *Irwin*, and the *Birmingham*. That afternoon the *Birmingham* came along the *Princeton*'s starboard side to fight the fire—"

"Port side."

"What?"

"We were on the *Princeton*'s port side," the admiral told Peggy.

In the candlelight, her face looked stricken. "Then you saw?"

"I was a communications officer aboard the *Birmingham*."

"Were you . . . ?"

"Some shrapnel in the back was all. I was one of the lucky ones. When the *Princeton* blew up, more than two hundred of our own crew were killed."

"Oh, Charles . . ." Suddenly, her arms were holding him. "I didn't know. I'm sorry. I'm so sorry."

Tenderly, he put his arms around her, saying nothing.

Distant thunder, as from long-forgotten battles, echoed as the storm moved out to sea, away from them.

But holding one another, neither of them heard.

7

Although his eyes remained closed, he had a sudden sense of light. When he opened his eyes, he discovered bright sunlight streaming in the space between the living room curtains. Turning his head, he found a freshly made mug of coffee sitting on the low table near the sofa. A man's plaid wool bathrobe was folded over the end of the couch. From the slightly frayed cuffs and the thinness of the fabric, he assumed it, too, had belonged to Peggy's father.

He stood up and put it on quickly. Then he picked up the mug of coffee and sipped it. From the kitchen he heard the sounds of dishes being moved around on the countertop.

He called out, "Good morning."

"Good morning, Charles," she said as she came in. "I see you found your coffee."

"Yes, thank you." He saluted Peggy with his mug.

"I know you like it with some cream," she said. "But this

restaurant happens to be out of cream this morning. I used milk."

"Milk's fine."

"Your shirt and shorts are in the bathroom. They're pretty dry, considering how wet they were last night. Your shoes weren't so lucky. I'll fix us breakfast while you change. Would you like cereal?"

"Oh, no thank you. Toast and coffee's plenty. Juice, too, if you have it."

"I do. That's Continental breakfast number one at this establishment. Plus jam or marmalade."

"Jam, please."

"Done."

"One question," he said. "Since you don't like calling me Admiral, I know I can't address you as Commander. So what name should I use—Peg, Peggy, Margaret, Pegs?"

"Peggy is fine," she said, and went back in the direction of the kitchen.

"Then Peggy it shall be!" he called after her. He turned and headed toward the bathroom.

He reemerged a short time later, dressed in his shirt and madras shorts and carrying his shoes. The table in the living room was set, there was a plate of toast, and Peggy was pouring orange juice.

He sat down opposite her, glancing out the window. "It looks like a nice day."

"Clear skies, good breeze from the northwest. A perfect day for sailing."

"My boat!" he realized. "It's still down on the beach!"

"It may or may not be," Peggy said. "Earlier, while you were asleep, I called the boatyard."

"What did you tell them?"

"That I was out walking on the beach this morning and found a boat from Dodge's Boat Yard pulled up on the sand. Noah said he'd send one of the boys down to tow it back."

The admiral still looked concerned. "I'd better call them myself. When they discover it's my boat, they might think I was lost at sea during the storm."

Peggy shook her head. "I doubt it. There was nothing on the local news." She smiled. "Concerning your whereabouts last night, that is. But maybe you should call the boatyard anyway. Their number is beside the phone."

He went quickly to the kitchen. As he dialed, Peggy rose from the table and went to the glass doors leading to the deck. She slid them open and stepped out. The sky was a bright summer blue, cloudless and benign. The only hints of last night's storm were scattered leaves and a few broken branches strewn around the lawn. From the kitchen she could hear snatches of the admiral's conversation. "Yes. Admiral Deering . . . That's right. Safe and sound . . . out for an evening sail and got caught . . . car passing on the beach road gave me a lift . . . Sorry for the inconvenience."

Peggy heard him hang up, and she stepped back into the living room. He was standing in the doorway of the kitchen.

"It's eight thirty," he said. "I also remembered I have a sailing lesson in an hour. I should call my instructor and delay it."

He turned back into the kitchen. She heard a piece of paper rustling, then the sound of dialing followed by a lengthy pause. Finally, the phone was hung up and the admiral returned to the living room.

"No answer," he said, frowning.

"Then I'll drive you to your cabin," Peggy said. "But let's finish breakfast first."

She refilled the coffee mugs and both sat down at the table. The admiral reached for the jar of beach plum jam and began spreading great globs of it on his toast.

"About last night," she said at last. "I'm sorry. I mean, sorry I—behaved the way I did. When you asked me about the *Princeton*. A lot of memories are locked up in that ship, and until last night, I thought that, like the ship, they were sunk too deep to ever surface after all these years. I guess I was just vulnerable."

"To be vulnerable to memories is not a vice."

"I know. But I was brought up to be strong. My parents taught me that. Since then, people have expected me to be that way."

"Who, for instance?"

"The patients I took care of as a nurse. Other people."

"Including you?"

"I guess . . . How are your sailing lessons coming?" she asked him, changing the subject.

"Very well." He took a swallow of coffee. "I'm surprised—pleased, really, that I still remember as much about sailing as I do. But I guess it's like a lot of things you learn to do and very much enjoy. Even if you haven't done them in a while, it doesn't take long to pick up the technique again."

"Such as what things?" Peggy asked.

What came to his mind first was making love. He shrugged. "Oh, you know. Golf, bridge, tennis—things like that."

"I guess," said Peggy. She sipped her coffee. "By the way," she went on. "I saw you out on the river yesterday. At least, I wondered later if it was you."

"I saw you too, then." The man beamed. "But if you saw a blue Lightning caught up in stays, that was *definitely* me. It was a dumb mistake on my part."

"It can happen to us all," she said, passing it off.

"But I'll confess," he said, "there's still one thing I'm uncertain of sometimes. A simple thing."

"What's that?"

"When to change my heading. There are moments when I think I'm getting nowhere fast."

"You know the basic rule of sailing," Peggy said. "If

you're going nowhere, put some wind behind you, reset your sails, and change course. Just remember all those 'ready abouts' I called out the other day when we were sailing back after your, uh, mishap."

"You're charitable to call it a mishap. I capsized and fell overboard. And you saved me." He put down his coffee mug and looked at her. "Last night, you saved me a second time."

She didn't answer, instead picking up her coffee mug and drinking from it.

"Maybe you should write a sailing book yourself," he added, lightly.

"What should I call it?"

"Oh, I don't know. Something simple and direct. Like *Peggy's Book of Sailing*."

"If I did, I'd include a special chapter entitled, 'Be Aware of Changing Conditions All the Time You're Sailing."

"That's pretty long for a chapter title."

"Then maybe just 'Changing Conditions—Be Aware."

"Conditions such as?"

"Wind, tide, currents," she said. "Anything that can affect your boat. If you know sailing, you know nothing stays the same as when you started out."

"I'd like to read *Peggy's Book of Sailing*. And I should take you with me the next time you and I go sailing. Seriously, would you like to?"

"Sure. Sometime."

"Tonight?" he asked.

"Moonlight cruise, like the one you planned last night?"

"The forecast for tonight is, what shall I say? More promising," he reassured her. "The only thing I won't promise you is ukelele music. How about it? Will you sail with me?"

"Yes, Charles. I think that would be very nice."

"Wonderful!" He lifted his coffee mug, saluting her. "I'll sail my boat down and be here about six thirty."

"This time, why don't I make the sandwiches? What kind do you like?"

"Anything but so-called 'luncheon meat.' It reminds me too much of the Spam I ate during the war."

Peggy laughed. "I agree with you. No luncheon meat." Her face changed, suddenly. "My God—we've got to leave." She stood up and began to clear the table.

"What's wrong?"

"I just remembered Mrs. Doberman is coming here this morning."

"Who?"

"A local lady. I'll explain in the car."

"When's she coming?"

"I don't know. But knowing how she gossips, I don't want her to find you here. Particularly having breakfast."

He downed his coffee. "Busy grapevine around Hasty Harbor, is it?"

"Very busy." Peggy hurried to the kitchen with the empty plates and glasses. She returned with her car keys. "And in the case of Mrs. Doberman, the tendrils of the vine would grow immediately."

"Then let's go. I'm ready." He got up from the table and followed her to the front door.

Less than a minute later they were headed north along Lonely Point Road, Peggy's small car careening around the curves. The road was a single lane of aging asphalt; where there were shoulders they were of sand and beach grass.

"Down!" said Peggy suddenly as she accelerated out of a sharp curve.

It was too late. Approaching them, assuming the entire center of the road, came the large yellow Cadillac of Mrs. Doberman.

Peggy wrenched the Pinto's steering wheel, and shot past the Cadillac along the sandy shoulder. She glanced up at the rearview mirror as she sped on. Mrs. Doberman had come to a dead stop, turned her head, and was staring after Peggy and the admiral, her mouth agape.

Seated at the office desk, Sarah put a piece of boatyard stationery in the typewriter. "Dear Mr. Rumplemyer," she typed: "Once again, we must remind you that the payment of your mooring fee for May remains outstanding. Dodge's Boat Yard is of the opinion that a power cruiser of the size of yours, which, as you know, is referred to around Hasty Harbor as 'the Supertanker' requires considerable anchorage, and therefore—"

"Hi," said a falsetto voice.

Sarah stopped her typing. Leaning against the doorframe was a large clam with round eyes and eyelashes painted on its upper shell. In fact, measuring two feet across, it was the largest clam Sarah had ever seen. It also appeared to be made of plastic. Sarah remembered seeing similar versions in the toy section of the five-and-ten in town.

"Hi," the clam repeated, flapping its shells open and shut.

Sarah didn't know whether to be annoyed or amused. The clam went on. "Let me introduce myself. My name is Clementine Clam."

"Clementine Clam?" Sarah asked.

"Or Clem for short," the clam said. "Be that as it may, I am here for three reasons. First, to assure you, Sarah Dodge, that you're considered a true friend of the clam. Therefore, on behalf of all clams everywhere, I wish to thank you for your attention and support. Because of you and others like you, the Save the Clam movement is alive and well."

Joe's forearm appeared briefly between the clam and the doorframe, then withdrew. "The second reason I am here," the clam said, "is to apologize for my friend, Joe Marino."

"He's a friend of yours?" said Sarah.

"Oh, yes." The clam bobbed up and down in what Sarah took to be a vigorous nod. "For years he's taken pleasure in our company in a variety of forms—raw, fried, and casino. And he wants to apologize to you if what he said the other day sounded like anything less than total admiration for our species."

"Why didn't he come and apologize himself?"

"Because he's shy," the clam answered.

"I wouldn't have suspected that."

"He is, though. Very shy," the clam assured her. "He'd be very embarrassed if he knew you and I were talking about him person to clam, as it were."

"And what's the third reason you're here?" Sarah asked.

"That's the best part," Clementine Clam said. "Joe and I would like to invite you to—excuse the expression—a clambake."

"A clambake?"

"Shh," the clam cautioned. "Among us clams, the word is almost never uttered. But a few of my cousins have agreed to sacrifice themselves for the pleasure of Joe and his friends. Tomorrow evening. Saturday. Sixty Bismarck Street in Whitby. Ground floor apartment. But come around the side to the back yard. How does seven o'clock sound?"

"I—"

"Don't say it," the clam interrupted. "You're thinking about my buddies at the mud flats. But low tide is four fifty-one in the afternoon on Saturday. I checked. You can still get to the party by seven. How about it? Will you come?"

"How big will the party be?"

"Oh, very small. Select. Just Joe and the two other navy ensigns he rooms with, plus their dates."

"I'd—I'd like to think about it," Sarah said. "But thank you for the invitation."

"My pleasure," the clam answered, opening as wide as possible. "I await your response with baited shell."

Sarah thought a moment. "There are two messages you can give Ensign Marino when you see him."

"Really? What?" The clam opened wide again.

"You can tell him he's a terrible ventriloquist."

"He knows that. What's the other message?"

"The admiral's sailboat was found this morning down near Lonely Point. Empty."

"What!" Joe stepped into the office, the clam hanging from his hand.

"Don't worry," Sarah said. "He called later to say he'd gone out for a sail and got caught in the storm. He beached the boat and somebody gave him a lift home. But he did leave some things in the boat. The boys found them."

"Like what?"

"A picnic hamper . . . and a ukelele." Sarah reached under the desk and brought up the small hamper. Then she held up the instrument, its strings limp from exposure to the water.

"What was he doing sailing with a ukelele?" Joe took it with his free hand and checked the side, where the veneer was peeling off.

"He's your student," Sarah said.

"Where's the boat now?"

"At the dock. The boys towed it back. It's probably full of water, though."

"Of course it is," Joe said. He sighed. "I spent an hour bailing it out two days ago. No reason I shouldn't do it now."

He started out the door. "Sailing in a gale with a picnic hamper and a ukelele! Unbelievable!" He raised his arms, the clam still dangling.

* * *

It was about a half an hour later when Joe finally finished emptying the water from the sailboat. As he set the bailing bucket on the dock, he saw the admiral striding rapidly across the pier. Joe said nothing.

"Sorry I'm late," the admiral told Joe as he came down the ramp. "They conveyed my message, I assume."

Joe was visibly annoyed. "Let me ask you something. Did you listen to any marine weather forecasts yesterday?"

"Well, yes, but—"

"And you heard the predictions of a squall line for last night?"

"Yes, but it came sooner than I thought. The storm, I mean. I thought I could get a sail in beforehand. Just to get more practice."

"Did you read the weather signs, at least?" Joe pointed skyward. "By evening, thunderheads were everywhere."

"You're right. I'm sorry," said the admiral. "But I was prepared. I had my life vest—"

"And a ukelele. Did you plan to use the ukelele as a paddle if the sea got rough?"

"Oh, that. Well, that's another story."

"And not one that has anything to do with sailing practice."

"No," the admiral admitted.

"I should probably punish you by making you tie sailor's knots all afternoon," Joe said. "But I won't. Just don't do it again. Come on, let's hit the water. You take the helm."

The admiral stepped into the boat and began raising the sail, as Joe prepared to cast off the lines that held *Invincible* to the dock.

"By the way," Joe said, after he had settled into the cockpit. "Were you expecting any visitors today?"

The admiral looked puzzled. "Visitors? No, why?"

"It seems there are three gentlemen observing us who are very interested in how you sail."

"What do you mean? What gentlemen?"

Joe pointed to a sandy area near the boathouse, where a number of vessels had been pulled up out of the water. Three men sat on an overturned dinghy. One was bearded, one wore yellow waders, and the third man had a finger in his ear.

"They came down to the dock," Joe said, "while I was bailing out the boat. They asked about you. They said they heard you were staying in the area and doing lots of sailing here."

"I never saw them before," the admiral said.

"Well, if they want a show, we'll give 'em one," Joe said. He pushed the boat away from the dock. "Cast off—and hard alee!"

"Aye-aye, sir!" the admiral replied. He pulled the tiller, the mainsail swung out and billowed, and the boat responded smartly to the wind.

Still seated on the upturned dinghy near the boathouse, the three men watched until *Invincible* was well into the harbor. Then, as one, they turned and shared a nod.

Peggy had never been so high before—at least, not on her own house. But before this afternoon she'd never had reason to sit on the peak of her roof. In one hand she held a large screwdriver, in the other, a shiny copper weather vane. The figure on the weather vane was an angel holding a long trumpet out before him as he flew. He was the Angel Gabriel, the owner of the hardware store had told her. That morning she had gone to Whitby, seen the weather vane in the window of the store, and liked it. So she bought it.

From where she sat the view afforded her was breathtaking. The expanse of water was vaster than she'd ever been aware of from ground level. There were boats everywhere, in the river and out into the Gulf of Maine. Far to her right the Kidds Rock Light was a slash of white on a blue canvas. Directly ahead and for several miles seaward were scattered outcroppings of rock too small to qualify as islands, but which bore fanciful names such as Big Momma, The Wicked Rock, and Casper's Thumb.

She heard a car, and looking to her left she saw Sarah's red VW hurrying down Lonely Point Road. It slowed as it approached the house, turned, and pulled into the driveway. There were two short beeps of the horn. Peggy watched as the girl got out, glanced around briefly, and then went up the steps to the front door. "Peggy?" she called in through the screen.

"I'm here!" Peggy shouted down.

The girl backed down off the steps. "I hear you. But where are you?"

"Up here!" Peggy told her. "On the roof!"

Sarah stepped onto the lawn and looked up, shading her eyes against the sun. "What are you doing on the roof?"

"Putting up a weather vane." Peggy held it aloft. "It's the Angel Gabriel. I was painting near the peak of the roof yesterday, and realized this house has never had a weather vane. It should. So when I was in town this morning, I saw Gabriel—and here he is."

"What's that he's holding out in front of him?" the girl asked her.

"It's his trumpet. He's announcing a new life for one and all."

"He must have started with you first," Sarah said.

"You're right. Today I'm on top of the world, or close to it."

"When I talked to you the other night, you sounded really down."

"I was," admitted Peggy. "But that's changed."

"And how's your knee? The one you fell on."

"Cured. No problem." Peggy patted it. "Must be the influence of the Angel Gabriel."

"Well, I'm on my way to the mud flats. I want to see what last night's storm did to my clams. But I can stop by on my way back," the girl added. "If you're not doing anything tonight, we can have dinner."

"Sorry, Sarah. But tonight I've got a date."

"A *date*?"

"Don't act so surprised. I bet this puts me ahead of you for summer dates. And if you want to know, it's going to be my *second* in two days."

"You just never said anything before."

"There wasn't anything to say."

"Who is he? *Tell* me."

Peggy shook her head. "I can't. Not yet."

"Not Mr. Fogerty."

"Are you kidding?" Peggy scoffed. "Since his wife died, he's been acting like an eighty-year-old ram. Let him chase the lambs, the younger ones. I'm sure he thinks of me as a mutton."

"Then have a good time with your man of mystery!" Sarah called up. She waved and started toward her car. As she backed out of Peggy's driveway, she beeped the horn twice again. Then she turned and continued on down Lonely Point Road.

Peggy watched until the girl's car was out of sight. She held up the weather vane again.

"Gabriel," she said, "you're right. A whole new day has dawned."

In his logbook the admiral wrote:

> Friday afternoon, July 22. Great day for sailing—crisp N.W. wind of 20 knots, and not as many swells as I expected after the storm. That storm really cleared things out. Speaking of which, Joe was right to be upset at me for what I did last night. Still, I couldn't tell him that I have another evening sail planned. (Unlike last night, the weather will be fine.)

> As for tonight, I'm trying not to think about it. What a wonderful woman Peggy is. All day I've been on Cloud 9 (999!). If tonight is half as wonderful as last night was, I just may

He paused. Then he added:

> —but that's for tomorrow's log.

He chuckled to himself, put down the pen, and closed the book. After a moment's thought, he opened the logbook to the same page.

> P.S. As I was about to leave the boatyard this afternoon, three men approached me. Joe and I had seen them when we sailed out. Seems they'd like me to contribute to some sort of community event next week. They wanted to give me the details then, but I was in a hurry and suggested they stop by the cabin sometime when they were in the area.

He looked up from the book to see three figures standing at the cabin door. *They just arrived,* he wrote.

When Peggy finally came down from the roof, it was past four o'clock. She showered and dressed quickly so there would be ample time to prepare the picnic supper. That morning when she had gone to Whitby to buy groceries, she'd purchased a small can of Spam, and now she wrapped it in gift paper to give to Charles as a joke. From the state liquor store she'd also bought a split of champagne. She got beer and soda, too; both customary for a summer picnic. But the champagne seemed romantic somehow, and though Peggy acknowledged to herself that she was no expert on romance, the idea seemed appealing. In the plastic food bag she packed a pair of crystal flutes, from which the two of them could sip the champagne. Then she thought better of it and replaced them with paper cups. Even at the beginning of a love affair, there were times when romance had to give way to practicality.

She had just put extra napkins in the food bag and was searching in the cupboard for the box of plastic forks, when she saw the truck. It pulled into her driveway and stopped. On the door of the cab were the words SMILEY'S GARBAGE SERVICE. This isn't trash collection day, she told herself. What's Smelly Smiley doing here? She also noticed two other figures in the cab, whom she assumed were Jimmy's sons. It surprised her when she saw Able Fenstermacher emerge from the passenger's side followed by Cabot Lodge. Jimmy Smiley got out the driver's door.

Peggy closed the cupboard and went into the living room as the men started up the steps.

"Hi, Peggy!" Able called, from outside the screen door.

"Hi, Peggy!" Cabot said.

Jimmy Smiley waved.

"Got a minute?" Able asked her.

"Only a minute," Peggy said. "What can I do for you?" She did not open the screen.

"As you well know," Able began, "we are the race committee for this year's summer festival."

"I know," said Peggy.

"The race is eight days off, to be exact about it," Cabot said.

"I know that, too."

"And being such a long time resident of Hasty Harbor," Jimmy said, "you'll agree the Hasty Harbor Cup Race is the highlight of the festival."

"I thought Emma Wilmott's covered dish, Baked Bean Surprise, was," Peggy said.

Able made a face. "The food committee is asking Emma to try something less surprising this year."

"As you know also," Cabot said, "last year's race got sort of out of hand. That's why we decided on a two-person race this year."

"A two-*man* race is what you told me," Peggy said.

"Yes, well . . ."

"Peg, you're the best sailor around here," Able went on.

"Best woman sailor, anyway," Cabot confirmed.

"And we want you to be one of the racers," Jimmy said.

"No."

"Peg, before you make your mind up," Able said, "think of the advantages."

"Such as?"

"Getting your name engraved on the cup itself."

"Since when have you engraved the winner's name on the Hasty Harbor Cup?"

"We thought of starting this year," admitted Jimmy.

"The answer is still no."

"Give us one good reason why you won't," asked Able.

"I'll give you two," she told them. "The race may be the high point of the festival, but it's a joke. And even if I did accept, you might not find another racer to compete against me."

"To point number one," Able acknowledged, "maybe last year's cup race was a joke. But we want to change that. We want to show everyone that Hasty Harbor is a little town that can make a big splash in the yachting world. As for point number two—"

"We got the other racer lined up," Cabot blurted out.

"That is true," continued Able.

"Who is he?" Peggy asked. "If he's from around here, I—"

"Nope. He's from Maryland," Able said. "Ex-navy, like yourself."

A queasy feeling started in the pit of Peggy's stomach, quickly spreading through her as the men went on.

"It's that admiral who spoke at last week's launching," Able added.

"Seems he's staying up at Kare Free Kabins," Jimmy told her.

"We saw him sailing with a younger navy fella," Cabot said. "For an old man, he's pretty handy with a sailboat."

As each man spoke the woman stared at them in turn, her face blank. A pause followed. The three looked back at Peggy, hopeful and expectant.

It was Able, finally, who filled the silence. "We talked to him this afternoon and explained what the race was all about. We did tell him one little fib, though. We said—we said you'd already agreed to be the other racer. When he heard that, he said he'd race too."

"Now what do you say, Peg?" Jimmy asked her.

There was another pause. Again she looked at each of them in turn. Then she said softly, "Get your truck out of my driveway, Jimmy. There's somebody I've got to talk to. Now."

Noah stood on the boatyard pier. He heard the sudden squeak of brakes and turned to see Peggy spring out of her car and hurry over. She stood before him, hands on her hips, her face drawn. "Has the admiral been here yet?" she demanded.

"He told me he was going to try another evening sail," Noah said. "He's here now."

"Where?" Peggy glanced down toward the floating dock and saw the Lightning tied up beside it, empty.

"Probably in the boathouse." Noah pointed to the large corrugated metal structure a short way beyond the pier. "He said he wanted to replace some line before he sailed."

"Thanks." Peggy turned and started for the boathouse.

"Peg—" She stopped. "You seem upset," he said.

"I am. Those three stooges who call themselves the race committee may just have ruined my life."

She ran in the direction of the boathouse, hopping over the steel rails that led up from the water to the drydock area, and went to the huge sliding doors of the building, which stood open. At first all Peggy could make out inside were sailboats, with and without masts, a few resting on their wooden cradles. Then to one side she saw a mane of gray hair moving in the labyrinth of rigging, and she threaded her way among the hulls toward the admiral.

As she approached, she watched him measuring a length of rope, some of which was coiled in his hand. Suddenly he saw her. "Peggy!" he said, startled.

"I went to your cabin. When you didn't answer, I thought you might be here. Charles, we have to talk."

"Fine." He looked at the coil of rope in his hand. "I was going to bring this along as extra line, in case we want to moor in shallow water." He gave a chuckle. "Can't have us sinking on our moonlight cruise tonight."

"We may be sunk already."

"What do you mean?"

"You've got to tell that so-called race committee you've changed your mind. Tell them you can't."

"Can't what?" he asked. "You mean the sailing race?"

"Of course, the race!"

"But they told me you'd agreed, so naturally—"

"What they told you was a lie, a trick to get you to say yes!"

"A trick? Then what was it they said to you?"

"That doesn't matter. What you've got to do is find those men, any one of them, and tell them you will definitely *not* be in that race."

"Now, Peggy." The admiral placed the length of rope on the workbench next to him and made an openhanded gesture. "Actually, the race sounds like it might be fun."

"Fun?"

"I mean, this morning when we talked, you said you'd sail with me."

"*With* you," Peggy told him. "Not *against* you."

"Peggy—"

"Do you know what some people are going to call us out

there? The Old Fogies Flotilla. The Alzheimer's Armada. The real reason everybody will be there on race day will be to watch two gray-haired sailors going head-to-head to prove they're not quite ready for a nursing home."

The admiral looked down at her for several moments. "My age doesn't bother me. I'm proud of it, in fact. And I didn't think it bothered you."

"It doesn't. But there's still going to be lots of publicity. The newspapers."

"What newspapers?" he asked. "The local weekly?"

"To begin with. And the Whitby *Sentinel*."

"Has a Portland newspaper ever covered the race before?"

"Not that I know of."

"Boston?"

"No, but—"

"Peggy, there are a dozen summer festivals around the state this time of year, just as there are in every state. I don't anticipate what you call publicity."

"But when word gets out you're one of the contestants—"

"Me?" He shook his head. "I told you, I'm an old retired salt the world passed by a long time ago." He grunted. "In the time that I've been here, the media has hardly sought me out for interviews."

"Okay. All right—" It struck her that her hands were now in constant motion, and she grabbed the rigging of a nearby sailboat to quiet them. "All right," she went on more slowly. "But can't you see? Some people are also going to make this race into a man-versus-woman thing."

"Need I remind you," he began, and then realized how pompous that sounded. He started again. "Just let me say that the man-versus-woman thing, as you call it, has been going on for centuries. But in our case, it's not a man and woman battling for the supremacy of their sex. We're just two skippers, one male and one female, competing in a little race. That's all."

She shook her head. "It's more than that to me."

"Well, if the race is that important—"

"That's not what I mean. I mean . . . whatever was beginning, was beginning just between us. I thought maybe in time—" She stopped, looking up at him. He saw that her eyes were wet. "That's ended now."

"It's not."

"It is. Thanks to the race committee of the Hasty Harbor Summer Festival, you and I are about to become a public spectacle."

"Peg—" He reached for her shoulders, but she backed away. "Peg," he said. "I gave my word I'd race."

"Your word," she repeated.

"Yes."

"Thus spake the admiral, whose words can nevermore be changed."

"Peggy, sarcasm does not become you," he said gently.

"Well, I'm so sorry, sir. *So* sorry."

"Peg, it's just a little local race. These people around here—"

"'These people'? I live here. 'These people' are my neighbors. 'These people' are *me*!"

"What I mean is, in a week or so all this will be over. You and I will sail for a couple hours on race day. One of us will win some tacky trophy, and the whole thing will be forgotten by the time the clambake starts."

"And after that?" she asked him.

"We'll pick up where we left off."

"No."

"Peggy, please." He put his hands on her shoulders.

"Don't say anything," she said. "You gave your word you'd race—then so will I. I'll race against you. And until the race is over, we will not see one another, we won't speak. I may be an old retired sailor myself, but in a sailboat, I'll beat you. I will race against you, and I'll beat you."

"Peggy," he began again.

But before he could continue she had twisted from his grasp and begun to fight her way out of the boathouse through the maze of boats.

8

SAILBOAT RACE IS HIGHLIGHT OF FESTIVAL WEEK

The headline leapt at Peggy as she opened the newspaper at her doorstep the next morning. Although she was a subscriber of the paper, she had a low opinion of it. *The Peninsula Pilot* was a local weekly, which, according to its masthead, covered "All the Doings Round 'n' About" the small communities of the peninsula. The newspaper's publisher-editor-printer was a former newspaperman from a defunct New York City journal, who had retired to Maine and felt compelled to bring enlightenment and culture to the natives.

Peggy carried the paper into her kitchen and read it as she ate her breakfast. Below the headline it said:

Famous Admiral and Local Lady
To Square Off at Sea

The article followed:

> All the peninsula is agog with anticipation at the impending sailboat race that will be the featured

event of this year's Hasty Harbor Summer Festival, scheduled for Saturday, July 30. Mr. James G. Smiley, spokesman for the race committee, said, "We're proud as h— to have someone like a famous admiral like Admiral Deering pitted against our Peg." (Editor's note: "Our Peg" is Miss Peggy McCoy of Lonely Point, Hasty Harbor.) As is well known, Admiral Charles T. Deering has been called the Father of Modern Navel Communications, and he . . ."

Peggy had just taken a mouthful of coffee and choked briefly when she caught the misspelling of the word *naval. The Peninsula Pilot* was not known for its copyediting, which was done by the publisher-editor-printer's wife.

She went on reading. The story was mostly a profile of the admiral and an account of his career. When she thumbed through the rest of the paper she saw that much of it was devoted to the festival as well. There was a diagram of the race course that had been crudely copied from a navigational chart, with lines and arrows drawn across it. On the same page a brief piece about "the hazards confronting our two stalwart competitors" mentioned the Sawteeth and the dangerous submerged rocks during high tide around Big Momma. The piece was followed by a schedule of festival day events:

Parade: 9:30 A.M.
Auction & Prize Drawing: 11 A.M.
Prerace Ceremony: 11:45 A.M.
Race: noon until finish
Presentation of the Hasty Harbor Cup: after race
Clambake and Ladies' Auxiliary Supper: 6 P.M.
Fireworks: 9 P.M.
Dance: 9:30 P.M.

On the Let Our Voices Be Heard page of the newspaper was Mrs. Carswell Firkins's "Down East Doodlings" column, a grab bag of recipes and back-fence gossip, which today was full of tidbits and trivia about the festival. It mentioned that the theme of the dance to be held in the social hall of the Old Church was Seafarers Past and Present. It also announced that Emma Wilmott's memorable Baked Bean Surprise would not be offered at the clambake and supper this year.

Enough of this, thought Peggy. She drained the last of the coffee from her mug and stood up. As she did, the ship's clock in the living room struck two bells: nine o'clock.

The telephone began to ring. Peggy started for it and then stopped. It could be Sarah or her father, or one of Peggy's acquaintances. On the other hand, it could be Mrs. Doberman, who Peggy had successfully avoided since yesterday. Or it could be someone else who'd seen the story in the newspaper and wanted to offer their opinions or advice.

The telephone continued ringing. Could it be he? she thought. She stood looking at the phone, letting it ring until it stopped.

Then she opened the front door and hurried out as the telephone began to ring again.

Noah Dodge couldn't understand it. As he always did about nine every morning except Sunday, he went to collect his mail at the post office in T. C. Dabney's store. Usually there weren't more than two or three people in line at the grille window, behind which Dabney himself stood. Granted, in July and August the summer people sometimes caused a small line, buying stamps for postcards or conveying change-of-address information, but they rarely came so early in the day.

Yet this morning when Noah stepped into the store, he had to stop abruptly to avoid knocking over old Hetty Joy, leaning patiently on her cane. Ahead of her were eight other Hasty Harbor residents he knew, including Casper Fister, Fletcher Knox, and Wally Wonderman. Noah nodded an acknowledgment to Hetty Joy, who returned it and began counting the contents of the change purse she was carrying.

It wasn't until there were just three people in front of Noah that he noticed everyone was handing money through the grille and receiving nothing in return. After some quiet conversation, T. C. Dabney would accept the offered money, make a quick note on a postal slip, and wish the person at the window a good day. No one received stamps or envelopes or money orders. Nothing.

Finally, Noah himself stood before the grille.

"You, too, Noah?" T. C. Dabney asked him.

"T.C., what's going on here?"

"Taking stamp orders, that's all," Dabney said. "As of this morning the navy hero stamps are selling for six cents and the lady suffragettes for two. But of course, that's subject to change. I can give you either or both. Just tell me what you want."

"I want a roll of one hundred regular first-class stamps with the American flag on 'em," Noah told the man.

"That's it?"

"That's it."

"Okay. But you're missing a bet." Dabney chuckled and reached into the drawer below the counter.

Noah was ready to ask what was so special about navy hero and lady suffragette stamps, when the answer became clear. He leaned toward the grille and signaled Dabney to come closer. "T.C.," he asked, "are you bookmaking on the sailing race next week? Six to two odds for the admiral? Is that it?"

Dabney put a finger to his lips. "Careful, Noah. You never know when there might be a postal inspector in the line behind you. But in answer to your question; you're a businessman, and I'm a businessman. And if a lot of folks around here want to place a wager on the race next week, I'm just happy to oblige."

Noah frowned. Since last night when he'd heard about the race, the news had troubled him, more for Peggy's sake than anything. And already it had turned the citizens of Hasty Harbor collectively into a bunch of shameless gamblers.

"Say you want to order two dollars' worth of lady suffragette stamps," Dabney went on. "You give me the two and if Peggy wins the race, I give you back six dollars. Simple as pie."

He pushed Noah's roll of stamps toward him under the grille. "Will that be all?" he asked, and winked. "Or would you like to place a order for special stamps too?"

Noah sighed and reached into his wallet. "All right, here's for the roll of first-class stamps. And put me down for ten dollars' worth of the lady suffragette stamps."

T. C. Dabney smiled his weasel smile, accepted Noah's money, and wrote the information on a slip. "I figured that's how you'd go," he said. "Being a friend of Peggy's, and all."

"I still don't like the idea," Noah told him.

Dabney shrugged. "Lots of your friends around here don't agree with you. Just look behind you."

Noah turned. He saw the line behind him now stretched out the door of Dabney's Store.

It was the end of that same line Peggy saw as she made the turn off River Road and drove on toward the boatyard. She assumed it must be another scam the storekeeper-postmaster was perpetrating, and dismissed it from her mind. Arriving at the boatyard pier, she first checked to make sure that *Free Spirit* was waiting for her at the floating dock. The boat was there. Peggy started for the office when she saw Noah walking down the boatyard road. He hailed her.

"Morning, Peg," he said as he approached.

"Hi, Noah. What's the sour face for?" Then Peggy realized. "You heard."

"I heard. All of Hasty Harbor's heard. Peggy, why on earth did you agree to it?"

"For a lot of reasons. Maybe some I don't even know myself."

"Peg, we've been friends for a long time. And I think your judgment's pretty near perfect. But to agree to this damn fool sailing race—"

"I agreed, and that's that," Peggy said.

"I just don't want to see you hurt. And one way or another, you will be, you know."

"I've been hurt a lot of times in my life. That's nothing new."

"I mean, this race is a no-win situation for you," Noah said. "You beat the admiral, and you humiliate a revered old navy man. *And* bruise a lot of male egos at the same time."

"And if he beats me?"

"Some people'll say it proves men are better at everything, including sailing. And that one more uppity woman who tried challenging a man has again been shown her place. Peg, please, back out while you still can."

"I can't."

"You can."

"And say what?" Peggy asked. "That I was afraid? That I changed my mind—just like a woman?"

"I know you're the best sailor around here," Noah said. "Everybody does. But it's because I care about you—"

"So do I," she told him. "I care about me too. Maybe that's one of the reasons I'm sailing in this race. For *me,* and for all those other uppity women who don't quite have the gall I do. And maybe also I am doing it to bruise some male egos, some of the egos that *need* bruising."

Noah dug into his pocket and brought out the roll of

stamps. "Know what these are?" he asked, holding up the roll.

"Stamps, of course."

"And did you see the line outside Dabney's Store?"

"Yes, but I thought—"

"What'd you think?" Noah asked her. "That T.C. was having a sale of his wife's baked goods? He's not just selling real stamps in his post office, he's got a whole betting operation going, on your race against the admiral. He's making book on you."

"He's *what*?"

"He's taking 'orders for stamps'; navy hero stamps, and—I think you'll like this—stamps featuring a lady suffragette. The odds, by the way, are six to two against you. But as T.C. says, that's subject to change."

"The bastard!" Peggy said.

"By day's end, I'm guessing, everyone in Hasty Harbor will have gone to T.C.'s post office to place a bet."

"And what about you?" Peggy asked him. "Did you place a bet too?"

Noah pursed his lips, then nodded. "I've got ten dollars on the lady suffragette."

"Thanks," Peggy told him. "And I promise you this, Noah. You're going to win some money on her. On that lady suffragette."

The navigational chart lay spread out across the table in the admiral's cabin. It was held down at its four corners by the cans of beer Joe and the admiral were drinking, by one of the admiral's books on sailing, and by a souvenir ashtray from Annie's Truck Stop in Skowhegan. The chart was number 13295 of the U.S. National Ocean Survey, and was titled "The Newell and Kerrenac River Entrances." Drawn in pencil on the face of it were three straight lines connecting to form an irregular triangle. The northernmost point of the triangle represented a buoy with a flashing signal near the entrance to Hasty Harbor and the Sawteeth. One line extended in a southwesterly direction from the buoy to a gray-shaded object identified on the chart as Osprey Rock, but referred to generally as Big Momma, since to the mariners who named it years ago, it resembled at a distance the outline of a large recumbent woman. From there another line went east for two miles to a buoy marked Gong-R 4-CL. The final line ran north-northwest from buoy 4-CL for just over four miles, ending once more at the Hasty Harbor entrance.

Joe took a sip of his beer, placing one hand on the corner of the chart to keep it from curling up. The admiral continued to peer down at the chart as he moved a pencil along the lines of the triangle.

"Well?" Joe asked him. "What do you think?"

"I think I can do it."

"Of course you can do it," Joe said. "The question is, can you sail the course fast enough to win?"

The admiral looked up at him. "What do you think?"

"What I think doesn't matter. Do *you* think you can win?"

"Yes," the older man said simply. Then he added, "If I go faster than the other boat."

"And that's what we're going to spend the next week working on." Joe tapped a finger on the chart. "Okay, one more time. Let's make sure you know the course."

He took the pencil from the admiral's hand and put the tip of it at the point of the triangle beside the harbor entrance. "The start-finish line is here, at the flashing buoy just beyond the Sawteeth. The first leg of the race is from the start line down to Big Momma. You know about the currents there, and the dangers at high tide from underwater rocks."

The admiral nodded. "I see the asterisks around it: wrecks. I don't intend to make my boat another asterisk."

"Glad to know that. It'd really put a damper on the race." Joe moved the pencil eastward. "You'll probably have an easy run to your next mark, the red gong buoy, here." He touched the pencil briefly to the diamond-shaped symbol, then moved it slowly along the third line of the triangle. "After that, it's home you go. In all, it's a distance of about ten miles."

"If there's very little wind it could take hours."

"It might," Joe agreed. "Are you in a hurry to get back for the clambake?"

"Not particularly. By that time, I may even be seasick."

"And if you lose the race, *I* may be," Joe said. "But you won't lose. We'll make sure of that."

"No, I won't lose," the admiral repeated. "I just wish it was a different sailor I was racing."

"Why? Because your competition is a woman?"

"Because my competition is *that* woman."

"Just think of her as the opposition," Joe said. "Remember the war games you played in naval training. It was your ship against the enemy ship. She's the enemy."

"I'll try to keep that in mind," the admiral said. But he didn't look particularly happy about it.

"So, do you have any questions about the course so far?" The admiral shook his head. "No."

"Good." Joe rose from the table. "Now that we've sailed it on paper, let's see how you do on water."

Several hours later, as the *Invincible* struggled to make headway against a swift incoming tide, the admiral discovered he was not doing well at all. Seated amidships, Joe said little as they sailed. But even his few comments—"You know you can set the jib faster than that"; "Do you plan to sail all the way to Boston on this tack?"—told the admiral that Joe felt the same way.

As they approached their first mark, the rock known as Big Momma, the admiral made a wide cautious turn around it, keeping at least fifty feet away. He glanced at Joe. "I know I should have gotten closer to that rock." All he could think of was the ring of asterisks encircling the rock on the chart.

"Timidity does not win races," Joe told him. "I'm guessing your competitor will get a *lot* closer. I've seen her sail."

"So have I," the admiral admitted. "But one thing just occurred to me. Now that we *are* competitors, what's to prevent us from practicing out here at the same time?"

"Don't worry, I've already worked out a schedule so that you and Miss McCoy will practice at different times. I talked with her second."

"Her second? I never heard that word used except in connection with a duel or a boxing match."

"There are some similarities," Joe said.

"Who is it? Her second, I mean."

"Miss Dodge."

"Oh, that girl at the boatyard." The admiral nodded with approval. "She seems very nice. And very pretty. You should make her acquaintance."

"Uh-huh," was all Joe said. He was about to say more but thought better of it. Instead he shifted his position at the cockpit rail and looked east toward the second mark.

"We've got a following breeze," the admiral said after a few moments. "I'm going to wing out the jib and raise the spinnaker."

"Good thinking," Joe agreed. "You got the whisker pole?"

"Right here." The admiral picked up a wooden pole about four feet long and moved forward. He hooked one end of the pole to the mast and the other end to a lower corner of the jib. With the jib now drawing wind from the side opposite the mainsail, he raised the large red-white-and-blue spinnaker sail at the bow. As all the sails billowed forward, the boat quickly gathered speed.

They continued running with the wind behind them toward red gong buoy 4-CL. Occasionally, Joe checked his watch and wrote something on the clipboard he carried.

At first the admiral wondered if Joe was critiquing his performance at the helm. But that wasn't Joe's style. If Joe had any remarks to make, good or bad, he would make them at the time, not later. The admiral liked that quality in the young man.

In fact, the more time he spent with Joe the more he liked him. He'll make a fine naval officer some day, the admiral thought. If he lacked physical stature, it shouldn't matter. Lord Nelson hadn't exactly been a giant, nor had John Paul Jones. Joe would command respect because of the more important qualities that he possessed; intelligence, assurance, competence, and that intangible instinct that marked a born sailor—a true feeling for the sea.

Because the wind had picked up, *Invincible* had increased her speed further, and as they approached the gong buoy the admiral felt as if he were at the throttle of a power launch. Now twenty-five feet from the buoy, he kept coming straight for it. Twenty feet . . . ten . . . seven, and he tacked around it in a neat, sharp turn.

Joe looked back at the admiral and relaxed his hold on the railing. "Clean and close. No wonder you were called Daring Deering."

On the final leg of the triangular course, the admiral reset his heading toward the Sawteeth and the harbor entrance. With the wind coming directly from the port side, the admiral found he had to tack more frequently. But *Invincible* did not appear to slacken speed. There were also more boats out across the water than there had been earlier. At one point they found themselves on a parallel course with another Lightning class sailboat, and the admiral was pleased that he outran her.

"By the way," the admiral said. "You mentioned you worked out a schedule for our practice sessions. What time tomorrow?"

"In the afternoon," Joe said. "Two thirty. Is that okay?"

"Fine. I just remembered I'm going to a church service

in the morning." He saw Joe's expression and explained. "Not to pray I win the race next week—although maybe I should. It so happens that a gunnery officer I once served with lives in Brunswick, and he learned I was in Maine. He reached me through Captain Carnes and asked if I could visit him and his wife for church and lunch on Sunday. And I accepted."

"Old navy reunion, huh?" Joe asked. "I bet you'll be glad to see each other."

"I will, but he won't," the admiral said. "He's blind. A shell exploded as he was loading an aft battery off Kwajalein. He was one of the more fortunate. The other men were killed." The old man looked at the young man. "War is an abomination, Joe. An obscenity. Pray God, you'll never have to fight in one."

Joe simply nodded and shifted his position at the rail. He looked down at his watch. Then he turned forward and stared out in the direction of the final mark, which neither of them yet could see.

As the admiral gazed across the water he recalled his own days as a young naval officer, recalled how at the beginning of the war he and his fellow officers, comrades in arms, had been filled with the patriotic fervor of the time. Proudly, almost passionately, they had gone off to fight. For some, all that their passion got them was a plot at Arlington, or in memoriam, their name in raised bronze letters on a plaque somewhere. As a career officer, the admiral had come to detest war. War had taken him from his new bride only days after their wedding; war still filled his dreams with scenes of death and carnage; war had killed his only son. Looking at the young man for whom he felt a growing fondness, he prayed that Joe would never have to fight and die, as Chip had.

Chip . . .

Sometimes the recollections of his son came flooding back. He'd had his mother's light blond hair and clear blue eyes. Full of youthful spirit, and an honors graduate of the academy, he had opportunities ahead of him that seemed endless.

Instead, the end came in the instant that it took the mine to detonate against the hull of Chip's patrol boat off the Vietnamese coast. When the admiral was in Washington, D.C., he often visited the long black-marble wall that bore the names of those killed in that tragic war. Each time he stood for a few silent moments as he read the name—Charles T. Deering, Jr.—and saw his own reflection mirrored in the wall before his eyes began to mist.

At last *Invincible* reached the flashing buoy near the Sawteeth. The admiral lowered the jib and started through the channel into Hasty Harbor. The harbor itself was less crowded than the admiral had expected: he would have an easy run across it to the boatyard dock.

Once inside the harbor, the admiral spoke again. "Joe," he began, "I'm not doing anything this evening. If you have no plans, would you like to join me for dinner?"

Joe hesitated but looked pleased. "Thanks. Maybe a rain check. Tonight my two roommates and I are having a little cookout. Just the three of us, plus dates. A back yard sort of thing."

"It sounds like fun," the admiral said. "Your date, if I may ask—is she a local girl?

"Yeah," Joe said. "She's a local girl. But she hasn't said yet if she'll come."

"I'm sure she will. It should be fun," the admiral repeated. Still, he couldn't help wondering just what kind of girl Joe had found. He wanted to ask more about her, but did not. He hoped, though, for Joe's sake that the girl came from a good family and wasn't the cheap sort who saw all navy men as easy prey.

The admiral approached the boatyard dock, came about, and let *Invincible* be carried broadside up against it. Joe leapt out and began securing the sailboat to the mooring cleats. Two of the teenage boys who helped around the yard were on the dock, and they took over the remaining chores of laying up the boat. Together the admiral and Joe walked toward the ramp up to the pier.

As they went up the ramp Joe said, "I've got to admit, after a slow start you really put the pedal to the metal. Maybe you'll win, after all."

The admiral grinned. "I told you, I intend to."

"Well, we have seven days to practice, barring weather problems. But if you sail on the afternoon of the big race the way you did today, you should be shooting through the water like a loose torpedo."

"They're talking about rain tomorrow. All day."

"So I hear," Joe admitted. "But if not, I'll rent another Lightning for myself and be your sparring partner."

"Pretend you're Miss McCoy, eh?" The old man grunted. "Just be sure you're as aggressive as I know *she'll* be."

Never a sailor.

Sarah had said that to herself, been told that by her parents, for as long as she could remember.

Never a sailor.

Some of them might seem gentlemanly, but they had only one thing in mind. She recalled how schoolgirl friends would giggle when the stories were exchanged. One had it on the best authority that the navy added huge amounts of saltpeter to the food all sailors ate to stifle their voracious lust—to no avail. Sarah thought back to the girl who sat next to her in junior English, who got pregnant by a sailor and had to go away somewhere, no more to be spoken of or seen.

Never a sailor.

So why was she doing what she was doing now? Why had she decided suddenly to accept Joe's invitation and attend the cookout? Maybe it was curiosity. He seemed nicer than a lot of the shipyard navy men she'd met. And he had a sense of humor. But he was still a sailor. And if he thought she was just another of the Whitby town girls who chased the fleet, he was in for a rude shock.

Sarah backed her car out of the driveway of her parents' house and waved briefly to her mother. At least her mother had finally accepted that there was no way she could change her daughter's mind. As for her father, Sarah had defused his disapproval by explaining that it was just a cookout; other girls would be there, and she'd be home early. And besides, she hadn't had a date all summer.

But if not a sailor, who then would she finally fall in love with? There'd been that fellow student at the university who had also majored in marine biology. She'd liked him and had thought that he liked her; they'd shared their notes, and she had helped him cram for his senior finals more than a year ago. But he'd moved on to graduate work in Florida and had never answered the four chatty, friendly letters she had written him. Lately, she admitted to herself, she'd fantasized about being on an oceanographic expedition doing her own postgraduate work. She would be on a research ship in the South Seas, and among the scientific team would be a handsome young doctor on a fellowship. Their fields of study would be mutual; they would begin to work together, and . . . It *was* a fantasy, Sarah reminded herself. But a pleasant and harmless one. And maybe, she decided, that was all she wanted, all she needed. Still, no matter who it was, the man could *never* be a sailor.

Crossing the Newell River into Whitby, Sarah took the first exit past the bridge and zigzagged among local streets until she came to Bismarck Street. It was in an older section of the town. Many of the houses had been built years ago by prosperous sea captains and shipwrights, but most were now divided into apartments or multifamily dwellings with toy-strewn lawns, motorcycles parked in the driveways, and laundry drying in the back yards.

Sixty Bismarck Street, then, was something of a surprise to Sarah as she neared it. She parked across the street and studied the large solid structure of brown-painted wood, with a porch running the width of the front and curving gracefully around the side. The lawn sloped off behind the house, and Sarah guessed that the entrance to the ground-floor apartment was in back. A hedge of privet and bayberry, neatly trimmed, separated the sidewalk and the lawn, and a broad walkway led up to the front porch.

Sarah took a breath, picked up her purse, and got out of her car. She stood for several moments on the sidewalk, smoothing the rose-colored summer dress that she was wearing. As she started up the walk, she heard a mix of voices and laughter coming from behind the house. She turned and followed a narrow flagstone path toward the sound.

At the far end of the backyard, diagonally opposite her, a metal barbecue on wheels was sending up a column of white smoke. Near it a card table was set up as a makeshift bar. Beside the table stood two young men dressed in shorts and sports shirts, a tall thin girl in a white sleeveless blouse and white flared slacks, and a short blond girl in a low-cut orange polka-dot dress that displayed more than enough of her ample bosom. Joe himself was near the grill. Around his waist he had an apron that said HAVE YOU HUGGED THE COOK TODAY? The two girls held paper cups; the young men were drinking from beer cans. As he talked, Joe waved a pair of cooking tongs, using it occasionally to poke the grill.

The girl in the polka-dot dress glanced over. She nudged Joe and gestured with a tilt of her head. Joe looked, saw Sarah, grinned, waved the tongs, and excused himself from the group.

He came toward her with arms open as if to embrace

her, but then thought better of it. "Hi," he said instead. "Welcome to Palazzo Marino. No trouble getting here, I hope."

"No."

"I wasn't sure you'd come."

"I wasn't either," Sarah said.

"Well, I want you to meet the two jokers I room with, and their dates." Joe started back across the yard, with Sarah following, to where the others were regarding her.

"Sarah, this is Ensign Sandy Whittemore." Joe indicated the young man who stood beside the girl in white. "And this is Gayle Holyoke."

The young man nodded and said, "Hi, Sarah." The girl beside him responded with a quick, thin smile.

Joe turned to the other young man, who had his arm around the blond girl's waist and was grinning boyishly. Joe went on, "This clown is Ensign Billy Buxson, and the young lady who is unable to escape his grasp is his new and very good friend, Corky Canty. Everybody, this is Sarah Dodge."

There were some murmured greetings. "Now mix it up," Joe said. "I'll get us some more liquid pacifiers. What'll yours be?" he asked Sarah.

"Oh. Something soft. Please," Sarah said.

"Soft? You mean water? How about some wine, at least?"

"All right. A little. Thank you."

"Hey, Sandy see that Sarah gets some wine while I check the kitchen." He turned and headed toward a door at the back of the house. Sarah watched him go, suddenly feeling abandoned and uncomfortable.

The tall ensign whose last name Sarah had already forgotten went to the card table. He picked up a gallon jug of wine, filled a paper cup and returned to Sarah with the cup and presented it to her.

"I was going to say here's your vino blanco, but Joe's the only one around here who's allowed to speak Italian. Or who wants to." He laughed and wrinkled his nose, as if the thought was odoriferous. "Joe says you're from down on the peninsula," he went on.

"Yes. Hasty Harbor," Sarah said.

"Where Joe goes sailing with Admiral Hornblower."

"With Admiral Deering. Yes."

"Are you vacationing there?" he asked her.

"No. I live there. I've lived there all my life."

The girl in white joined them. She slipped a hand over the young man's in a gesture of discreet proprietorship. "I find that part of the peninsula quite charming, really," said the girl. "We've taken our boat into Hasty Harbor several times this year."

"What kind of boat is it?" Sarah asked her.

"A new Barnegat. We wanted something that slept more than our last boat. My family summers at Boothbay. Do you sail?"

"Some. But I haven't much this summer," Sarah said.

The other couple had now joined them. Billy Buxson's arm was still around Corky Canty's waist, and Sarah noticed that the girl was chewing gum at the same time she drank from her paper cup.

"Dodge, Dodge," Corky Canty chimed. "How come I know that name from down around there?"

"My father has a boatyard," Sarah answered. There was silence. Because of the expression on the face of the girl in white, Sarah said no more.

"I see," the girl said at last.

"*Attenzione!*" Joe called, returning with another jug of wine and a six-pack of beer. He set them on the card table. "Everybody have yourself one more. In five minutes I start barbecuing the lobsters." He was about to start back to the house when he saw Sarah watching him. "Did I say something wrong?" he asked. The other couples had already abandoned them.

"No," Sarah told him. But her look of puzzlement remained.

"I know, I know," Joe said as realization dawned. "Nobody in his right mind would barbecue a lobster. But I decided I needed our large pot to do the pasta in. So as a result I've got to barbecue the buggers. Can you stand having them that way?"

"Of course."

"I mean, in the year I've been assigned here, I've found out that Mainers only eat their lobsters one way: boiled. But tonight you're going to live dangerously. In fact, Chef Marino's complete menu for tonight is Lobster Barbecue Diablo, Pasta alla Whitby, and Insalata Mista." Joe opened his hands toward her and shrugged in what Sarah guessed was probably a typical Italian gesture.

He smiled. "You'll also be glad to hear I decided against serving clams."

She smiled back. "I'm glad to hear. May I help you?"

"Thanks, but I'll just be a minute." Joe turned and headed toward the house, leaving Sarah standing by herself once more.

An hour and twenty minutes later, with the dinner guests seated in a circle on a variety of kitchen chairs, a deck chair, and a steamer trunk, the cookout wound toward its conclusion. Once more Joe poured wine into the women's paper cups and tossed beer cans to his fellow officers, who opened the tops and held a brief competition to see who could chug his beer faster holding it at arm's length above his head and pouring it into his mouth.

Throughout the dinner, Sarah had listened as Sandy Whittemore expounded on the proper uses of a pitching wedge and nodded as Gayle, the girl in white, delighted in her recent purchase of a bathing suit that she was saving for the winter season in Cancún.

Billy Buxson and his date, blond Corky, sat saying very little. In the fading light Sarah observed that his arm remained fixed around Corky's waist. The girl still had her gum, and she continued chewing and drinking from her cup. But mostly it was Joe who talked, engagingly and easily, often addressing his remarks to Sarah. For her part, Sarah remained generally mute.

When dinner ended Joe and Billy cleared the empty plates and headed back to the apartment, while Sandy and Gayle entertained Sarah and Corky with an anecdote about skinny-dipping in some wealthy person's lake.

"Music!" Billy Buxson shouted as he and Joe started back across the lawn. In one hand he carried a huge portable tape player; in the other, some cassettes.

"It's cel-e-bra-tion time!" he sang out. "Everybody's gotta dance!"

"You're *baaad*!" Joe told him.

"*Baaad*!" sang Billy, prancing briefly, his left hand dropped.

Billy thrust a tape into the player, but what boomed out didn't sound much like music to Sarah. Obviously, others in the neighborhood agreed, since she heard the windows of adjacent houses slamming down. Immediately the other couples sprang up and began gyrating, feet stomping, elbows pumping, heads bobbing.

"Care to dance?" Joe asked. Sarah turned to find him standing before her with his hand outstretched.

"I—no, thank you."

"Come on. I bet you're a fantastic dancer."

"I'm used to—other kinds of dancing, really," Sarah told him.

"I understand," Joe nodded sympathetically. "I haven't seen a single New Age club in Hasty Harbor. But it's time you broadened your horizons." With that he took hold of both her hands and pulled Sarah to her feet. "Now kick off your shoes."

Sarah did so.

"That's it," Joe said. "Do your thing."

Sarah tried a few steps but felt ridiculous. She stopped. "If you don't mind, I'll sit and watch."

"No problem," Joe said. "I'll sit with you. If you want to know the truth, I think this kind of dancing was invented by Saint Vitus, anyway."

Sarah sat down on the steamer trunk and Joe straddled a chair opposite. In the growing darkness, the manic actions of the dancers made them look like participants in some tribal rite. Finally the tape ended, and Sandy and Gayle staggered to chairs as Billy Buxson and Corky fell onto the grass.

It was Sandy who rallied first. He stood up. "Great party, my friend. But I think Gayle and I are going to take a little drive to cool off."

Gayle stood up also and offered her hand to Joe. "Wonderful party, Joe. You can cater for me anytime."

"You think so?" Joe said. "Maybe in Cancún this winter."

Billy Buxson sat up on the grass. "Man, it's a good thing Sandy and me have sea duty starting Monday. After tonight's party, I'm gonna need a rest." He came to Joe. "You're the host with the most, Giuseppe. But I think Corky and me are going to, you know, take a drive, too." He winked at Joe. Corky Canty staggered to her feet and hiccupped once, then giggled.

Joe walked with the two couples to the corner of the house. Then he returned and sat down again across from Sarah.

"Thanks for coming tonight," he said. "I'm sorry we didn't get much chance to talk."

"I should be going soon myself," she told him.

"But not yet." Abruptly he reached down, slapping at his ankles. "Damn! These Maine mosquitoes must eat elephants alive! Listen, I've got a spray can of repellent inside. I'll get it."

Before Sarah could respond, Joe had risen and was making his way hurriedly across the lawn to the house.

Perhaps it was the wine; perhaps the mellow sweetness of the summer night. But Sarah realized she couldn't just say good night to Joe and leave. Throughout the dinner she'd felt awkward and estranged from the others. Yet now that they were gone, she was surprisingly at ease.

No, she should go. She must.

She found her purse and stood up just as the door of the apartment opened and Joe started back toward her, carrying a spray can and a lighted citronella candle in a little glass.

"Something I can get you?" he called out as he approached her.

"I—no, nothing," Sarah answered. And she sat down on the trunk.

Joe came to her, spraying himself liberally with the repellent. He put the candle in the grass and sat opposite her once again. "Whew! They call this stuff Backwoodsman brand. No wonder the guys who use it have to live in the backwoods—the minute they put it on they're banished from society."

He offered the can to her. "It won't smell as pretty as your perfume, but it does the job."

"No, thank you," Sarah said.

"So," Joe said. "Since you *did* make the decision to come to my party, let's get to know a little more about each other. We'll start with names. Tell me about Sarah middle-name-or-initial Dodge."

"Sarah Alice Dodge. Alice was the name of a great-aunt."

"A nice name, but an awful monogram," Joe said. "People will take one look at your luggage and say, 'Sad.'"

"I never use the Alice, though."

"Good thing. Any brothers? Sisters?"

"No."

"And you'll be in your senior year of college where?" he asked her.

"Orono."

"Is that a city or a cookie?"

"Orono, Maine. That's where the state university is."

"And you're studying marine biology. Then after college, what?"

"Graduate school, I hope. Maybe out of state."

"Out of state? Have you ever been out of state before?"

"Of course I have." She sounded mildly indignant at the question.

"Again, where?"

"Boston. And New Hampshire. And twice we were in Canada. The Maritimes."

"But you wouldn't exactly call yourself a world traveler."

"Not exactly," Sarah nodded. "But I hope I will be someday."

"You could always join the navy. If you did I might think of reenlisting."

"Did you always want to be in the navy?" she asked, hoping to turn the conversation in his direction.

"Maybe so," Joe answered. "When I was a kid we lived two blocks from Sheepshead Bay. That's in Brooklyn, which, in turn, is in the city of New York. Sometimes a few friends and I would find a wooden cargo pallet washed up on the shore and we'd go rafting."

"How did you get into the naval academy?"

Joe caught her tone of voice. "You mean, how did a Brooklyn boy get himself included in the august company of future admirals? I have my grandfather to thank for that."

"Your grandfather?"

"Since both my parents worked, I spent a lot of time at my grandparents' apartment in Red Hook. They were immigrants from Napoli—Naples—and they took a great chance coming to America. As my grandfather used to say, 'We dared to live!'

"As for Annapolis, my grandfather had a shoe repair

shop, and the cousin of a local congressman always had his shoes fixed there. One day my grandfather told the man he wouldn't give him back his shoes until the congressman wrote a letter on my behalf to the academy. After that, I was a shoe-in, you could say. Good grades I had in school helped, too, I'll admit."

He reached into his back pocket and drew out his wallet. "I've got a picture of them, my grandfather and my grandmother. I'll show you."

Joe picked up the citronella candle and sat down beside Sarah on the steamer trunk. He flipped among some plastic-covered photographs and found the one he sought. As Joe held the candle up, Sarah looked at the aging snapshot of a young couple wearing very formal clothes. Their wedding picture, Sarah guessed.

Joe pointed to the woman in the photo. "She was beautiful when she was young. Of course, I didn't know her then. But she was the artistic talent in the family. Along with the pictures of Jesus and the Holy Virgin, she had reproductions of old paintings on the walls of the apartment."

"Which artists did your grandmother like?" Sarah asked him.

Joe laughed. "She liked Leo and Mike a lot."

"Who?"

"Leo D. Vinci and Mike L. Angelo. Maybe you've heard of them."

"I've seen their work." The girl smiled.

"I once thought I'd become an artist, because of seeing all that great art. When I was in fourth grade, I sat for an hour on the stoop outside our building, drawing a picture of the fireplug beside the curb. And the whole time I was drawing, not a single dog came by. Obviously they were great respecters of my talent. I will modestly admit that that picture won me first prize in the elementary school student art exhibit at P.S. Twenty-six."

"I'm impressed," said Sarah. "Mike and Leo must be very proud of you today."

As the candle flickered, Joe moved closer to her on the trunk. "There's something else I'd like to impress on you," he told her. "How much do you know about *il bacio*? Not a lot, I'll bet."

"Il bacio? Is he an Italian painter too?"

"*Il bacio* isn't a painter," Joe said, facing her.

As Sarah waited for his explanation, Joe kissed her softly on her lips.

"That is what *il bacio* is," he said.

9

Very early in the morning, after the Sunday sections of the Portland *Press Herald* and the Boston *Globe* had been assembled, T. C. Dabney stepped onto the porch of his store carrying a felt eraser. A light rain had begun to fall, but Saturday's grocery specials were still chalked on the blackboard next to the front door. Dabney wiped the blackboard clean. He thought a moment, and then wrote:

SIX
DAYS TO
FESTIVAL DAY

underlining the *six* for emphasis. He now added at the bottom of the blackboard (6/2).

They were the current odds on what had become known around Hasty Harbor simply as The Race. Since yesterday, when Dabney had decided on them, they had remained six to two in favor of the admiral. The disparity was not based on any feeling that the admiral was the better sailor. In fact, throughout the area Peggy's skill was acknowledged and respected; whatever ability the admiral possessed was virtually unknown. The reason the odds were weighted in the admiral's favor was that almost all of the initial bettors had been men. Those same men, smug and confident of the preeminence of their own sex, had been absolutely certain that a man could beat a woman anywhere, at any time, at anything. What's more, the rank of admiral itself led them to assume that he had mastered every vessel from a dinghy to a battleship, and that skippering a small sailboat around some buoys off the coast of Maine would be child's play for him.

But as Dabney had assured his clientele, those odds were almost certain to change between now and the following Saturday. He had already enlisted half a dozen of the local lobstermen and fishermen to report what they observed of the practice sessions of the two competitors. The storekeeper even had the rough time of their trial runs the day before.

Dabney studied the numbers (6/2) at the bottom of the board. Finally, he erased the 2. He picked up the piece of chalk that hung down beside the blackboard on a string, and in place of the 2 he drew a 3.

The admiral stood morosely at the window of his cabin looking out at the rain that fell. At last he turned back to the table. He sat down, opened the logbook, and began to write:

> Sunday, July 24. 3:30 P.M. There is not a single thing that I can say about today, as far as sailing goes. The weather is a bust—steady drizzle in the morning; rain this afternoon. But Joe said keep a log, so I will keep it, even on a lay day. I will note that I can't afford many such days this week. Peggy may not need the sailing practice, but I do.
>
> And I confess I still vacillate about whether I did

the right thing in agreeing to this race. I want to win, and yet I don't—not if winning means I will lose the chance to see her again. But I'm committed to go through with it. Even my neighbors in the other cabins are asking me about it. I was also wrong to think it would remain a quiet local event. This morning, I went up to the 7-Eleven on the highway and bought the Sunday papers. To my surprise, there was a piece about the race in the Brunswick "Times." Now, Brunswick, Maine, is not exactly New York City, and the Brunswick "Times" is not "The New York Times." But Brunswick is a good bit larger than Hasty Harbor, and twice the size of Whitby, for that matter. So I'm afraid the word is definitely O-U-T.

FIVE
DAYS TO
FESTIVAL DAY

(6/3)

The phone had begun ringing at six thirty in the morning, and without thinking Peggy had made the mistake of answering it. The caller had been some gravel-voiced woman who had identified herself as the president of a militant feminist organization in Ogunquit known as the Legion of Lysistrata. The woman informed Peggy that she had heard about the sailing race next weekend and wanted Peggy to speak before her group concerning the natural superiority of women in sports. Peggy had said nothing for a moment. Then she'd compounded her mistake by offering her own belief that the particular field in which women had true natural superiority was child-bearing, although she herself was not prepared to offer any insights. The caller hung up before Peggy had a chance to.

Now, two hours and four unanswered phone calls later, Peggy finished her final mug of coffee. She rose from the kitchen table and picked up from the countertop the single small heel that remained of the loaf of oat bran bread. For several days Captain Bligh had not appeared. Yet every morning, she had left scraps of bread out on the deck, and every evening when she checked, the scraps were gone.

Peggy went out onto the deck again, tore up the heel of bread, and tossed the bits around. She glanced up at the sky for any sign of the seagull. There was none. Peggy closed the sliding doors, returned to the kitchen, and began to wash her breakfast dishes.

She had just put her cereal bowl in the dish rack when she heard a familiar squawk coming from the deck. She turned off the faucet and listened. The squawk was followed by a staccato tapping on the sliding doors. Captain Bligh had obviously arrived, eaten the heel of bread, and was demanding more.

Peggy thought of trying to ignore him, but the tapping became more insistent. Finally she took a box of cornflakes from the kitchen cabinet and headed for the deck. The gull saw her and flapped its wings briefly as she slid open the doors.

She stepped out, closing the doors behind her. "Sorry, Captain, but there's no more bread. How about cornflakes? They're fortified with niacin and riboflavin. Very healthy for a growing bird."

She shook some flakes into her hand and scattered them in Captain Bligh's direction. The bird leapt forward as they fell, devouring several in midair.

"So, did you finally hear about the race and come to wish me luck?" she asked the gull. "You know, you remind me of another bird, the albatross. Did you ever read that poem, Bligh? I guess not. In the poem the albatross came to a sticky finish, and he brought bad luck to the sailors who had done him in. But that won't happen to you here. You're safe with me, Bligh. And I will consider you my *good* luck bird."

The seagull gave an impatient squawk, and Peggy tossed more cornflakes.

"Now, tell me," Peggy asked him, "have you and the other gulls made any bets on who is going to win the race? But maybe that's the reason that you're here, to see if I'm worth betting on at all. Well, let me say, the answer's yes. I'll admit—and this is just between the two of us—I'm nervous. More than that, I'm scared. Not about losing, but because I feel trapped. The race is suddenly a great big deal. Everybody's taking sides, and when the admiral and I head out onto the river Saturday, it'll be worse. People will be cheering us, or jeering, as if we were two gladiators in a struggle to the death.

"But do you know what's died already? Something nice. Something the admiral and I had just begun to find. It made me happy. . . . And it's over now. This stupid race has made us public adversaries. The admiral and I didn't kill the albatross, the race did. But it's *our* bad luck."

Peggy knelt. The seagull didn't move; it simply stared at her as if it understood and sympathized.

"Even so, I'm going to win, Bligh. No—I *have* to win. So bring me luck. Will you do that?"

The gull continued to look up at her. Peggy held out her empty hand. The bird took a step toward her, then another, and another. For several moments, it stared at Peggy's hand, then it lunged forward and gave the hand a quick peck before backing off again.

Peggy smiled. "Thanks. I mean it, Captain Bligh. I do intend to win that race."

She stood up. "Still, the next time you fly over Dabney's Store," she said, "you might just want to check the odds."

Ahead, the traffic light turned red; Joe slowed his car and stopped. The Monday morning rush was over, but the highway was still busy. The digital clock on the dashboard showed nine twenty-nine. He was due to meet the admiral at the boatyard about ten, but he had left his apartment earlier than necessary, hoping he would have some time alone with Sarah in the office before the admiral arrived.

Waiting for the light to change, Joe noticed that the parking lot of a sizable shoe store outlet beside the highway was already filling up. The outlet's name was Moosey Mocs, and there were a dozen similar stores scattered up and down the state of Maine. Above the building was a huge sign featuring a grinning moose with moccasins hanging from its antlers. Whoever ran the chain assumed correctly that tourists associated Maine with moose and moccasins. Some probably even thought the moccasins they bought at Moosey Mocs were really made of moose hide, laboriously worked by local Indians who had preserved their tribal crafts, rather than vinyl-coated canvas machine-stitched in Taiwan.

The traffic light turned green and the dashboard clock blinked to 9:30. As Joe began to move again he turned on the car radio. He was assaulted at once by a hyperkinetic voice.

"Howdy howdy howdy! On this bee-*yoo*-tiful morning, to everyone from Kennebunk to Quoddy Head, and up and down east, ha! ha! ha! This is your on-air buddy, Bangor Bob, Maine's *fay*-vorite deejay!"—Joe reached for the radio dial—"And here's a seafaring note from the good folks in Hasty Harbor."

Joe listened.

"Seems they're having a real wing-dingy, you might say, of a sailing race—*dinghy*, get it? Ha! ha! ha! It's gonna be this Saturday as part of their summer festival. And the nautical nabobs competing are *none other* than two retired navy officers—an admiral and a commander. But it may be a case of 'Blow the Man Down,' because—get this!—the commander is a *woman,* name of Peg McCoy, who was a commander in the Waves. And she's racing against Rear Admiral Charles Darling—"

"It's *Deering*, you jerk!" Joe told the radio.

"So why don't all you salty sorts scrape off your barnacles and haul your keels down to Hasty Harbor come this Saturday. In other news, put on your sunbonnets, ladies, 'cause it's snap bean pickin' time at Darrett's Farm in Orrington—"

Joe switched off the radio, frowning. He didn't like the increasing publicity the race was getting, and he wondered if the admiral felt the same way. Of course, there wasn't much either one of them could do about it now. With five days left to practice before the race, the single thought, the lone objective was the winning of the race itself.

Except, Joe had to admit, his mind was also occupied with something other than the race. Some*one*. Sarah Alice Dodge.

Since the cookout two nights earlier, she had been on his mind constantly. With the rain yesterday, Joe had not come to the boatyard. But today he looked forward to seeing her again and asking for another date. Saturday night had been only the beginning. Seated beside her on the steamer trunk in the darkness of the summer night, they had talked until almost midnight. And in that time he had discovered a young woman who was bright as well as beautiful, and who knew—or thought she knew—exactly what she wanted out of life. But innocent. Oh, was she innocent. His two roommates were away for a month's sea duty; Joe had the apartment to himself. Might it be possible . . . ? Joe quickly scotched the idea, as pleasant as it was. Sarah wasn't a town tart to be bedded. In fact, the other night confirmed what Joe felt when he'd first seen her; this girl was different. This girl had class.

As Joe slowed the car and turned onto the boatyard road, another thought occurred to him. It was a thought that both exhilarated and surprised him. Maybe, just maybe, he, Ensign Joe Marino, was in love.

Still deep in thought, Joe suddenly saw he was about to drive onto the boatyard pier and stopped the car at once. He caught his breath and looked around. The admiral was nowhere to be seen. Joe got out of the car, adjusted his officer's cap on his head, and marched in the direction of the boatyard office. Outside the door, he took another breath and started in—and stopped.

Seated at the desk was a large woman with a flat round face and a full head of hair pinned up in a bun. She saw Joe and smiled. "You must be Ensign Marino. I'm Mrs. Dodge. Sarah's mother."

Joe hoped his disappointment was not too obvious. "Hello, yes. Pleased to meet you. By any chance, is Sarah . . . ?"

"She'll be in Portland for the day. She was just helping here temporarily," the woman added. "Is there something I can do?"

"I'd like to rent another sailboat. A Lightning. I booked it starting Sunday, actually. But it rained."

Mrs. Dodge seemed puzzled. "Aren't you and the admiral sailing together?"

"Yes. But I want him to get the feel of the boat without me in it."

Mrs. Dodge gave Joe another friendly round-faced smile and began flipping through the card file on the desk. "It should be quite a race on Saturday," she said.

"Yes, ma'am."

"We even got a call from someone from *Yachting* magazine about it."

"Is that so?" Joe said. Privately, he cursed. More and more, Hasty Harbor, Maine, was sounding like Newport, Rhode Island, at regatta time.

Mrs. Dodge drew a card out of the file. "Here it is. Another Lightning. It's probably at the dock already."

"Good. Thanks. Thank you." Joe started out again. He hesitated. "By the way, would you please tell Sarah . . . I said hello." He touched the brim of his hat and closed the door behind him. But as he did he wondered if the girl's absence was her way of saying good-bye.

Shortly after dawn on Tuesday morning, T. C. Dabney began picking up the empty soda cans, discarded beer bottles, and general assorted trash that he found strewn about the porch and turnaround area in summer. Giving the cans and bottles a quick count, he calculated that with deposits he would net four dollars and thirty cents. There was even a single penny that his foot had scuffed up in the gravel just beyond the porch.

Putting the penny in his pocket and slinging his collection bag inside the store, he went to the blackboard next to the front door. He erased it and in place of what had been there, he wrote:

FOUR

DAYS TO

FESTIVAL DAY

What he had not erased, he realized, were yesterday's odds on the race: (6/3).

T. C. Dabney pondered. He then spat on his index finger and with it wiped away the number 3. With the heel of his hand, he rubbed dry the small area. Next, he picked up the piece of chalk, and where the 3 had been, he made a 4.

Peggy regretted she had sailed in the morning. By afternoon the heat had begun to build, and she would have preferred to be on the water now enjoying a sea breeze, rather than where she was—halfway up a ladder painting the north wall of her house. In fact, the weather forecast was predicting a heat wave stretching through the next three days. July was still behaving like July, even in Maine.

She had just reached up with the paintbrush to begin painting under the rain gutter of the roof, when she heard the sound, a faint and fitful sort of crying. She'd been awakened by it the other night, and in her soporific state she had assumed it was some nocturnal animal—a raccoon, a skunk, or even a stray cat—that occasionally went in search of food around the yard. But any such animal would not be making its rounds at three thirty in the afternoon.

The sound ended, then resumed, then stopped. Peggy stood on the ladder, listening. When it began again, she realized that what she heard was more mechanical than animal. And it seemed that it was coming from the roof. . . .

It was the weather vane she had put up several days before. She hadn't oiled any of the moving parts, so that on days or nights when the winds were changeable or gusty, the vane was squeaking as it turned. It amused Peggy to think she could leave it as it was and pretend it was the Angel Gabriel practicing his horn. But it didn't sound much like the clarion of an archangel, and besides, she was sure it would increase soon to the point of annoyance.

Peggy set the paintbrush on the can of paint, descended the ladder, and went around to the storage shed beneath the deck. From the shed she took a can of oil. She returned to the ladder, and climbed back up. The ladder was extended beyond the lower edge of the roof, so she was able to climb onto the roof itself with reasonable ease. Although the shingles were hot, Peggy crawled upward toward the peak of the roof, and then along it to the weather vane. As she approached the weather vane, a sudden wind gust caused it to swing—and squeak.

Sitting astride the peak, she spun the weather vane while

squirting oil down into the shaft holding the supporting rod. She gave it one last application of oil for good measure, then twirled it again. The squeak was gone. With a flourish, Peggy spun the weather vane a final time, wondering as she did so in what direction the arrow would point when it stopped. The arrow slowed finally and came to rest on a line parallel with Lonely Point Road.

It was at that moment she saw Mrs. Doberman's yellow Cadillac as it glided imperiously down the road toward Peggy's house. Since last week Peggy had succeeded in avoiding the woman: if Mrs. Doberman had called or even visited the house, Peggy had been lucky enough to be somewhere else. But now her luck had ended. Worse, she couldn't escape, trapped up on her own roof as she was.

As the Cadillac approached her driveway, Peggy made a plan. Although the ladder was still raised against the wall, it was the wall at the back of the house; the ladder wouldn't be visible from the driveway or the front door. If she could press herself down flat enough against the roof, the woman might not even think of looking up.

Peggy climbed off the peak of the roof as quietly and as quickly as she could and waited. She heard the car door close, and a short time later, the heavy tread of feet on the front steps.

"Yoo-hoo!" she heard Mrs. Doberman call out. "Peg-*gee!* Are you home? I tried phoning you *so* many times, my dear, but you were never here. . . . I've caught you now though, haven't I? I see your door is open, and your car is right here in the driveway, parked in front of mine."

There was silence, as if Mrs. Doberman half-expected Peggy to appear before her and confess that, yes, the woman had caught up with her at last.

Peggy heard the screen door open. Obviously, Mrs.

Doberman had taken it upon herself to search the house. For the next several minutes there followed a series of "Yoo-hoos!" as the woman snooped her way from room to room.

At last the screen door could be heard opening again, and the thump of feet on the top step. When Mrs. Doberman spoke, her voice revealed her uncertainty.

"Well . . . perhaps I was in error, after all. You could be here, and not here. I mean, you could be walking on the beach, or somewhere in the area." Mrs. Doberman seemed to be talking to herself and addressing the absent Peggy at the same time.

"What I wished to tell you," Mrs. Doberman went on, "is that there is no need for you to feel you should make a contribution to the auction for the festival. The contribution you're making just by being in the race is more than any of the rest of us could give. Some people may think I'm a silly woman, but I *am* a woman. And a single one, like you. And I know the courage it took to accept the challenge of that race. I'm very proud of you, my dear. All of the women who I know are proud of you, whether they admit it to themselves or not. You're going to win on Saturday. I *know* you will. . . ."

Once more, there was silence. Peggy heard footsteps descending to the walk, and soon after the car door opening, then closing. The engine started, and the gravel of the driveway crackled as the car backed out onto the road.

As the sound of the car was fading off, Peggy raised her head. What she saw was a flash of yellow and chrome as the Cadillac disappeared around the corner of the road.

Slowly, Peggy raised herself and sat up on the roof, still looking in the direction the car had gone. From that day on, thought Peggy, she would have a very different attitude toward Mrs. Doberman.

THREE DAYS TO FESTIVAL DAY

(6/5)

"It still seems odd with you in another boat," the admiral called over at Joe. *Invincible* and the sailboat that Joe had rented were drifting side by side. Downriver of them was the flashing buoy near the Sawteeth that would mark the start and finish points of the race.

"That's a rule of the race," Joe called back. "Only one sailor to a sailboat."

"But suppose during the race I run into trouble, like foundering or capsizing? What do I do then?"

"Don't worry. I'm sure a member of the spectator fleet will rescue you," Joe told him. "If not, then swim for shore, and try not to look embarrassed."

Just then there was the roar of an approaching powerboat. Thirty yards beyond Joe's sailboat a large sleek runabout with half a dozen teenage girls passed, sending up a hefty wake. As the runabout went by, the girls waved, and some blew kisses in Joe's direction.

Joe quickly grabbed the tiller of his sailboat to stabilize her; the admiral did the same. The wake rolled past them, and again the sea was calm.

"Ah, the appeal of the navy uniform," the admiral said after a moment. "How well do I remember my own days as a young officer. Before I was married, you understand. What's the expression—a girl in every port? And I remember some of those ports, too. Tangier, Albufeira, Brest—now there's a well-named city, judging by the endowments of the girls who gathered on the dock to greet our ship. And my oh my, did our white summer uniforms impress those girls then."

Joe smiled. "Sometimes when I wear my summer whites, I feel like the Good Humor man."

"Nothing wrong with that," the admiral said. "Just keep ringing your bell, and watch the girls flock to taste the goodies that you're offering."

The two men laughed together. By now they had approached the flashing buoy. With his free hand, the admiral gestured toward it.

"Will they fire a starting gun at the beginning of the race?" he asked.

"I assume so," Joe answered. "I'll check that with the race committee. Since Miss McCoy has a somewhat smaller boat, they may decide to give her a handicap and let her start ahead."

"And will they give *me* a handicap for inexperience?"

Joe shook his head. "I doubt it. Some people consider you the expert. Although the Hasty Harbor postmaster-hyphen-bookmaker seems less sure of it than he did yesterday. He's narrowed the odds to six to five."

"I've heard what's going on," the admiral said. "To be honest, I'm not sure what upsets me more—to be bet on like a racehorse or to have those newspaper people who've been coming to the dock all shouting questions at me."

"Forget them. And forget the betting, too. Don't think of anything except the race. And keep repeating to yourself, 'I'm going to win. I'm going to *win*.'"

"'I'm going to win. I'm going to win'," echoed the admiral. "I sound like the Little Sailboat That Could."

"Okay, enough of ship-to-ship communications," Joe told him. "We're using up our practice time." He came about and began to put some distance between them. "Come on," he called back. "Avanti! Let's get sailing!"

And for the next three hours, sail they did. The day was even hotter than the preceding day had been, and the wind was steady from the west. For half an hour they practiced crossing the imaginary starting line beside the flashing buoy. Each time Joe would call out a warning, each time both men would put their sailboats in readiness to make the starting run, and each time they would turn and race downriver toward the buoy, maneuvering to gain the advantage and be first across the line.

When Joe finally signaled with a wave of his hand, they continued down the opening leg of the course in the direction of Big Momma. Approaching the first mark, Joe led by two boat lengths. It was then the admiral jibed suddenly, swinging in behind Joe's boat, closer to the rock. The move caught Joe by surprise, literally taking the wind out of his sails, and the admiral shot past him as *Invincible* made a hairbreadth turn around the rock.

At the moment he assumed the lead, the admiral looked back at Joe and beamed.

"Well done!" Joe shouted to him.

With the wind astern of them, both sailboats now pointed eastward toward the second mark, gong buoy 4-CL. Running downwind as they would be for the next two miles, their spinnaker sails set, Joe knew there wasn't much point in attempting any fancy sail handling: both boats would travel at approximately the same speed no matter what their skippers did. So he just sat beside the tiller, played out the mainsail as far as possible to catch the wind, and let his sailboat run free. Now and then the admiral gave Joe a backward glance from his position several lengths ahead, as if uncertain why the young man hadn't challenged him.

Joe simply shook his head, and gave a gracious "You go first, I'll follow" gesture. Once they were on the final leg of the course, Joe reassured himself, he had a surprise or two of his own.

The admiral tacked around gong buoy 4-CL, dropped the spinnaker, and began sailing upriver toward the buoy near the Sawteeth. With both sailboats now pointed closer to the wind, Joe decided it was time to play his game of cat and mouse. Gradually, in a series of small, frequent tacks, he began to gain ground on the admiral. At first the admiral seemed unaware that Joe was closing on him; when he realized it he made a number of quick countermoves to keep ahead.

The admiral was only partially successful. Less than a mile from the flashing buoy, Joe was now a boat length astern of the *Invincible*.

Okay, thought Joe. Now's the moment for the cat to catch the mouse. Abruptly he swung his boat sharply away from the line the two were sailing. The wind immediately billowed his mainsail and jib. Joe tacked again at once, aiming his boat squarely in the direction of the admiral's.

The older man saw Joe's boat coming for him at great speed and was dumbfounded: instinctively he tacked off to avoid a collision—as Joe came about again and took the lead.

Joe crossed the finish line four boat lengths ahead of the *Invincible*. He slowed his sailboat and brought it around in a wide arc to where *Invincible* was drifting, her sails slack.

The admiral shouted over to him. "What was that trick you just used to get by me?"

"It's what I call the Marino Maneuver!" Joe shouted back. "I'll give you the details later."

"Well, what do we do now?" the admiral asked. "We've sailed the course once."

"Are you up to doing it again? Or is the heat getting to you?"

"A bit," the admiral allowed. "But I'd rather be out here than back on land."

"Spoken like a true sailor. All right," Joe said. "We'll make one run at the starting line, and then around the course again."

"Fine," the admiral said. "But I warn you, I won't allow my boat to get whipped again—even if you do try the Marino Maneuver, or something equally sneaky. So let's sail!"

The admiral tacked sharply with a flourish, ready for another duel to the starting line.

By that afternoon temperatures were in the nineties. Those tourists and visitors who could do so had taken to the water or the beaches, or escaped into the cool solace of the Whitby movie theaters. Even the stray dogs that scavenged in the Hasty Harbor turnaround or at the dumpster behind Dabney's Store had sought the shady sides of buildings, where they lay with lolling tongues.

So when Peggy drove into the boatyard road she was not surprised to see more cars than usual parked along the side, and she guessed that Noah was doing a brisk business in boat rentals. What did surprise her, after she had parked behind the line of cars and begun walking toward the pier, was that several of the cars bore the names of newspapers in the area: the Portland *Press Herald,* the Augusta *Sentinel,* the Rockport *News*. Peggy had stopped answering her telephone, assuming that some of the calls, at least, came from inquisitive newspeople.

As Peggy crossed the pier, she saw men and women she was sure belonged to the press cars; some held notepads while others focused cameras, and most were engaging Noah Dodge in earnest conversation.

She gave Noah a small wave before she started down the ramp to the floating dock. He looked in her direction but did not acknowledge her further. At first she was surprised and slightly hurt; then she realized his inattention was meant to spare her. Unlike the admiral, no picture of her had appeared in print; the press people buttonholing Noah now had no idea who she was when she walked past them. And she hoped they never found out.

Free Spirit was waiting for her when she reached the floating dock. Peggy stepped into the boat, cast off, and quickly raised the sails. Today her practice session had been scheduled for the afternoon, and as the temperatures rose she'd looked forward to being on the water when the heat was most intense. Even so, the wind had lessened, and she knew that it would take her longer to complete a circuit of the course.

With the breeze behind her, Peggy sailed out across the harbor, through the channel, and past the Sawteeth in the direction of the flashing buoy. When she was well upriver of the buoy, she reached into the pocket of her shorts and took out a stopwatch. The metal case was worn and nicked around the edge. She couldn't remember how many years she'd had the watch, or why she'd bought it in the first place; probably in connection with her duties as a nurse. But it had come in handy this week, helping her to time her starts and telling her how long it took to sail each leg of the course.

She wound the watch and set it running. Giving herself a two-minute signal, she made several runs at the starting line. On her fourth try, she found that she had judged her speed and distance perfectly, hitting the line exactly two minutes later, when the starting gun would sound.

Peggy clicked the stopwatch back to zero, restarted it, and headed southward toward Big Momma. Arriving there soon after high tide, she saw that only the top portion of the rock was visible. Attempting a close turn around it was inviting tragedy; jagged sections of its seaward face lay just below the surface of the water, waiting to tear apart the boat of any foolhardy sailor who approached too near.

She rounded the rock at a respectful distance and started eastward toward gong buoy 4-CL. She checked her stopwatch, discovering that her time on that first leg had been faster than she had anticipated, given the light wind. But now the wind was squarely at *Free Spirit*'s stern, and with the spinnaker raised, it would be an easy, even boring run to the next mark.

As she had suspected, sailors in all sorts of craft could be seen, including one intrepid figure in a kayak, paddling furiously toward the open sea. She also noticed, several hundred yards away and to her right, a large darkish object, and next to it a smaller one of the same shape. Suddenly a spray of water filled the air, followed by another, smaller one. Peggy knew at once it was a mother whale and her calf. It amused her to consider the panic they would cause if they showed up amid the fleet of spectator boats during the race on Saturday.

She rounded gong buoy 4-CL and set her heading toward the harbor entrance and the finish line. Unless her boat—or the admiral's—had an unchallengeable lead on Saturday, this would be the leg in which the race was won or lost. Spurred on by the thought, she trimmed *Free Spirit*'s sails and reset her heading, seeking every bit of speed her sailboat could give.

Peggy observed a drifting lobster trap directly in *Free Spirit*'s path; for amusement she decided to pretend the admiral was sailing it. As she was about to overtake the trap, she made a sudden turn, shot past it on the windward side, and sped ahead. Savoring the moment, Peggy raised her arm in triumph. Touché, Charles! I'm ahead! I'm going to beat you to the finish line!

Then, slowly lowering her arm, she knew how meaningless the exercise had been. The lobster trap was not the admiral's boat—it was not *any* boat. It was a flimsy frame of wood and chicken wire bobbing in the waves.

She also realized that seldom in her life had she sailed with another person, either as her passenger or in a companion boat. But in the three days that remained before the race, she admitted, it would help to have a real sailboat she could compete against, a second boat to simulate the actual conditions of the race itself. But who? Of course. She would ask Sarah Dodge to sail it. Since her mother had returned to working in the boatyard office, the girl had gone back in earnest to her studies in marine biology. But certainly over the next few days she could find time to sail with Peggy during practice runs around the course.

At least, thought Peggy, it would give the girl something to think about besides her clams.

"Clams?" Joe asked.

"Deep-fried, with tartar sauce," the girl said. "The way you like them."

Joe raised himself on his elbows and blinked. After his practice session with the admiral that morning and working outdoors around the ship works in the afternoon, the heat had so fatigued him that he had come back to his apartment, removed his shirt and shoes, and fallen asleep on the living room couch. He had awakened to the sound of the screen door swinging back. He opened his eyes to see Sarah standing in the doorway. She was dressed in a blue halter top and a short white skirt.

As Joe stared she went on standing there, the sun at her back, a cardboard container with a wire handle in one hand and a small grease-stained paper bag in the other. A bottle of rosé wine was tucked under her arm.

Joe sat up on the couch. "What time is it?"

"Six o'clock."

"Which day?"

"Wednesday."

With a start, he realized that he was bare above the waist. He ran a hand across his chest. "Sorry I'm not better dressed. But neither was I expecting a young lady to burst into my apartment unannounced."

"I knocked. You were asleep."

"Just catching a few Zs." He shook his head to clear the cobwebs.

"May I come in?" Sarah asked him.

"Of course." He gestured to the room. "I also apologize for the way the place looks. Sandy is the housekeeper around here. With him and Billy gone, I have to do my own cleaning. Which begins and ends this side of sloth. Come in."

Sarah came into the room and at once disappeared into the kitchen. Joe could hear cabinet doors opening and plates and glasses being set on the table. There was the sound of a corkscrew at work. A moment later, she called out, "Have you heard from your roommates yet?"

"Are you kidding? Their sea duty only started Monday. They're partway to the Azores by now. I won't see them for two weeks."

Sarah returned to the living room. She was carrying a wineglass in each hand. She handed a glass to Joe and sat down beside him on the couch.

"Thanks," Joe said. "So were you in Portland again today?"

"No, Brunswick. At the Bowdoin College library. Have you ever seen Bowdoin?" Joe shook his head. "In one of the buildings they have rooms dedicated to Robert Peary and his arctic expedition. He was a Bowdoin graduate."

"I could have used some arctic air today."

"It's still very hot," Sarah said. "I think it's the hottest day so far this summer. That's why I got us some chilled wine." She sipped her rosé.

"Let me see if there's an electric fan around. I can go up and ask my landlord." Joe started to rise.

Sarah shook her head. "I'm fine. After the frigid winter that we had, real Mainers never complain about spending a day or two in heat."

Joe was amused at her choice of words, but didn't say so. "Well," he went on, "were you working on your thesis?"

"Uh-huh."

"And did you pick up any further tidbits about clams that I should know?"

"No, unless you plan to become a marine biologist. But

I did come across some in-depth research about their hearts."

"Really? You mean clams have hearts too?"

"Why shouldn't they?"

"Oh, they should, by all means. Especially if they have feelings, like you said. In fact, it makes them seem almost romantic. I can picture their tiny clam hearts going pitter-pat whenever they touch shells."

Sarah smiled. "You're teasing me again. But I don't mind."

"A couple days ago you took offense at my clam jokes. Is this a whole new Sarah Dodge I'm seeing now?"

The blue eyes fixed their gaze on him. "Yes," Sarah answered. "Maybe it is."

"I tried to call you several times the last few days," Joe said.

"Yes, I know. I guess . . . I needed time."

"For what?"

"To think," she said.

"And now you've thought?" he asked her.

"Yes." She took a sip of wine. "So how did the sailing go today?"

"Very well. The old man's really getting into it. He notched good times on every leg of the course, in spite of the temperature. When I complained about the heat later, he told me nothing could be hotter than being in the South Pacific under Japanese Naval fire."

"He's quite a person, isn't he? I mean, besides being sort of famous and all. Does he have a family? A wife or anyone?"

"Nope. He had one son, who was killed in the Vietnam war. His wife died of cancer a couple years ago. But you wouldn't know all that just to talk to him. Most of the time he seems on top of the world."

"Do you think he'll win the race on Saturday?"

"He might. He's a good sailor. But so is Miss McCoy,

from what I hear. Still, I'm doing everything I can to *help* him win. The rest is up to God and sea conditions." Joe grinned. "As a matter of fact, today I showed the admiral a racing technique I developed when I was on the sailing team at the academy. I call it the Marino Maneuver."

"It sounds tricky."

"Not really. It's just a good way to surprise your opponent and seize the advantage. But I don't suppose I should be telling you these things. Aren't you on the side of the opposition?"

"Peggy's a friend. But I'm trying to stay impartial," Sarah said.

"Look, why don't I put on a shirt? I feel sort of funny talking to you half dressed this way."

"Don't do it on my account," she reassured him. "I've seen bare-chested men before."

Joe raised an eyebrow. "Oh? From hanging out in male topless bars?"

"What?"

"Nothing. My crude humor again." He leaned forward on the couch. "Let me ask you another question. Why did you bring me the fried clams?"

"I thought you might be hungry. It's almost suppertime."

"But why clams? I got the idea you considered it a sacrilege to appreciate clams in anything but their natural state."

"Maybe I'm broadening my horizons," Sarah said. "And trying to understand the attitudes of other people. That's what you told me I should do."

"True. Very true," Joe agreed.

"I also brought some french fries. They're in a paper bag in the kitchen. With the clams."

"Great. Why don't we have something to eat now? You'll join me, won't you?"

Sarah looked uncertain suddenly. "I don't know. I probably should be getting home."

"Didn't I hear you putting out two plates before?" he asked.

She looked at him. "Not much gets by you, does it, Ensign Marino?"

"Not if I don't want it to," he said.

Sarah stood up. "All right, I'll fix a plate of clams and french fries for you. And I'll just have the fries. I haven't reached the point where I can eat the subject of my year's research. Especially deep-fried with tartar sauce."

She turned and walked quickly to the kitchen. Joe leaned back on the couch and put his arms behind his head. From the kitchen he heard the sound of drawers opening and utensils rattling.

Joe closed his eyes. For the first time in a long time, he realized that he was greatly puzzled. Yesterday he was prepared to write off any hope of making headway with this girl. All this week she had been absent from the boatyard at the times that he'd been there. The tentative phone calls he'd made to her home had gone unreturned.

And yet now, tonight, she'd showed up in his apartment unannounced, and bearing *clams*. Other girls Joe had known had sometimes brought him gifts. But fried clams hadn't been among their offerings. That wasn't Sarah's style, anyway. She was still guileless, an innocent. The only thing her visit proved was that she wasn't giving him the brush-off, as he'd thought.

Joe smiled to himself. In fact, she likes me. She *likes* me. Maybe even—

At that moment, Sarah reappeared, carrying the bottle of rosé. "Would you like some more?" She indicated the wineglass at his feet.

He nodded and checked her glass on the side table. "Sure. How about you?"

"Sure." She picked up his glass and topped it up, then

refilled her own. "I'll bring out the plates," she added, and headed back into the kitchen.

They ate side by side on the couch, Joe dabbing his fried clams into a small paper cup of tartar sauce while Sarah nibbled her french fries.

"I've got to hand it to you," Joe said finally. "You deserve a lot of credit."

"Why?" She turned, her pale blue eyes fixed on him once more.

"Number one, because these clams are terrific. They could have been deep-fried by Escoffier himself."

"Who?"

"Georges-Auguste Escoffier. He uh—he's a French-Canadian who runs a fish house outside Portland." She looked at him expectantly, waiting to learn more. Joe felt embarrassed. "I'm kidding. He was a great French chef. The godfather of la cuisine française."

Now it was Sarah who appeared embarrassed. "I'm sorry. I guess I'm not very bright. There are so many things I don't know."

"You're very bright," Joe said at once. "You're just—well, you just have some more living to do. Learning about life. That's all."

"I want to."

"And you will. In a year or so, when you're out in the big world, you'll—"

"Before then," Sarah said. "Sometimes I think I don't know much about life at all. Will you help me learn?"

Joe took a sip of wine to ease the sudden dryness in his mouth. "Well . . . maybe we can go down to Portland some night. If you're free."

"Do you know why I came here tonight?" she asked him softly.

"Why?"

"Because the other night when you told me about your grandparents, you said that in order for anyone to make their life complete, they had to 'dare to live.' Do you remember?"

"Yes."

"When you said that, it came to me that I was the most undaring person in the world. All my life I've been afraid to take a chance on anything. Until now."

And now? Joe was about to ask, but he didn't.

The blue eyes that still regarded him remained serene. Joe put his plate of clams and french fries on the table next to the couch. He took Sarah's plate and did the same. The wineglasses, which were empty, he did not refill. Instead he put them on the floor. Then, stretching an arm behind her along the back of the couch, he touched her long blond hair. With his fingers, he separated the hair gently and began to stroke the nape of Sarah's neck.

For what seemed an endless time, the girl merely stared at him, her lips slightly apart, her tongue now and then caressing, wetting them.

"Is this also a Marino Maneuver?" she asked quietly after a moment.

"One of many," Joe said. "One of many."

TWO
DAYS TO
FESTIVAL DAY

(6/5)

On Thursday morning the admiral rose promptly at dawn. He had always been an early riser, but as the race approached, the less relaxed and confident he felt and the more fitfully he slept. Last night was no different. Until midnight he had tossed in bed with only a sheet over him, and the heat had not seemed to abate. Morning presented a new problem: when he began to fix his breakfast, he found that he was out of coffee, and the single egg remaining in the carton broke as he removed it, oozing sticky egg white everywhere.

He wasn't scheduled to meet Joe at the boatyard until afternoon. He could get breakfast at a diner on the highway and spend the morning doing other things.

Thus, half an hour later, he slid onto a counter stool at Rocky's Roadside Rest. In general the topic of the diner patrons was the heat wave. To his right two truckers were exclaiming on the demolition of the Red Sox in a game the night before. To his left sat a trooper from the state highway patrol, a plate of scrambled eggs and sausages in front of him. The trooper was trying unsuccessfully to bisect a rock-hard bran muffin with a knife.

A mug of steaming coffee suddenly appeared before the admiral. He sipped it tentatively. It was good, but very strong, and he decided if he didn't drink it soon it would probably dissolve the glaze on the inside of the mug.

When the counterman approached him, the admiral requested two eggs, scrambled, with sausages and toast. Although he'd taken only three sips of coffee, the counterman refilled his mug to the brim.

The order seemed to come almost at once, and the admiral began to eat. It was not until he'd started on his second sausage that he became aware of voices rising from a booth behind him. There were murmured phrases: "That's *him*." "That one?" "I'm sure it is." "Well, why don't you find out?"

Several moments later the admiral felt a large hand come down squarely on his shoulder. He turned to find a squat man in his fifties grinning at him. The man was dressed in an orange sweatshirt. On his head was a fisherman's hat with a variety of colored flies hooked around the band.

"Hubert Wiggim," the man said. "Put her there." He grasped the admiral's hand and pumped it. "I know who you are. You're that admiral. Am I right, or am I right?"

"I'm Admiral Deering. Yes."

The man turned back in the direction of the booth. "It's

him, Dot!" Hubert Wiggim shouted to a woman sitting there. "I'm right!"

He looked at the admiral again. "Come join us. I'll buy you breakfast. We was just about to eat."

"Thank you, but I'm nearly done."

"Another cup of coffee then," the man said. "I told my grandsons you was a navy hero. A damn living legend. They won't leave this place until they meet you."

With that Hubert Wiggim picked up the admiral's plate and carried it to the booth. The admiral had no choice but to follow him, carrying his coffee mug. Wiggim waited till the admiral sat down, then squeezed in beside him. As the admiral sat, he found himself face to face with a woman who looked like a female clone of Hubert Wiggim. She also wore an orange sweatshirt, but instead of a fisherman's hat she had a golf visor with a green plastic bill encircling her head. Seated next to her were two small boys, both with prominent front teeth. They were staring at the admiral.

Hubert Wiggim made the introductions. "This is my wife, Dot. And these are our grandsons, Rod and Tod." He gestured to the admiral. "And this here is the famous admiral—what's your name again?"

"Charles Deering."

"Salute the admiral, boys," Mrs. Wiggim said. Simultaneously, both boys attempted a salute, although one boy—the admiral wasn't sure if it was Rod or Tod—accidentally stuck a finger in his nose and began to cry.

It was then that the admiral looked up and saw Captain Carnes, in uniform, entering the diner. "Excuse me," the admiral said to Hubert Wiggim, "but a gentleman from the military is here to confer with me." He kept his voice low. "It's necessary that I speak with him alone."

Hubert Wiggim regarded the admiral. "The military? Where?"

"He just came in the door." The admiral gestured with a

spoon. Captain Carnes remained standing just inside the door, scanning the diner.

"I see him," Wiggim said in an equally low voice. "There's another diner down the road. We'll go to that. You stay here and keep the booth so's the two of you can talk."

Hubert Wiggim stood up. "Dot, kids—atten*shun*. Fall out!" On command, his wife and grandsons stood and stepped into the aisle. "Now, 'bout face—and forward march!"

The woman and the boys turned and headed toward the door. Wiggim remained standing at the booth. He looked down at the admiral again, removed his fisherman's hat, and placed it over his heart. "Admiral, I just want to say God bless America, God bless the U.S. Navy, and God bless you on Saturday!"

Several patrons turned and stared at them. "Thank you," muttered the admiral. Hubert Wiggim put his hat back on his head, turned, and marched in the direction of the door.

Captain Carnes stepped aside to let him pass and then moved down the aisle. In his hand was a folded newspaper. He slid into the booth opposite the admiral, offered a "Good morning, sir," and gave a quick salute.

The admiral returned it. "Better take some saluting lessons from those kids who just left, Carnes, or they might have your job." He smiled. "So what brings you to Rocky's Roadside Rest this morning?"

"I . . . hoped that we could talk. Sir."

"Fine. Care for some breakfast? I recommend the scrambled eggs and sausages. Forget the muffins. What'll it be?"

"Nothing. Thank you."

"How about some coffee then? It's strong, but you look like you could use something."

"Tea will be fine."

"*Tea*? What's the navy come to?" The admiral gave the captain a wry look. "Would you prefer Darjeeling or oolong?"

"Whatever, sir."

The admiral gestured to the waitress. When she arrived he ordered tea for the captain and a refill of coffee for himself. Then he leaned back in the booth and studied the younger man. "First of all, how did you find me?"

"I stopped by your cabin. One of your neighbors told me that you came here for breakfast sometimes."

"But why did you want to see me?"

The captain took a breath. "Sir," he began, "yesterday I received a communiqué from the office of the secretary of the navy. It seems their press people have been receiving increased attention from the media. Inquiries."

"About what?" the admiral asked, although he was fairly sure he knew.

"Coffeeanatea." The waitress set the two mugs on the table. She peered down at Captain Carnes. "Zadit?"

"Yes." Captain Carnes nodded. "That's all, thank you." He seemed about to add, "sir." The waitress shrugged and walked away. Gingerly, the captain lifted the teabag from his mug, looking for someplace to deposit it. He finally settled on the ashtray.

"To continue," said the admiral, "what else did the communiqué say?"

The captain pursed his lips. "Well, it appears the navy is getting rather nervous about your little sailing race on Saturday."

"Miss McCoy and I don't consider it a 'little' race, and neither do the residents of Hasty Harbor. In fact, they're making it into something of a big deal."

"And so are a lot of other people, I'm afraid." Captain Carnes picked up the newspaper he'd been carrying, and unfolded it across the table. "Have you seen today's Boston *Globe*?"

"No. Should I?"

"There's an article in it about the race."

"Which section? Sports or entertainment?"

"Regional," the captain said. "The point is, it was a wire service story. It's going out across the country."

"So? Do they expect the country to attend the race?"

"Sir, the Department of the Navy feels . . . uncomfortable."

"Uncomfortable?"

"If you lose the race, it will trouble certain, uh, older members of the military. And if you beat Commander McCoy, it could discourage our recruitment efforts among women. Either way the department sees the potential for adverse publicity for them—and for you."

"I can handle mine," the admiral informed him. "As for the Department of the Navy, that's what their so-called press people get paid for."

"Admiral." The officer looked deeply pained. "In fact, the navy respectfully requests, sir, that you don't race on Saturday."

"I beg your pardon? I don't believe what you just said."

"Sir, as I understand it, there have been calls about the race from all the major networks. I'm told that *Sports Illustrated* has asked the America's Cup skipper to come here and write up his personal impressions of it. Furthermore—"

"Wait, wait." The admiral held up a hand. "If the race is getting all this attention, how can I back out of it without looking like a coward. Or a damn fool?"

"The navy has considered that."

"And?"

"And they have several fallback positions you can take."

"You mean, lies that I can tell the press." The admiral snorted, took a swig of coffee from his mug, and set it down again. "So what are they? These fallback positions?"

"First, the physical condition of a man your age—"

"I'm in fine health. Excellent. If you're suggesting I use that as an excuse, forget it."

"Second, a family crisis could arise."

"Captain Carnes, perhaps the navy doesn't know it, but I have no family. My wife and son are dead. On the other hand, my closest friend—my bulldog, Halsey—is alive and well and in a high-priced kennel that costs more than my cabin does. So the navy can forget that excuse too."

"Well, if you insist on racing, then at least they hope you will . . . go easy."

"You mean, lose the race?"

"I didn't say that."

"Then what *are* you saying, damn it?" The admiral saw several patrons look around again; he leaned across the table, lowering his voice. "So what does the navy recommend I do? Not raise my sails? Sink at dockside? Sail backwards from the starting line?"

"Just . . . give the lady the benefit of every doubt, sir."

"Back off, in other words. I can assure you, the lady will not give *me* the benefit of *any* doubt. Your tea is getting cold, Carnes. You want some more?"

"No." The captain shook his head. "No, thank you, sir." For several moments he stared into his mug, running a finger up and down the handle.

Here it comes, the admiral thought. Here comes the final salvo, the appeal to my navy loyalty and pride. The young man will look me directly in the eyes. He will say, Admiral. Sir . . . Then he will pause. And then the rest will follow. The admiral felt he knew the words by heart, he'd heard them many times before.

Captain Carnes raised his head and looked the admiral directly in the eyes. "Admiral. Sir," he began. He paused. "Sir, you are a respected—no, more than that, you are a *revered* officer, almost a legend in the modern navy. As a young man you chose the navy above all other services. You gave it a great deal. But the navy gave you much in return—an education, a career, a purpose and direction for your life. But most important, it provided you the opportunity to serve your country in the best way any person can, defending freedom as a military officer. And now the navy asks something of you in return."

"Lose the race."

"Well, not exactly, sir, but . . ." Having made his speech, Captain Carnes was unsure how to go on.

"I appreciate your effort, Captain. But I suggest you send a communiqué *back* to the Department of the Navy telling them that I am going to race. And that I'm going to win. Unless, of course, they have one of their PT boats torpedo me out there on Saturday. As for being—what was it you said? a legend?—if I am, it's *in spite of* some of those swivel-chair sailors in the Pentagon. In the forties, when I told them that the navy would one day communicate by means of satellites in space, they thought I was a crackpot, a crazy man. In those years, we had semaphore and short-wave radio. The communications officer was generally called Sparks, because everybody thought of radio as zigzag bolts of lightning that arced across the sky.

"I believed in communicating through the skies too. But in a different way, with sophisticated electronic instruments put miles up in space by rockets." The admiral raised a hand skyward, at which the waitress brought the coffeepot over, refilled his mug, and walked away.

"May I go on?" the admiral asked Captain Carnes.

Captain Carnes nodded.

"The rest is history. Suddenly, the Russians launched their sputnik, and satellites weren't Buck Rogers gadgets anymore. And a new invention, which for want of a better word they called a computer, was just coming into being. And all the while, I kept writing letters, memos, lobbying anybody I could find to try convincing them that *that* was where the future of communications lay, not just for the navy, but for *everybody*. Don't you see?"

The admiral paused. He leaned back against the leatherette seat back of the booth and gazed out the window. Finally he turned back to Captain Carnes. "Naturally, there is a postscript to all this. It was a Pyrrhic victory for me. I fought the battle too hard, and I rubbed too many gold-braided feathers the wrong way. Because of all the static I was making, they began transferring me to shallow-water ports, and then they retired me before my time. It was only later that they found those letters and memos, tried what I'd suggested, and discovered I was right. Someone leaked the memos to the press, and the next thing I knew I was on my way to becoming 'the father of modern naval communications.' And, of course, whenever the navy wants to brag about how technologically advanced they are today, they reverentially invoke my name.

"And what do *I* do these days to keep active? I don't reread my press clippings, I assure you. I play golf with some friends, walk my bulldog twice a day, and now and then accept an invitation from the public affairs office of the navy to give a speech, help launch a ship, or review a graduating class of fresh-faced OCS naval officers.

"As you know, it was my own decision to remain in Maine after my shipyard speech a week or so ago. But I'll tell you, since then life for me has been anything but boring. In that time I've been told off by a Wave commander, fallen out of a sailboat, and been rescued by that same woman, and in two days I will race against her in a race that is gathering 'increased attention from the media.'

"So please, Captain. Don't ask me to go easy. There are no fallback positions I need to fall back on." Now it was the admiral who looked the younger man directly in the eyes. "I intend to win that race on Saturday. And that is *that*."

The admiral checked his watch. "Time flies; I've got some other business to attend to. Excuse me, Captain."

He rose and signaled to the waitress for the check and

dug into his pocket for some coins for the tip. The waitress handed him the check; he thanked her pleasantly and looked at Captain Carnes once more.

"By the way, Captain, if you happen to be passing by the Hasty Harbor post office today, I'm told the current odds are six to five, my favor. Just in case you want to place a bet."

The admiral winked, turned, and headed toward the cashier's desk.

ONE
DAY TO
FESTIVAL DAY

(6/6)

T. C. Dabney had debated with himself before posting today's odds. On Wednesday he had made them six to five in favor of the admiral. They had remained six to five on Thursday. Now that it was Friday, Dabney felt he had no choice but to make them even. Fishermen and others who'd observed the practice sessions of both racers had come back with stories of Peggy's skill and speed around the course. It was especially so now that Noah's daughter, Sarah, was helping her by sailing in a second boat. But the admiral looked just as good, they added. It was even-steven, the observers said.

Even money made sense for other reasons, too. It made the outcome of the race seem more uncertain, spurring the increased activity of bettors. Also, it should put an end to the complaints of the Hasty Harbor women, who throughout the week had scolded him for siding with the admiral. So six to six it would be. And unless something unexpected happened, it would probably stay that way until the race began.

Dabney studied the blackboard again. He took the piece of chalk and with it broadened one 6, then the other.

Finally, with a bold stroke he punctuated the numbers with an exclamation point. Yes sirree, he told himself with satisfaction, today the Hasty Harbor post office would be busier than it had ever been.

Neither the admiral nor Joe were aware of the new odds when Joe had arrived at the Kare Free Kabins about seven thirty. They had eaten a quick breakfast, which the admiral had fixed, and afterward had spent some time looking over the nautical chart and reviewing strategy for the race. An hour later they had started for the boatyard, with Joe at the wheel of the navy car.

As Joe turned onto the main highway, the admiral spoke up. "I could have driven myself to the boatyard, you know."

"After what happened yesterday," Joe answered, "you need me to run interference for you."

The admiral grunted and said nothing. Instead he reflected on the rapidly increasing press attention that the race was getting. Maybe Captain Carnes had a point, after all. Early in the week, only one or two reporters from small-town area newspapers had been waiting at the boatyard when the admiral arrived. Being naturally gregarious, he had enjoyed chatting with them; he was even a bit flattered they had sought him out. But as the week went on the number of newspeople had increased, and they had begun to come from out-of-state. What's more, their questions had become more trivial and more personal; had the admiral stayed on the pier to answer them, he and Joe would have had to forfeit the practice time they had.

The moment he had set foot on the pier the day before, he'd been surrounded by a pack of noisy reporters and photographers assaulting him with still more questions on the race. When Joe had appeared several minutes later, it was all the two of them could do to get free, reach the safety of their boats, and sail to the river. As they were casting off, they had seen one of the photographers trying to rent a motor launch from Noah Dodge so as to pursue them out into the river. Fortunately, the boatyard owner had claimed no boats were available. That night the admiral decided he would do nothing more than wave and smile at the reporters and photographers—and get away from them as quickly as he could.

Joe slowed the car and turned off the main highway onto the peninsula road. For most of the ride he had been silent, not the usual loquacious Joe the admiral had come to know. When Joe looked over at the admiral and began to speak at last, the young man's face was serious.

"Sir, do you mind if I ask you a question? Two questions, really," Joe said.

The admiral looked curious. "No. Go ahead."

"Yesterday when I got home after our practice, I found a letter from the navy, telling me my request for a transfer to San Diego had been approved."

"Congratulations. San Diego is a fine facility. It shows the navy has its eye on you. Ever been to California before?"

"No sir."

"You'll like it. Talk about the girls." When Joe said nothing, he went on. "You've accepted, I'm sure."

"No." Joe shook his head. "I mean, not yet."

The admiral studied him. "There's not a problem, is there?"

"Not really, but . . ."

"Something personal. Is that it? A young lady?"

"Yes sir."

"Local?"

Joe nodded. "We sort of . . . got together . . . several nights ago. When it was very hot."

"Obviously," the admiral said. "Sorry. I didn't mean to make a joke of it." He thought a moment. "It's after the fact, I know, but there's an expression I recall: never plant depth charges in your own harbor. I've seen it happen more than once. A young navy officer who showed great promise got involved with some local woman. Sometimes, he even made her pregnant. If so, because he was an officer and a gentleman, he legitimized the union. Usually, he found it very difficult to raise a family and pursue a navy career at the same time."

The older man shook his head. "If you had to become fond of a local girl, Joe, why couldn't it have been somebody—well, somebody like that girl at the boatyard? Sarah."

Joe looked at him. "Why did you mention her?"

"Because she doesn't seem the kind to, how shall I put it? Indulge in things like that. Not that she won't show passion, mind you, when the right man comes along. But right now, from what I can remember, she seemed much too serious—I might even say, too virginal. Would you agree?"

Joe made a noncommittal sound and kept his eyes on the road.

"Anyway," the admiral went on, "this girl you speak of. You may believe you love her. But if you want to make the navy your career, just be aware of how difficult it's going to be if you should marry her and have to support a child."

The admiral leaned his head back against the headrest and was silent. Finally he said, "Of course, if I'd taken my own advice many years ago, I'd never have married the wonderful woman I did." He turned to Joe. "So forget what I just said. You're a bright young man, and any girl who loves you and whom you choose to love must be quite special. Very special."

"She is," Joe said, still looking at the road. "She is."

They drove on in silence, Joe lost in his own thoughts, the admiral gazing idly at the scenery. At the junction of the state highway and River Road, the admiral observed for the first time the banner that hung across the intersection.

HASTY HARBOR SUMMER FESTIVAL
SATURDAY, JULY 30
WELCOME ONE AND ALL!

Once more the admiral wondered just how far the welcome extended. For the first time he felt his stomach tighten with anxiety in anticipation of the race.

"Hell," Joe muttered suddenly under his breath.

"What's wrong?" The admiral saw Joe studying the rearview mirror.

"Guess what's on the road behind us."

"What?"

"A mobile unit," Joe informed him.

"A what?"

"One of those big television vans," Joe said. "The kind you see parked outside of sports events, or at the scenes of big news stories, like disasters."

The admiral turned in his seat. Several hundred feet behind them a trailerlike vehicle was following them down River Road. He looked at Joe again. "If they're here to televise the race, maybe they expect it to be both a sports event *and* a disaster." And he felt his stomach grow still tighter.

As they approached the turnaround in front of Dabney's Store, Joe slowed the car. He turned into the boatyard road but stopped abruptly. "I figured that," he said. He pointed down the road ahead of them. A dozen cars were parked along both sides of it.

"The boatyard's popular today," the admiral muttered.

"The race is. *You* are," Joe said. "Listen, your boat should already be at dockside. Once we get to the dock, run to it, cast off, and sail for the river presto. I'll try to clear a path for you, but I don't know how much good I'll be. Try broken-field running, if you have to."

"Maybe you didn't know it," the admiral said, "but I was on the varsity football team at the academy."

"Really? No kidding." Joe looked genuinely impressed. "What position?"

"Halfback. In my senior year we whipped the Army seventeen to zip."

Joe smiled. "Daring Deering strikes again, huh? So let's see what you can do now."

"Ready whenever you are."

Joe gripped the steering wheel. "Okay, you mothers. Here we come." He put the car in gear, pressed the accelerator, and shot forward down the boatyard road.

Shortly after noon Peggy left her house, went across the road and down to the shore, and walked northward half a mile to a small protected cove. Extending into the cove from the water's edge for a distance of twelve feet was a dilapidated dock. Many of its planks were missing or the victims of dry rot. The dock had been built years ago by the summer people who had owned the property, but last year the land had been put up for sale, and because of its remoteness interest in it had been slight.

On the other hand, for Peggy and *Free Spirit* the cove was perfect; a safe harbor in which to moor the sailboat away from the press and the merely curious who had descended on the boatyard in the last few days.

The woman stepped cautiously out onto the dock, boarded *Free Spirit,* and raised the sails. Sheltered as the cove was from the wind, neither the jib nor mainsail filled. So Peggy picked up a paddle and maneuvered the boat into the river.

As *Free Spirit* found the open water and her sails billowed, Peggy studied the horizon. A mile off the starboard bow the jagged outline of Big Momma could be seen. Because the cove was nearer to that rocky outcrop than to the other predetermined points of the course,

Peggy and Sarah had agreed to meet there and begin their practice runs. Sarah had raced against her in a second sailboat for two days, and Peggy had been glad to have the competition. Considering the fact that Sarah sailed only now and then, she was a proficient sailor. Several times in practice yesterday she'd even beaten Peggy's time between the marks. Each time Peggy knew her own mistakes had been the reason: an errant turn, a jib line that had fouled, a heading that had cost her time.

But even so, the girl had always used those mistakes to her own advantage and pulled her sailboat into the lead. The rapport between them had been good; each challenging the other as they sparred tack for tack, stealing one another's wind, then losing it, then stealing it again.

Still, there was something in the girl's whole demeanor recently that puzzled Peggy. What it was she couldn't quite describe. Outwardly, Sarah was the same sensible and friendly girl Peggy had always known. But now it was as if Sarah had been made privy to some precious secret; she seemed invested with a sly, enigmatic quality, a cat-that-swallowed-the-canary look.

Last night she had thought of asking Sarah candidly if there was anything that troubled her. But the girl didn't appear troubled. Quite the opposite, in fact; she seemed serenely happy. But happy or unhappy, Peggy knew the girl would eventually tell Peggy what the reason was—or would she? For the first time, Peggy wondered if she really knew the girl half as well as she believed she did.

This afternoon was not the time to think about such things in any case. Tomorrow at this hour, she and the admiral would be battling each other on the first leg of the course. Until tomorrow, no other thoughts, no personal concerns she had or those of anybody else should be permitted to distract her. Until tomorrow all her concentration, all her efforts would be fused into a single goal—win the race.

Friday, July 29. 9 p.m. Final log entry of the sailboat "Invincible," by her captain, C. T. Deering. Well, we have reached the end. The lessons and the practice runs are over. Tomorrow is the race. I should probably say the BIG race, judging by the gang of rowdies at the dock today, and since that's what everyone is telling me it's going to be. Unfortunately, what began as a small community event has become a "human interest story" that the media has magnified beyond all bounds. It just shows how little real news there is in summertime.

As for this morning's practice, Joe was very pleased. He told me afterward that my course times overall were better than I'd ever done. We had a good wind from the S.W. helping us, especially on the leg between Big Momma and gong buoy 4-CL. Joe also told me I've been an outstanding student; he says I've learned more about the art of sail racing in a week than most people do in a year's time. It just shows that you can teach an old dog new tricks. But Joe has been an excellent teacher, too—though I'll admit he's seemed preoccupied these last two days. Must be the transfer to San Diego.

The marine forecast for the race is perfect—W. wind about 15–20 knots, with an incoming tide. Tonight my head is full of all the racing techniques I've learned from Joe, plus some special tricks I might use to outfox my opponent, Miss Mc

The admiral stopped writing.

My opponent. Just over a week ago, she was someone who I thought I might even be in love with, he admitted to himself. Now, she is Miss McCoy, my opponent.

He rose from the table, crossed over to the kitchenette, and reheated the remainder of the coffee left over from dinner. Looking out the window above the sink, he could see lights shining in the other cabins. Only the curtained windows of the cabin next to his were dark. But from behind them he could hear a man and woman laughing. The laughter gently quieted, to be followed by a woman's voice saying, "Oh, now, Willie," to be followed by more laughter.

The admiral refilled his coffee mug and carried it back to the table. He put it down beside the open log and sat. He took a sip of coffee. Picking up the ballpoint pen again, he completed the name *McCoy* on the page. He paused, and then continued writing.

> Since this is my last entry in the log, I will add a word or two about myself, and why I am participating in this race. Of course, there is the reason I gave Captain Carnes and others; that once I committed myself to being in it, I was too determined—or too stubborn—to back out. But there is another reason too. I am in my seventies. Clearly I should be content to settle for old age. But the word "content" has never been a part of my vocabulary. Old age is something that happens to my friends, not me; it's always five years ahead of whatever age I am. And this I know about myself—I still have too much zest for life, but nobody to share it with. I might add also that I have too much love to give and nobody to give it to. Last week I thought Peggy might have been that person—I still think so. Now she is Miss McCoy, my opponent.

For several moments, the admiral looked down at the page. Then, he set aside the pen and slowly closed the book.

10

FESTIVAL DAY!

wrote T. C. Dabney across the blackboard of his store at dawn.

Precisely at nine o'clock in front of Hasty Harbor Fire Station #1, the drum major of the Peninsula Regional High School marching band blew his whistle, and the festival parade began. The line of march was led by the twenty-member band in their blue and gold uniforms, flanked by two female twirlers twirling red-white-and-blue batons. They were followed by the community's lone fire engine. Behind it came a white Rambler convertible, driven by the president of the Hasty Harbor Lobstermen's Association. On the top of the back seat of the convertible sat the two other officers of the association, jovially waving live lobsters at the crowd. Walking gamely in their wake were the dozen women of the Ladies' Auxiliary, a smattering of Legionnaires, the Boy Scouts, the Girl Scouts, the Cub Scouts and the Brownies, and four members of the sewing club, the Busy Bees, riding in a horse-drawn surrey. Bringing up the rear came Jimmy Smiley's garbage truck, festooned from hood ornament to dumpster guard with bright multicolored crepe paper.

Along the parade route that led from the firehouse to Dabney's Store and back, dozens of people stood or sat in camp chairs, watching the paraders. With the attention Hasty Harbor had received the last few days the parade organizers had anticipated a larger turnout, and perhaps television coverage. But the crowd lining the route made up in spirit and enthusiasm what it lacked in numbers.

Upon the conclusion of the parade, the auction began on the side lawn of the Old Church. Reverend Clapp himself presided as auctioneer. There was considerable bidding on a number of donated items, including an antique rocking chair that had been in Mavis Hooker's family for a century and was purported to have been sat on by Calvin Coolidge when he was still governor of Massachusetts.

Peggy McCoy herself was not among the celebrants, either along the parade route or at the auction. On the morning of the race she had awakened early, tossed some bread crumbs on the deck for Captain Bligh, and fixed her breakfast while she listened to the marine weather forecast on the radio. The sky was blue and bright; already a breeze was building from the west that was expected to reach twenty knots by race time. Low tide was about ten o'clock, high tide at a quarter after four. Thus the race would be run entirely on an incoming tide. Slow for the first leg of the triangular course, Peggy figured, from the harbor entrance southward to Big Momma, but faster on the last leg, from the gong buoy back to the harbor entrance and the finish line.

As she ate her breakfast she reviewed the pre-race procedures to be followed. She and the admiral were to arrive at the town pier at eleven thirty and be welcomed by the race committee. They would then be escorted out of the harbor into the river, to the vicinity of the starting line beside the flashing buoy. As for the race committee's recommendation that the competitors "affect attire suitable to the event," Peggy had already chosen her outfit: a pair of navy blue shorts and a simple white T-shirt. But certainly she'd bring along her sailor's hat. At the thought of it she glanced up to where it hung on a hook beside the kitchen door. Today it would be her lucky talisman.

Peggy finished her breakfast and brought the dishes to the sink, gazing out the kitchen window while she washed them. Sunlight sparkled off the surface of the water, and a few boats were visible, most of them commercial fishing craft. She wondered how many more boats would be out there by the time the race began. She put the question out of her mind, dried her hands, and went out onto the deck again. Last night she had given *Free Spirit*'s sails a good rinsing, and they now lay stretched out across the lawn, large white Dacron triangles drying in the sun. They would be filled with wind several hours from now, and depending on how skillfully she played them, they would carry her and *Free Spirit* to victory or—

No, she would not even think the other word.

At exactly the same moment the admiral was peering down at the navigational chart spread out across the table in his cabin. The experience reminded him of the days when he played football at Annapolis. Before each game he would pore over the playbook, studying the diagrams and running the plays in his imagination. Still staring at the chart, he repeated aloud to himself, "From the flashing buoy outside the harbor entrance southwest to Big Momma, east to the gong buoy, north-northwest to the flashing buoy again."

The admiral looked at his watch. They had agreed Joe would arrive at the cabin about eleven. Last night the young man had insisted he pick up the admiral and drive him to the Hasty Harbor pier to spare him coping with the crowds alone. Joe had added with a smile that a contingent of other navy officers, all Joe's friends from the ship works, had agreed to form a kind of honor guard to lead them to the pier, and to provide protection for the admiral and Joe in case the need arose.

The admiral quickly reviewed in his mind the basic sailing tactics that he planned to use, plus several tricks that Joe had taught him. He made a fist and banged it squarely at the center of the chart. "All right, Deering!" He remembered the words of the football coach at the academy so many years ago. "Get out there! And let's see if you have the stuff it takes to win!"

Peggy gripped the door handle of the police cruiser as it turned onto River Road. The whole thing was silly and unnecessary, she thought; a waste of public money. Shortly before she was to leave her house a state police car had appeared in her driveway. The pleasant young officer had informed her he'd been sent to drive her into Hasty Harbor. Peggy had protested; she was perfectly capable of driving her own car. If there were crowds—and he insisted that there were—she'd simply ignore them and go on her way.

But as the car rounded the last curve and started down toward the village and the pier, Peggy understood the officer's concern. Lining both sides of the road were more people than she'd ever seen before in Hasty Harbor. Parked next to Dabney's Store was a trailer with the call letters of an Augusta television station emblazoned on the side. Other cars identified by press signs on their dashboards were parked on both sides of the turnaround. But it was the number of spectators that surprised her most. Already some people along the road had spotted her, and they now cheered and waved at the police car as it passed.

The car descended slowly toward the turnaround,

where more policemen stood. Long yellow wooden barricades had been set up at the perimeter of the area, encircling it and keeping it clear of people who might otherwise have thronged it. As the car drove into the turnaround, more applause and shouts ignited, quickly rising to a roar.

The police officer stopped the car at the entrance to the pier. An officer standing nearby stepped forward and opened Peggy's door.

"'Morning, ma'am," he said, adding something that was drowned out by another burst of cheering from the crowd. "Follow me, please." He gestured toward the pier.

Peggy stepped out of the police car. She took a deep breath, pushed the sailor hat down firmly on her head, and keeping close behind the officer, followed him to the pier.

Less than a minute later two dark blue sedans, both bearing the insignia of the U.S. Navy, also descended toward the turnaround. In the lead car were four young naval officers, all from the navy unit at the ship works. In the second car, with Ensign Joe Marino at the wheel, was the other competitor in the Hasty Harbor Cup Race, Rear Admiral Charles Deering.

Again the crowd broke into applause and cheers as the two navy cars drew up to the entrance to the pier. The four men in the first car stepped out at once and moved to surround the second car.

The admiral looked over at Joe. "I guess this is the moment of truth, isn't it?" He gave the young man a nervous smile.

"Good luck." Joe held out his hand.

The admiral grasped it. "Thank you, Joe. Thank you for a lot of things. Where will you be during the race?"

"At the harbor entrance, near the finish line. Waiting with a bottle of champagne to greet the winner." Joe added, "You're going to win. I know you will."

"I'll try." The admiral withdrew his hand and opened the car door. "I'll try," he said again, and stepped out of the car.

Escorted by a state policeman and the four navy officers and accompanied by the ovations of the crowds, the admiral walked onto the pier.

As she stood before them, Peggy thought the three men of the race committee looked ridiculous. It was the only time she could remember seeing Cabot Lodge dressed in a jacket—or for that matter, a clean shirt and tie. But like the other two he was outfitted today in white linen slacks and a blue blazer. Incredibly, for the first time anyone could remember, he was actually even wearing shoes instead of the familiar yellow waders. Able Fenstermacher, as committee chairman, alone wore a yachting cap. Peggy's immediate impulse was to laugh. She didn't, but the sight of them helped relieve some of the tension she felt. It must have been all the publicity that had caused this transformation in them, she assumed.

"Hi, Peggy," Able Fenstermacher greeted her. "See you made it through the crowds." He looked past her to the entrance to the pier. "Appears the admiral himself has just arrived."

Peggy heard the ovation for the admiral but didn't turn around. Instead, she clasped her hands together and looked down. The sensation she experienced was curious and contradictory. On the one hand, she felt like a prizefighter who had entered the ring first and was waiting for the challenger. On the other hand, she also had the sense of panic a bride must feel in those few anguished moments after she had been escorted to the altar and left standing there before the vows began.

At least the wait wasn't long. The admiral appeared beside her; she nodded to him briefly, and saw that he was dressed in white slacks and a simple white short-sleeved shirt. He returned the nod, then shook hands with the members of the race committee, while around them cameras clicked.

"First off," Able said, "we'll have a little prayer from Reverend Clapp, so as to bless this race we are about to race."

Peggy didn't really know if one of Reverend Clapp's blessings would do any good, but if it made everybody happier it was all right with her. Reverend Clapp stepped forward from a gathering of townspeople on the pier. He opened his Bible and began to read from it in brisk dramatic bursts, as if he were still conducting the church auction.

While he bounded from one biblical verse to the next, Peggy looked out toward the harbor. Moored to one side of the pier was Cabot Lodge's scalloper *Persephone,* which would serve as the official boat for the committee at the start-finish line. Near it could be seen *Free Spirit* and *Invincible.* An hour ago a boy from the boatyard had come by her house and picked up *Free Spirit*'s sails and the sailing gear. Now with their sails furled to their booms, both sailboats bobbed gently side by side placidly unaware, Peggy thought, of the sea battle that was about to be waged.

Reverend Clapp closed his Bible and stepped back into the crowd.

"Okay, now," Able said to Peggy and the admiral, "you both know the rules and the course we got laid out. Us three committee men will get into the Percy-phone, and you two follow us into the river in your sailboats. And may the best man—the best sailor win."

He reached for Peggy's hand and shook it briefly and then shook hands with the admiral.

"How about a handshake between racers!" someone shouted from the crowd.

"Guess you ought to. How about it?" Able asked them.

The admiral's hand engulfed Peggy's. He looked down at her and smiled. "Good luck, Peggy."

She felt her hand tremble slightly as he continued to hold it. "Good luck to you," she said.

The crowd broke into sustained applause.

"Enough is enough," Able whispered to them. "Let's get going." With that he turned and, followed by the other members of the race committee, marched toward the *Persephone*.

With *Free Spirit* and *Invincible* astern of the committee boat, and a flotilla of boats of a variety of types and sizes following, the passage to the starting line began.

As Peggy crossed the harbor she cast her eyes over the spectator fleet accompanying them. Some of the larger runabouts were obviously occupied by members of the press. The majority of boats, however, seemed to belong not only to local people but to boat owners from a distance of a hundred miles up and down the coast of Maine. Peggy felt a sense of native pride to note the names of ports she knew: Orrs Island, Cape Elizabeth, Tenants Harbor, Owls Head.

By now *Persephone* had started through the channel leading from the harbor to the river, with *Free Spirit* and *Invincible* trailing in her wake. The committee boat moved past the Sawteeth, swung slightly to port, and hastened in the direction of the flashing buoy. Fifty yards beyond the buoy a bright cone-shaped orange float bobbed corklike on the waves. It had been placed there yesterday, and between it and the buoy was the imaginary line that marked the start and finish of the race.

As *Free Spirit* moved into the river, Peggy could see more boats, many more, in fact, but it was not until she passed the Sawteeth herself that the actual number was apparent. Up and down the river, on both sides of the course, a vast armada waited. Rowboats with small outboard motors were moored beside huge windjammers. There were canoes and cabin cruisers, Windsurfers and catboats, and a yacht known to be owned by an Arab businessman, which had a rock band playing on the afterdeck.

Peggy saw commercial fishing boats as well—the *Bluebonnet* and the *Jumping Jack,* and at a respectful distance upriver of the starting line, even the *Mary G.:* Link Mallott, the lobsterman, hard-shelled as he himself was, had relinquished half a day of work to watch the race.

Peggy's watch showed six minutes to twelve. If the race was to begin as scheduled, she had better start positioning *Free Spirit* upriver of the buoy. She swung the tiller and began to sail toward the area where she could begin her opening run at the starting line.

A short time later there was a loud bang. Peggy looked around at the committee boat and saw Able with his arm held in the air, a starter's pistol in his hand. The five minute warning had been given.

Because the starting line was reasonably broad, both boats could cross it without one blanketing the other's wind. In any case, Peggy chose to sail closer to the flashing buoy rather than the orange float. In a stretch of open water and with a stiff breeze blowing directly from the west, she put *Free Spirit* through some practice tacks and jibes. As she did she watched the sails. The jib appeared to be correctly set, but she noticed the fabric of the mainsail had loosened somewhat near the mast. She pulled it taut: any slackness in the setting could cost her dearly once the race began.

She looked over in the direction of *Invincible.* The admiral was also practicing his sail-handling techniques and making small adjustments to his sails. He had obviously been observing the movements of *Free Spirit* and had decided to put his own boat nearer to the float.

Another pistol shot rang out. Two minutes.

Peggy came about sharply and headed toward the spot she'd picked to start her run. She was glad the tide was not a factor. Still, since it was coming in at a reasonably rapid rate, both sailboats would have to push some at the start.

Peggy checked her watch. One minute. She took a deep breath. Then she swung *Free Spirit*'s bow around and headed directly toward the starting line. Out of the corner of her eye she saw Able Fenstermacher lift his arm skyward once again, the pistol raised.

Peggy gave *Free Spirit*'s hull a pat. "Come on, old girl. Let's show everyone what we can do." The starting line was rushing toward her now.

The pistol fired.

Horns and whistles of the spectator boats erupted with a din that filled the river and surrounding hills.

The race was underway.

"Bluebonnet, this is Jumping Jack. How do you read me? Over."

"Jumping Jack, this is Bluebonnet. I read you loud and clear. Over."

In the wheelhouses of the two commercial fishing boats nearest the starting line, the radios crackled. A week ago their skippers, as well as several other lobstermen and scallopers, had been asked by a Brunswick radio station to position themselves around the course and provide continuous reports on the progress of the race. *Bluebonnet* and *Jumping Jack* were chosen to observe the start and finish. Near the first mark, Big Momma, the fishing boat *Porpoiser* was anchored; near the second mark, gong buoy 4-CL, sat *Kathy's Pride*. And because she was a large tuna boat with a flying bridge on which a lookout could stand, the *Rockport Rocket* had been assigned to travel the perimeter of the course, providing color commentary.

"Jumping Jack. Jumping Jack. This is Bluebonnet. Looks like the admiral's out front! What'd you see? Over."

"Look like he is, Jack. He caught a wind gust as he crossed the line!"

The admiral grinned broadly; he hoped Joe had seen the way *Invincible* had hit the starting line. A sudden breeze had given her an extra push, but those hours of practicing his starts had paid off too. He didn't lead by much, he guessed; only a few seconds. But it gave him confidence that he *was* a skillful sailor—and that he just might win the race!

"Damn!" Peggy swore. From *Free Spirit*'s heading on the starting run she couldn't see the admiral. But the loud cheers she'd heard when she was several seconds from the line had told her he had crossed it first and was ahead.

Don't panic, she told herself. Take it easy. It's a long race. What's a couple seconds at the starting line?

Peggy gave *Free Spirit*'s deck another encouraging pat and pointed the boat closer to the wind. She checked the admiral's position in relation to her own. He was ahead, all right, and sailing at an angle toward her, probably hoping she would tack away from him and lose the wind.

Okay, she thought. If that's the way you want to play the game, then I'll play too.

Pulling on the tiller hard, she tacked—but in the opposite direction from the one he was clearly expecting, and at once *Free Spirit* found a burst of speed. The move surprised the admiral; he tacked abruptly in an attempt to cover her.

He was too late. Increasing her speed further, Peggy pulled ahead of him and seized the lead.

What followed for exactly half an hour was a tacking duel, each boat maneuvering to take advantage of the wind. Several times *Invincible* attempted to outtack *Free Spirit* and failed; every move the admiral made, Peggy countered. Her lead was never more than a boat length, but it began to irk him that he couldn't close the gap.

After tacking for what seemed the hundredth time, the admiral looked seaward. Down the course ahead of him he saw Big Momma. Around it several yellow patrol launches of the state police were also visible, holding back a large number of spectator craft.

Although Peggy had finally increased her lead to two boat lengths, the admiral suspected she would have to change her heading soon if she intended to sail close around the rock. He also knew his angle of approach was better. He could probably hold his present tack and maybe even catch her as she went around.

He decided it was worth a try. The tide, though rising, was still low enough to make the effort possible. It'd be a close shave, in any case. Briefly he recalled the asterisks that ringed Big Momma on the chart, wondering if any of those wrecks had happened in a sailing race.

He put the thought out of his mind immediately, made a slight correction in the sail trim, and sailed almost directly for the rock.

"Porpoiser, this is Jumping Jack. I'm handing off to you down at Big Momma. What do you see? Over."

"This is Porpoiser. Thanks, Jack. Big Momma's just a good spit from us . . . and I can see both sailboats closin' on it fast. . . . Free Spirit's still ahead, but—Invincible is comin'! Peggy's gonna have to move her butt to shake him off! . . . She sees him! Invincible's still coming'! He's inside! He's caught her now! Invincible has got the lead!"

I did it! The admiral wiped his eyes and looked back at *Free Spirit*. It had been a daring move: he'd cut inside of Peggy at Big Momma, skirting the rock so closely that *Invincible* and he were drenched as a wave broke over the rock just ahead of him.

Forget the self-congratulations, he immediately told himself. Astern of him Peggy had begun to raise her spinnaker. He'd better do the same. They were on the second leg now, with the wind behind them. In practice, this downwind leg had never been one of his strong points. He set the tiller and mainsail and scrambled forward to raise his own large red-white-and-blue sail.

With both huge spinnakers now ballooning out in front of them, the two sailboats sped toward gong buoy 4-CL.

Well, well. He certainly surprised you at Big Momma, didn't he? Peggy admitted to herself that his bravado at the rock had caught her unaware. It was a gutsy move. Had there been a sudden wind shift he'd have grazed the rock, disqualifying himself and doing damage to his boat—or worse. But now they were on the downwind run, and Peggy knew that there was not much fancy sailing either one of them could do until they went around the second mark.

For some minutes *Free Spirit* and *Invincible* sailed parallel to one another, Peggy's boat a length behind the admiral's and about twenty feet off to starboard. Now and then she heard applause from people on the boats lining the course, and several times she saw the admiral acknowledge the attention with a wave of his hand. She probably ought to do the same, but she felt awkward and embarrassed at the thought. She finally settled for a nod and a brief smile and hoped that would suffice.

Peggy switched hands on the tiller and adjusted her position at the cockpit rail. The run to gong buoy 4-CL would probably take another twenty minutes.

Again she heard a small burst of applause from the spectator boats she was passing. When she looked over she saw most of it was coming from a pair of large 6-meter sailboats at anchor. What surprised her was that although their sails were not raised, the anemometers atop their masts were spinning furiously. It meant one thing: a stronger breeze was blowing outside the course than *Free Spirit* was receiving where she was. In contrast, the wind farther inside, where *Invincible* was sailing, wasn't nearly at the same velocity.

Peggy eased *Free Spirit* farther to the outside—and at once she felt the extra push the wind gave her. Ahead, still maintaining his position on the inside of the course, the admiral seemed ignorant of what she'd done. Ignorance is bliss, thought Peggy. Beneath her, *Free Spirit* was beginning to build speed, and soon was racing like a steeplechaser through the waves.

"Kathy's Pride, this is Porpoiser. Looks like they're comin' up on the gong buoy. Over to you, K.P."

"Got 'em in my glasses, Porpoiser. I can't see who's leadin', though. . . . The admiral, I think. He better be! I got fifty bucks on the old man to win! . . . Now Peggy's comin' up on the outside. . . . They're comin'! Here they come: . . . Peggy's pulled up! They're dead even as they go around the mark! . . . They're in the home stretch now! The spinnakers are droppin' like an old maid's bloomers, as both skippers scramble to reset their sails!"

Around the course itself and within a radius of fifteen miles, other boats were monitoring the progress of the race. Near the flashing buoy at the entrance to the harbor, Joe sat in a rented runabout, a radio held to his ear.

He frowned, put aside the radio, and decided he should have worked harder with the admiral in practice on the downwind leg. Now there was one leg of the race remaining, a distance of about four miles. From where Joe had moored the runabout he could see that what had been the starting line an hour or so earlier was being transformed into the finish line. A short time ago two sloops had anchored in position at each side of the line. Their masts and riggings were arrayed with flags and streamers to welcome the winning sailor back to port.

Well, the admiral was not winning at the moment, Joe acknowledged, but he wasn't losing either. And on this final leg in practice, under similar wind and tide conditions, he'd done well. And a lot could happen that could give him back the lead. They might have cause for celebration, after all, tonight.

Tonight—

At that moment Joe saw her.

On the far side of the finish line, crowded in among the other vessels that were gathered there, was the boatyard skiff. Noah Dodge was at the helm. Behind him stood Sarah, her long hair wind-tossed at her back, binoculars held to her eyes as she looked down the course.

Joe turned away. Tonight he knew that he would have to tell her the decision he had made.

He thrust the prospect of it from his mind, picked up his own binoculars, and focused them downriver.

Peggy looked across her shoulder and allowed herself a smile. Soon after both sailboats had rounded the gong buoy, *Free Spirit* had successfully crossed over to the inside of the course and begun to edge ahead. At first her lead was imperceptible, in part because *Invincible* had gone far to the outside of the course to keep from being caught in her wind shadow. But by the time the two of them were halfway down the final leg, Peggy knew it would be difficult to take the lead away from her. And if his constant glances in the direction of her boat meant anything, the admiral knew it.

She had just begun to check the wind direction when well behind her to her right she heard a rising whirring sound. She looked back and saw a Coast Guard helicopter coming into view. Before the race had started the helicopter had begun circling the river, checking the activity and seeking to discourage any aircraft that might try to overfly it for a better view. Now hovering outside the course, away from the two sailboats, the helicopter pilot and his crewmate had decided to give themselves a perfect vantage point for the closing minutes of the race.

Peggy shaded her eyes against the sun to look up at it. As she did, she saw the pilot bank in her direction, giving her a thumbs-up sign. He thinks I'm going to win the race! she realized. In acknowledgment and thanks, she removed her sailor hat and held it high. *I will! I'll win!* her gesture reaffirmed.

The admiral was glad it was a Coast Guard helicopter that was watching them, not one belonging to the U.S. Navy. Had it been, he thought, the navy men aboard might well conclude all hope was lost, and bomb *Invincible* into oblivion, rather than allow navy pride to suffer the indignity of a defeat.

It was grim humor, the admiral admitted, but his situation was grim, too. Since the boats had rounded the gong buoy, he'd attempted a variety of tacks and other actions to increase his speed, or at least prevent *Free Spirit* from making it a runaway. But with two miles remaining in the race, Peggy held the lead now by as much as twenty feet, and she was not about to give it up.

In the distance he could faintly see what he assumed to be the finish line. Around it boats were clustered, and in one of them he knew, awaiting his return, was Joe Marino.

Joe! It came to him. Of course! Why hadn't he thought of it before? The trick Joe used on him in practice. What did he call it? The Marino Maneuver. If there was a time to try it, it was now.

Peggy, he observed, was facing forward, concentrating on the run for home. Moving deftly in behind her boat and trailing her as closely as he could, he waited for sufficient leeway on the inside of the course. He found it.

Now! He pulled the tiller fiercely with both hands; at once *Invincible* swung away sharply from the line that both were sailing, passing at right angles just behind *Free Spirit*'s stern and rocketing toward the spectator boats beside the course. As skippers and their passengers stared, gasped, and scrambled to avoid a collision, the admiral jibed now, and headed straight for Peggy's boat.

The crowd shrieked. Peggy turned and saw him coming and instinctively fell off to keep from being hit.

Instead *Invincible* cut back in the opposite direction and resumed her course, leading by a boat length on the windward side. A roar from the crowd followed; boaters who had caught their breath soon cheered as well.

The admiral now, finally, allowed himself a breath, and looked ahead. Three hundred yards upriver was the finish line.

"Bluebonnet to Jumping Jack. They're coming!"

"That they are, Blue! Two hundred yards I make it—and Invincible is leadin' by a length! . . . Free Spirit's tryin'! Peggy's pullin' up the centerboard. . . . She's pointin' sharper! And she's gettin' speed! A hundred yards to go! They're bow to bow! . . . Seventy-five yards! . . . Sixty! . . ."

The noise that surrounded them was rising to a crescendo. For a moment, sea spray clouded Peggy's vision; the boats around the finish line were no more than a blurry mass. But on the race committee boat she could see Able Fenstermacher stand and raise his pistol in the air.

Above the shouting of the crowd and the steady wail of boat horns the admiral heard nothing—but he felt the thud. The tiller jolted in his hand.

"Twenty-five yards! And Free Spirit's pullin' out ahead!"

Behind *Invincible* he saw it suddenly: a fragment of a fishnet that was held fast to the rudder. Frantically, he reached down to remove it—when the object floated free and disappeared as mysteriously as it had come.

"She's done it!!!"

There was a pistol shot and a tumultuous reaction from the crowd. *Free Spirit*, Miss McCoy at the helm, had won the Hasty Harbor Cup.

As the race committee had requested prior to the race, and as both sailors had agreed, there would be no post-race celebration at the finish line. Instead the committee boat would lead the procession back into Hasty Harbor, followed by the winning boat, and after her, the runner-up. The official ceremonies, including the presentation of the Hasty Harbor Cup, were to take place on the town pier.

Thus, a few moments after she had crossed the finish line and slowed *Free Spirit,* Peggy saw the committee boat swing toward the harbor entrance. At the same time, Able beckoned to her. Obediently, Peggy came about and slipped in behind the committee boat.

A chorus of horns, whistles, cheering and applause continued as *Free Spirit* slowly made her way after *Persephone*. Occasionally Peggy raised her hand in brief acknowledgment.

But what appeared as diffidence or modesty on her part masked the exuberance she felt. Several times she found it necessary to remind herself the race was over. She had won. Yet mixed with the sense of exhilaration was an emptiness; it seemed to Peggy the way a woman might feel soon after giving birth.

Free Spirit sailed past the Sawteeth and moved swiftly through the harbor entrance with the tide. It was not until she had reentered the harbor that she realized she'd totally ignored the admiral from the moment she had crossed the finish line.

Embarrassed, Peggy turned around. He was at the tiller of *Invincible*, trailing in her wake by thirty yards. She waved; he nodded and then waved as well. Above the noise of the crowd, he called, "Congratulations."

"Thank you," Peggy answered. Then, not knowing what else to say or do, she turned forward once again.

At last the *Persephone* drew up to the town pier. Led by Able, the members of the race committee disembarked. They were soon joined on the pier by Peggy, and a short time afterward, by the admiral. The crush of press people and spectators was even greater than it had been several hours earlier, causing the police to close the pier.

After some rearranging by the photographers, Peggy and the admiral were positioned on each side of the race committee. At the center Able Fenstermacher stood holding a large silver-plated object that looked like a cross between a soup tureen and a crematory urn.

When the shuffle of photographers had ended and the crowd had quieted sufficiently, Able stepped forward. "On behalf of the race committee of the Hasty Harbor Summer Festival," he announced, "I hereby present this cup to the winner of this year's sailing race: Miss Peggy McCoy, of Lonely Point, Hasty Harbor, Maine."

He thrust the cup at Peggy as the crowd broke into applause. She took hold of the cup by its handles and stared down inside it, as if she half expected something to pop out at her.

"Speech! Speech!" someone called.

"They want you to say something," Able whispered.

"What?" she whispered back.

"I don't know. Tell 'em since you won the race, you're goin' off to Disney World or something. Anything so we can all go home." He looked impatient.

"I . . ." Peggy faltered, and then began again, "I just want to say—"

"Louder!" people shouted.

"I just want to say thanks to everybody who believed in me, and who thought I could win. I thought so too—most of the time. But I had a good boat, and a good friend, Sarah Dodge, who helped me." She saw Sarah beaming among the crowd. "And thanks, too, to Admiral Deering. He gave us a good run." She looked over at the admiral, then looked away, addressing Able once more. "Anyway, I'm not used to making speeches. So I guess that's it."

There was polite applause.

"Admiral?" said Able. "Anything you'd like to say, seein' how you're the lose—the also-ran?"

The admiral nodded. He waited for the crowd to quiet. When he finally spoke his words were directed to Peggy. "While I was out there on the course this afternoon, two brief quotations came to mind. The first was, 'The race is to the swift.' Well, I also had a good boat, and a good friend to help me, Ensign Joe Marino." The admiral surveyed the crowd, but Joe was nowhere to be seen. He went on. "But neither I nor my boat were quite swift enough to win.

"The other saying that came to me is, 'Ships are but boards and sailors but men.' Now, years ago all sailors *were* men. But the sailor—the *fine* sailor in whose wake I trailed at the finish line is a woman. And a *fine* woman. She won. She deserved the victory. And I congratulate you, Miss McCoy."

He extended his hand toward Peggy; she accepted it.

"Aren't you going to kiss her?" someone shouted.

"May I?" he asked Peggy.

"Yes!" the crowd shouted in a body.

"I guess so," Peggy answered.

Gently, he took both her hands in his. Then he bent and

kissed her lightly on the cheek. There were hoots and whistles from the crowd, and shouts of “More!” “Again!”

“Forget the more again,” said Able firmly. “Some of us have been out on the water for three hours, drinking beer and standing up in boats without facilities. Let’s get this ceremony over with. One final note,” he said to Peggy and the admiral. “You both are guest of honors at the clambake supper on the beach tonight. Will you be there?”

“I’d like to. Thank you,” said the admiral. He turned to Peggy. “And I hope you’ll be there, too.”

She hesitated. “I guess so.”

Able clapped his hands together. “Okay. The ceremony’s over. All of you, go home.”

En masse, everybody began moving off the pier, Able somewhat faster than the rest. Reporters and photographers sought to surround Peggy and the admiral. But two burly state policemen were already escorting Peggy to the police cruiser, and the quartet of navy men formed a makeshift flying wedge around the admiral to get him through the crowd.

As the admiral approached the navy car, he saw Joe leaning against the fender, his arms folded across his chest. Without a word Joe opened the door for the admiral, then went around and slipped in on the driver’s side.

“I’m sorry,” the admiral said at last.

Joe shoved the key in the ignition and started the car. “What happened?”

“I lost.”

“That’s not what I mean.” Joe continued looking through the windshield waiting for the car in front to move. “Did she beat you? Or did you deliberately let up?”

“You mean, did I throw the race? No.”

“Then what *happened*?” Joe looked at him. “I was watching. You slowed down when you could’ve won!”

“The vagaries of wind and tide—” the admiral began.

"Wind and tide, my ass," Joe interrupted. "Something happened out there. Tell me what it was."

"First, let me ask you what you did with the bottle of champagne."

"After you lost I threw it in the river. It's floating out there in the Kerrenac somewhere." Ahead, the first navy car was pulling out. Joe put his car in gear and followed.

"That's not the only thing floating in the Kerrenac," the admiral said.

"What do you mean, not the only thing?"

"Joe, I'll tell you something. Several things," the admiral went on. "Principal among them is that Miss McCoy *is* a good sailor. An excellent one."

"Agreed. But so are you," Joe said. "That's not the reason you lost. What was it?"

The admiral felt weary suddenly. He leaned back against the seat and for a moment watched the scenery pass by. "Joe," he began again. "Both of us are navy men. Officers and gentlemen. What I am about to tell you goes no further than this car. I fouled on a net."

"A *what*?"

"A fishnet. A piece of it. The last thirty yards or so before the finish line, it caught the rudder. And it slowed me down."

"We'll file a protest!"

"We'll do nothing of the sort."

"You lost the race because of a lousy floating fishnet in the river, and you're going to let it *go*?"

"Yes."

"But you could have won! You *should* have!"

"Maybe. Maybe not. The race is over. Done." He paused. "Oh, we could bring a protest. Maybe even prove our point and have the result of the race overturned. But what good would it do? None. And it would hurt several people very deeply. Miss McCoy most—and her young friend who helped her, Sarah Dodge."

Joe drove along the road in silence.

"I'm sorry," he said finally. "I'm sorry I got mad."

"No reason to be." The admiral looked over. "As my coach and trainer, you're right to be upset. If I were in your position I'd be mad as hell."

"Sir . . . you're one of the best men I've ever met."

The admiral gave a little shrug as if to dismiss the remark and leaned back in the seat again. "I tried my best, at least."

He thought for several moments. "As it is, the race was only the first of today's challenges. The second comes tonight. And it may be a lot tougher for me than the race was."

11

What residents of Hasty Harbor referred to as their beach, two miles north of town, was not what someone other than a native of the state of Maine would think of as a beach at all. Along the water's edge there was a narrow margin of sand, which gave way almost at once to long horizontal slabs of granite rising tierlike to a crumbling macadam parking lot.

For purposes of the annual clambake and supper, nonetheless, the smooth flat rocks nearest the sand provided firm support for the tables of food that had been set up, around which fussed a dozen or so members of the Ladies' Auxiliary. Some members' husbands also had been pressed into service, tending to the steaming cauldrons that contained the lobsters and the barbecue grills on which were now roasting open clams and ears of corn. Spread out on the tables themselves was a display of dishes, all contributions of the ladies of the town. Among the offerings were three kinds of potato salad, a variety of garden vegetables, and baskets full of homemade breads and rolls. Sitting at a discreet distance from the other items was a new covered-dish surprise from Emma Wilmott, which she assured everyone would be even more memorable than her baked beans. But for a few daring souls no one touched it. Many ladies had made cakes; on a special table there were upside-down cakes, layer cakes, angel food cakes, devil's food cakes, shortcakes, pound cakes, bundt cakes, and a lone brown Betty. Coffee was available from four massive urns, as well as soft drinks for the children, and any others who desired them. As for the admission fee, those who supplied food or beverages to the supper were charged nothing; for the rest the cost was five dollars, half price for children under twelve, free for carriable tots.

When Peggy arrived at the beach parking lot at about six thirty, she neither brought food nor paid admission. She and the admiral, as Able Fenstermacher had insisted, were the "guest of honors." Ahead of Peggy, cars meandered back and forth across the lot, their drivers parking randomly despite the efforts of the lot attendants to direct them otherwise. Generally, the cars' occupants then leapt out, grabbed whatever blankets, folding chairs, or cushions they had brought, and headed in the direction of the wooden stairway that led down to the beach.

Peggy, at least, parked her Pinto in the designated spot. She took the boat cushion she planned to sit on and got in line with those already moving toward the stairway. Ahead of her she saw the three members of the race committee, still dressed in their white slacks and blue blazers, and still savoring their temporary notability amid a small attentive crowd. Among the townspeople who noticed her, most waved or called out their congratulations. Peggy did her best to thank them all with at least a smile or nod.

At the top of the stairway Peggy surveyed the scene, stepping to one side to let those behind her pass. There was more of a crowd than she had anticipated. Many were gathered near the water in a long line that wound its way in front of the food tables. Those who had been served already were standing in small groups trying to balance paper plates or sitting here and there on the rocks.

Peggy felt someone touch her elbow. She turned to find the admiral standing beside her.

"Good evening." He gestured at the scene. "Looks like quite a little shindig they've got going. Is it like this for every summer festival?"

"I don't know," Peggy said. "I haven't been to very many."

There was an awkward pause, as if neither of them quite knew what to say next.

"Yoo-hoo, my dear! Congratulations!" a voice from behind called out.

Peggy turned to see Mrs. Doberman approaching. Beside her was the randy octogenarian Mr. Fogerty, beaming happily and carrying a lavender beach blanket. As she passed Peggy and the admiral, Mrs. Doberman gave Peggy a broad wink that said, "You found your man; now I've found mine," before she seized Mr. Fogerty's free hand and started down the stairs.

"Well, how about some supper?" the admiral offered. "I'll get it for us. That is, unless you plan to be with your friends."

"No. I'm alone."

"Good," he said. "I mean, it's not good you're alone; it's good you're here. But I'm alone too. Shall we dine together?"

"Yes. I guess. That's fine."

"Fine," he echoed. "Fine. You get us a place to sit and I'll report to the chow line. Anything particular you'd like to eat?"

"No." Peggy shook her head. "Whatever looks good. I think I'll skip the clams, though."

"Fine," he said again. "But the line looks fairly long; it

may take me a few minutes. Do you have any idea where you'd like to sit? Just so I can find you."

Peggy looked around, then pointed to a spot high on the rocks that was still free of other people. "How about there?"

"In the box seats. Or is that the upper balcony? All right, I'll look for you there." He turned from her and started slowly down the wooden stairway.

Peggy also turned and began making her way up to the spot she had suggested. Arriving there, she placed her cushion on the flat expanse of rock and sat. She looked at the activity below her. The admiral was right. It was like being in the box seats of a theater; she, a witness to the drama, watching it with interest but avoiding participation in it. That's the story of my life, she thought.

The declining sun had begun to cast long shadows over the rocks. Only the tables of food and the people nearest them were still in daylight, bathed now in a kind of amber glow.

Peggy saw the admiral join the others moving forward toward the tables. Some among the line had recognized him and were offering their hands. She watched as he stepped up to the food tables bearing two large paper plates, one in each hand, and was served something from that cauldron, this salad bowl, that bread basket. If anyone sought to shake hands with him now, he answered with some friendly remark and held up the two heaping plates. Soon he was making his way back up the stairs. He stopped several times to get his bearings. Peggy waved; he saw her, called "I'm coming!" and continued on to where she sat.

Puffing, he handed her a plate. "Lobster, corn on the cob," he recited, "tomato salad, potato salad, bran muffins, courtesy of Mrs. Somebody, who insisted everybody over sixty needed roughage. We can have dessert later—if we've got room. Ah! I forgot to get us anything to drink! If you can start without it," he went on, still out of breath,

"I'll make the trip to get it shortly." He breathed heavily again.

"Don't worry," Peggy said. "Sit down and eat." She pointed to a flat space on the rock beside her. "Granite's not the softest seat. I'm sorry that I didn't bring a second cushion for you."

He patted the rock and sat down with his plate. "Believe you me, I have sufficient padding of my own. But thank you." He reached into his shirt pocket and withdrew some plastic forks and knives, then fetched a wad of paper napkins out of a trouser pocket and gave several to Peggy. "I brought plenty of these for the lobster. At our first dinner I learned how really messy lobsters in their shells can be."

"Some Mainers say the only way to eat a lobster is to take off all your clothes," she told him.

The admiral laughed. "That may be. But I am not about to disrobe for this crowd, summer festival or no summer festival."

Peggy smiled. "I just thought you might be interested in some of the native customs."

"I am." He paused, then said more seriously, "And to that end, I thought I might stay here in Maine a while longer."

"Oh?"

"I mean, rather than go back to Maryland tomorrow."

"I see." Peggy took her fork and began eating. "This is good potato salad," she said.

"Good." The admiral looked from her to his own plate. "But I think I'll tackle the lobster first. And I'll be less polite than I was at our first dinner." He tore off a front claw and slapped it on the rock until it cracked. Then he broke open the shell, and started sucking at the meat inside. "So," he said, "how do you feel now that the race is over?"

"Relieved," she answered. "Once more, I'm a totally anonymous person, I'm glad to say."

"Don't be so sure. You may be asked to skipper the next America's Cup yacht."

"I doubt it."

"Then the Hasty Harbor Cup will be the last addition to your trophy case?"

"Hardly," Peggy said. "What I'll probably do with it is fill it with topsoil, put it on my deck, and plant petunias."

They returned to their dinners. The sunlight was continuing to fade; the rocks and the beach itself were now in total shadow.

Finally, Peggy put down her fork and looked over at him. "May I ask you something?"

"Certainly. What is it?"

"At the end of the race, as we were nearing the finish line—you slowed down."

"Yes."

"Why?"

"One of those freakish things," he told her. "I lost the wind."

"But you were the windward boat," she said. "And I was close to you. I didn't lose it."

He made an openhanded gesture. "As I said, it was a fluke. You know things like that can happen when you sail. It just happened to me in a big race at the wrong time."

"I mean—you didn't let me win. Deliberately."

"Why would I do that?"

"To make me feel better."

"I thought you might think that. It's not true." He shook his head. "You won the race on your abilities. And believe me, I am not about to seek a rematch."

"Good thing. I don't think I could go through it all again."

The admiral set down his plate. "Now, how about some coffee for us both?" he asked her. "And dessert?"

"Just coffee. But are you sure you want to make the trip?"

"I may not be as young as I once was. But I'm not ready for the coronary care unit yet. Besides, it'll be dark soon. If I wait I may not be able to *find* my way back here."

"All right. I'll take my coffee black, please."

"Very good." He stood and turned to go. "Oh, my." He was looking at the people who were starting down the stairway.

"What's the matter?" Peggy asked him.

"Ensign Marino just arrived."

Peggy looked in the direction the admiral was facing. Joe and the girl had not seen them and continued downward toward the beach.

"There's Sarah too," said Peggy.

"Oh, my," the admiral repeated. "I'll get our coffee," he said after a moment, and headed down in the direction of the beach.

Joe did not want to be here. Not on this rock pile they called a beach, eating from a paper plate, sitting in the middle of a hundred or more Hasty Harbor citizens as they watched fireworks fall into the Gulf of Maine. Tonight, in fact, Joe wanted to avoid fireworks of any kind.

Where would he prefer to be? He wasn't sure. Maybe at a local restaurant, at an out-of-the-way table where the two of them could talk. It would be a friendly, candid conversation. He would quickly explain to Sarah what had happened. She would listen, and—maybe after a few tears—she would understand. What had occurred between them had been wonderful; what had been wrong about it was the timing. Certainly, she'd see that. Sarah was a sensible, a reasonable girl. She would understand.

Joe had suggested that they go to Galahad's for dinner. But Sarah had wanted to come here. Because of the race and general activity, Dodge's Boat Yard had been overrun with people, and Sarah had stayed late to help her mother in the office. At about seven thirty in the evening she'd gone home to change. Joe had picked her up at eight, and they had driven to the clambake.

Sarah led the way down to the beach, Joe several steps behind. Under her arm she carried a red beach blanket. When they approached the food tables at last, the line of people waiting to be served was short. But the dinner offerings were in short supply as well. Sarah and Joe each took a paper plate.

"I'm not really hungry," Sarah told him. "What about you?"

"I'll admit I am," Joe said. "I couldn't eat before the race. Afterward I didn't have much of an appetite."

"Maybe I'll just have the shortcake and coffee," Sarah said.

Joe took her plate. "Why don't I grab the food, and you can get coffee for us both. Black for me," he added.

Sarah started toward the tables where the coffee urns and soft drinks were set out. She joined the short line, and when she received two cups of coffee, she stepped back to wait for Joe. A short time later a man who had been in line behind her also stepped out holding two cups, and she saw it was the admiral.

"Good evening," he said, as he approached her. "You and Joe just getting here?"

"Yes. I guess we're late. I stayed to help my mother in the office."

He nodded amiably but said nothing, and Sarah wondered how much he might know about her and Joe.

"Is Peggy here?" she asked him quickly.

"We're sitting up above. Would you and Joe care to join us?"

"Oh, no. I mean, thank you, but I have a special place picked out for us. To watch the fireworks."

Joe came toward them now, carrying the paper plates;

one with shortcake, the other with a lobster and assorted salads.

The admiral greeted him. "I understand Sarah has a special place picked out for the two of you to watch the fireworks."

"Oh?" Joe looked from the admiral to Sarah. He passed it off. "Well, Sarah knows these parts a lot better than I do. If she says it's special then it must be."

"Enjoy yourselves." The admiral bestowed a smile on them and started up the steps with his coffee cups.

"What's this about a special place?" Joe asked Sarah when the admiral had gone.

"It's up the beach a ways," Sarah said. "I used to go there a lot when I was young."

"Okay. Lead the way."

They started along the sand, Sarah several steps ahead. For the first hundred yards they passed crowds of people, standing in small groups or seated on the sand. But as they continued, the spectators thinned.

"How far is this place?" Joe called to her.

"Not far," Sarah answered over her shoulder.

They walked on for some minutes without passing anyone. Finally Sarah turned away from the water and led them into a small sandy area among high boulders, surrounded on three sides by a steep rock face.

Joe stopped and looked around. The space was hardly more than twenty feet across and reminded him of the nave of a small church. Whatever afterglow of sunset still remained was lost within the shadows of the rocks.

Sarah set the paper cups down in the sand, spread out the blanket, and sat down. She patted the blanket next to her as Joe approached. "I hope you'll join me."

"You bet." Joe sat and handed her the plate of shortcake. "Bon appétit. Ah yes, the silverware." He reached into his shirt pocket and drew out some plastic knives and forks.

They began to eat, Sarah taking small bites of her

shortcake, Joe breaking sections of the lobster off with his hands and digging out the meat with his fork. When she was done Sarah put aside the paper plate and picked up her coffee. She sipped it thoughtfully, staring out in the direction of the water. By now the light had disappeared, and only the sliver of a waning moon reflected on the surface of the sea. Beyond them in the darkness they could hear the steady tumbling of waves against the shore.

"So, what time do the fireworks begin?" Joe asked, putting down his plate.

"Soon," she said. She pulled her knees up toward her and rested her chin on them. A gentle onshore breeze had sprung up, and with her fingers Sarah softly brushed aside some strands of hair that fell across her face.

Joe picked up his coffee, sampled it, and made a face.

"Sorry about the coffee," Sarah said. "It must've cooled off during our walk."

"It's fine. Well . . . how's your college thesis coming? Your paper about clams."

"It's coming."

"When do you go back? To college, I mean."

"In a month. I plan to do a lot of things my senior year."

"That's the spirit," Joe said cheerfully. "Seize the day. Live life to the fullest. Gather rosebuds while you can."

"I'm trying to learn that," Sarah said. "I guess that's one reason I came to visit you the other night. Joe–"

"Talking about school," he went on, "you must be looking forward to it. I mean, seeing all your friends and all, and planning your activities."

"Uh-huh."

"Like what?" So far so good, Joe thought. Just keep it chatty, conversational.

Sarah sipped her coffee. "The second weekend in October is homecoming," she said.

"Homecoming! Great! I bet you'll be invited to a lot of parties. Things like that."

"Maybe you can come up and visit me." She continued looking toward the water.

"Well . . . let's see how things work out. It's usually pretty busy at the ship works in October."

Sarah looked at him. "I thought October was a slow month."

"Well, some Octobers are, some aren't." He drank some coffee. "Anyway, they say this October may be busy."

Sarah accepted his explanation without comment. She lay back on the blanket, stretched out her legs, and put her hands behind her head. "There are so many stars tonight," she said.

Joe sat forward. "You're right. Look at them. There's the constellation of Andromeda. And that's Cassiopeia. And the Dippers, of course." He pointed east toward the horizon. "See those? They're called the Hunting Dogs. And to the left of them—"

Joe felt Sarah's hand touching him. "That constellation's called—"

"Joe."

"Berenice's Hair. . . ."

"I love you, Joe."

"I love you, too. . . . Sarah, something happened that I was going to tell you about."

"What do you mean?"

"A couple of months ago, before we met, I asked the navy for a transfer."

"From the ship works?"

"Yes. From Whitby."

"Why are you telling me this now?" In the dark her voice was uncomprehending.

"Because it came through the other day."

"Well, if it's to Portsmouth, or even Boston, I could still visit you. We—"

"It isn't. It's to San Diego. In California."

She sat up on the blanket. "I know where San Diego is."

"I'm sorry. I didn't mean it like it sounded." He sought to save the moment. "But it's a great chance for advancement. Everybody says so. I mean, not that I intend to make the navy my career forever, but—"

"How soon do they want an answer?"

"Please try to understand."

"How soon?"

"I gave them one."

"And?"

"I accepted it."

"When?"

"Yesterday. Sarah, the day you came to the apartment, I was going to tell you—"

"But you didn't."

"No. Look, you're the nicest girl I've ever known," he rushed on. "And I don't mean just nice, I mean kind-hearted, smart. Why, all those things you showed me about clams, they really—"

"When do you leave?" Sarah asked him quietly.

"Soon."

"How soon?"

"In a few days. Sarah, please try to understand."

"I understand." She stood and began walking slowly away from him toward the beach.

Joe also stood. He started to call out her name. He wanted to go after her, to tell her he had changed his mind, that he would stay.

But he did not.

Red-white-and-blue Roman candles burst one after another, and skyrockets showered down. The spectators applauded.

"They certainly bring back some memories, these fireworks," the admiral said to Peggy. "When I was seven a friend of mine and I found a whole box of them somewhere. Torpedoes, cracker bonbons, whiz-bangs. Everything. We invited some of the other boys over to Granddad Jennings's barn and had our own fireworks display. Except one of the rockets went astray and set fire to the barn. Talk about pyrotechnics." He chuckled, recollecting. "My father gave me quite a hiding for that episode, I'll tell you."

"Our family wasn't much for fireworks," Peggy said. "Sometimes on the Fourth of July we'd go over to the Waldo County fairgrounds and they'd have them. But the big displays were down in Portland, generally. Or on Old Orchard Beach."

"You love Maine, don't you?" he asked.

"Yes. I can't think of living anywhere else."

"What about Maryland?"

She looked at him. After a pause, she said, "I don't know. I've never lived there."

"Would you like to?"

"I—" Just then, there was a flash of fireworks above them. Both looked up. "I don't know," she said once more when the sound had died.

"Peggy, the race is over; all that nonsense is behind us now. Let's pretend it never happened and begin again."

"But it did happen," Peggy said.

"All right," he answered. "But we're still the people we were before the race. Peggy, when my wife died several years ago, I thought *my* life was over, too. I thought that all that Grace and I had shared could never be replaced. And it can't. I know that. But I've learned since that my own life *isn't* over, and that I can begin again with someone else. Someone such as . . . you."

He paused, expecting a reaction from her. There was none. While he had spoken, Peggy had sat rigidly beside him looking at the sky. An orange flare arced upward from the water's edge. Around them the crowd gasped at the bright foliating light that rained down in golden sparks.

"Damn it, Peggy," he stammered. "I won't beat around

the bush." He thrust a hand into his trouser pocket and produced a small object, which he held out to her.

"I want you to have this," he said. "It's my class ring from the academy. I gave it to Grace the night we were engaged. I want you to have it now."

She spoke softly. "Are you asking me to marry you?"

"Yes, I guess I am. Will you?"

Peggy shook her head. "No."

Her response flustered him. "Well, I know it comes as a surprise, but if you'll think about it—"

"I've thought about it, Charles. Since the day we met I've thought about it. And tonight. You're the most wonderful man I've known in years. If I were to marry anyone, it would be you. But you . . . this . . . Everything. It's all so sudden. Maybe if we'd had more time."

"True, it may be sudden. But at my age I can't afford the the luxury of time. Listen, if it's also money that concerns you, be assured I have enough. More than enough."

"It's not money."

"Then is it the thought of having to leave Maine? We won't. We'll buy a place here near the shore, and travel in the winter—Florida, the Caribbean. Name your port of call."

In the darkness Peggy took his hand. A cascade of rockets lit the sky, and he saw that she was looking at him with affection.

"You see, you *are* a wonderful man," Peggy said. "But I can't marry you."

"*Why* can't you?"

"Ghosts. That's one reason."

"You mean that flier you were engaged to years ago?"

"Yes."

"Ghosts can be exorcised. Sometimes they have to be, or else they'll hold you captive."

Peggy didn't answer. She looked up as a lone skyrocket

lifted into the air. Halfway to its apex, it misfired, embers falling, scattering into the sea.

"Are you happy with your life?" he asked her, once more when the sound had died away.

"I'm not unhappy," Peggy said.

"You mentioned other reasons. What?"

"I'm comfortable. I guess that's the only way I can describe it. Call it habit, status quo. The fact is that I've lived alone so long I'm used to it. I am responsible to no one but myself. I am committed to nobody but me. I am a single woman. For some women that is a stigma, but I've made a virtue of my singleness. And at my age I'm not about to change. I doubt I could."

"People can make changes in their lives at any age. If they want to," he added.

"I suppose so."

"Is it that you can't?" he asked. "Or are you afraid to try?"

She thought for several moments, but said nothing.

"When I visited your house the first time, I saw a little prayer you had in a frame on the wall."

"'Dear Lord,'" Peggy recited. "'Watch over me. The sea is so vast and my boat is so small.'"

"That says it, doesn't it? Intrepid sailor that you are, you've always sailed within sight of shore, afraid of facing those vast seas. Because beyond the beacons and the buoys it's uncharted waters. Out there, wind and storms and God knows what may await you and your little boat. But you know as well as I do that the sea can also be as calm and bright and beautiful a place as any on this earth. And its horizons can be limitless. Peggy, I am asking you to marry me."

He was about to go on when a kaleidoscope of brilliant colors filled the heavens, and the rocks beneath them shook. The spectacle of light and sound went on for several minutes. One after another the filaments of light from the exploded fireworks fell seaward; until finally the last spark was extinguished, the last echo gone.

There was a moment's silence. Then, as one, the crowd erupted in a roar of cheering and applause.

Soon flashlights began winking on across the rocks. Spectators stood up, stretched, and started gathering their possessions. Murmurs of conversation filled the air, and feet could be heard shuffling in the direction of the stairway.

The admiral and Peggy remained seated. Neither spoke.

Around them people were disbursing quickly. Above them in the parking lot the sounds of engines starting up and tires moving slowly over gravel could be heard.

Peggy said at last, "We better go."

"Peggy . . . marry me."

"No, Charles."

"Keep the ring, at least. Please." He took her hand and sought to press the ring into her palm.

"It wouldn't be right. No." She withdrew her hand. "We better go," she said again, and stood.

He joined her.

She picked up her boat cushion. Without a word they followed the departing crowd. When they reached the parking lot it was nearly empty.

"My car's over there." He pointed.

She pointed in the opposite direction. "Mine's that way."

He was about to ask her one last time: *Please, marry me.* He knew, however, it would do no good. In fact, much he'd planned to say to her tonight would go unsaid.

The headlights of a car swept over them. Then it joined the cars still exiting the lot, and they were left in darkness once again.

"Well," he began, finally. "Circumstances being what they are, I'll probably leave tomorrow after all."

"I understand," she said.

"Good-bye, Peggy." He embraced her gently, and he felt her arms encircle him. Then he touched her wet face with his fingertips and bent and kissed her lips.

"Peggy—"

"Please, don't say any more. . . . Good-bye, Charles."

"Good-bye." Reluctantly, he released her.

Peggy turned away and, carrying her cushion, she walked alone across the lot to where her car was parked.

12

The seagull stood thoughtfully on the planks of the deck. Lowering his head, he poked at a scrap of blackened toast with his beak. He studied it a moment, decided it was edible, and picked it up, swallowing it with some difficulty. Then he shook himself and looked up quizzically at Peggy.

"Sorry about breakfast, Captain Bligh," she said. "I'm not functioning too well this morning. I burned the toast, for one thing. And that's all the bread I have. Take it or leave it."

As if in answer the bird opened his beak. Peggy broke another charred slice into small pieces and tossed a few in his direction. Captain Bligh sprang at them, gobbling them up in rapid order. When he was done he threw back his head and uttered a loud squawk.

"Is that an expression of your gratitude?" she asked. "Or a complaint?"

The seagull squawked again.

"Go easy, Bligh. What I could use from you this morning is a little quiet. And some tender loving care."

Peggy knelt before him and held out her hand. It contained some large crumbs, and the bird pecked them from her palm.

"I have a confession to make, Bligh," she said. "I may have lost my last best chance at something that will never come my way again. From now on it will be just you and me. You'll be the only one who will greet me in the morning, the only one I'll share my breakfast with. Just two old birds together."

Captain Bligh observed her pensively. He opened his beak as if to ask a question of her, blinked, decided otherwise, and closed it again.

"So what plans do you have today?" she asked. "It's Sunday, you know. Is there going to be a seagull social hour at the dump this afternoon? Or, since this is a perfect summer day, there should be lots of picnickers at the state park. You could fly over there and get all the junk food you can stuff into your craw.

"As for myself, I'll probably do a little painting on the house this morning. And now that the race is history, I can show my face in Hasty Harbor. I might even buy some things at Dabney's Store. I wonder how much the old crook pocketed on me and the admiral."

She paused, then threw out another darkened scrap of toast.

"The admiral. . . . You never met him, Bligh. He was a nice man. A wonderful man. And I have the feeling that I made a terrible mistake. . . ." She drew a breath.

"In any case, this afternoon I'll go sailing. I know that's not big news to you. But now, at least, there won't be any crowds of people on the pier, no spectator boats, no finish line to cross. This afternoon it will be just me and my small boat."

Peggy tossed the last of the toast pieces onto the deck and stood up.

"That's it for breakfast, Captain. But come back for supper tonight. I thought I'd do a frozen pizza in the toaster oven. It's a brand you like. I'll save you some crusts."

The bird peered up at her, but did not move. For an instant she thought she saw a look of understanding in the gimlet eyes.

"Now, shoo," she told him. "Scram. I've got work to do. Come back later and I'll tell you all about my day."

She clapped her hands. The seagull blinked, and with a beat of wings he rose from the deck and headed seaward toward the sun.

The mud flats of Lonely Point were two miles south of Peggy's house. A quarter mile short of them the road ended in a cul-de-sac of hard-packed sand. Those wishing to go farther were obliged to park their cars and walk down a narrow path among cattails and tall weeds.

At ten thirty that morning, Sarah crossed the mud flats carrying a short clam rake, a bucket, and a metal scoop. Although low tide was not for half an hour, most of the dark sandy surface of the mud flats was exposed, making digging possible.

Sarah stepped around some isolated pools of seawater and knelt on the wet sand. She put the bucket and the clam rake down next to her and began digging with the scoop. Taking up the clam rake, she was about to dig deeper when she heard a sound.

Sarah stopped. Behind her she could hear dry rushes snapping underfoot along the path she had just traveled. She did not look around. Her fingers tightened on the handle of the rake.

"You forgot your blanket last night," Joe said.

Still kneeling, Sarah turned. Joe stood at the edge of the flats, the red beach blanket rolled up under his arm.

"It's almost low tide," he said. "I thought I'd find you here."

She stood and faced him. "You were right."

"Do you have a minute?" he asked.

"If you came here to return the blanket," Sarah told him, "my car is unlocked. You can leave it on the seat."

"That's not the only reason I'm here." Joe came toward her, stopping several feet away.

"How are you?" he asked.

"Okay."

"Last night after you left, I walked up and down the beach looking for you. Later on."

"I went home," Sarah said.

"I still had a couple things to tell you."

"I thought you told me everything before I left."

"Not quite," Joe said. "First of all, I'm sorry. I should have mentioned that I'd asked for the transfer the night of the cookout. But until two days ago, I didn't know if it would be approved. Or when." He paused. "At least I should have told you when you came to the apartment."

Sarah shrugged. "We didn't spend a lot of time in idle conversation."

"Well, for whatever it's worth, the University of California has a branch in San Diego."

"I can't change schools now, not in my senior year. I'd lose credits."

"There's also Scripps Institute in La Jolla. You could go there for your master's in marine biology."

"Would you like me to?" she asked him.

"Yes."

"I'll admit, I have thought about Scripps for postgraduate work," Sarah said.

"Sarah, I want us to be together."

She was silent.

Joe shifted awkwardly. "So, all that having been said, I guess I ought to go. I promised the admiral I'd meet him at the car rental agency at noon and drive him to the airport."

"He's leaving?"

"He called this morning and said he wanted to go home."

Joe hesitated, then patted the beach blanket. "I'll leave this in your car."

He turned and started toward the path among the reeds, leaving a trail of soft footprints in the sand.

"Joe—"

He stopped and looked back at her.

"When you get to San Diego, will you send me your address?"

"Sure. If you'd like. Sure."

"And maybe some information about Scripps."

"You bet."

"And thank you," she added.

"For what?" He looked surprised.

"For helping me to start to gather rosebuds."

"Yeah, well. . . ." He seemed suddenly at a loss for words. "Right now, you look pretty busy gathering clams. So I'll ship out. Take care."

"You too. Good-bye." Sarah raised her hand to wave to him. But all she could see was the red beach blanket disappearing through the reeds.

When Sarah returned to her car a short time later, she found the folded blanket on the driver's seat. Lying in the center of it was Clementine Clam. Between the plastic shells of the toy was a note:

Dear Sarah,

I hope you will take care of me now that Joe is gone.

Love,
Clementine

P.S.: I know that clams have hearts. But I wish I didn't, if my heart could ever be as sad as Joe's heart is today.

Sarah picked up the clam and held it close to her. "So is mine, Clementine," she whispered. "So is mine."

The admiral was already waiting outside the car rental office in Whitby when Joe arrived shortly before noon. Joe parked the car, got out, and went around to the trunk. As he unlocked it, the admiral began picking up his luggage, which consisted of three suitcases.

Joe reached for the bags. "Here, let me help you."

"No need for that. Thank you." The admiral lifted the suitcases and placed them in the trunk. "Would you believe it," he told Joe, "when I arrived several weeks ago, I had only one suitcase. After I decided to stay on, I bought more things, and so I needed more suitcases to carry them back home in."

He placed the last suitcase in the trunk. "I even bought some souvenirs. A rawhide bone for my bulldog, a scented pillow with a picture of a pine tree for my cleaning lady, and a windup toy lobster for her son. She wouldn't have let me back into my own house if I'd forgotten her. I debated between the pillow and a monogrammed oven mitt. Of course," he added, "as tacky as it was, the Hasty Harbor Cup would have been a nice prize to return with too." He let Joe close the trunk. "For that matter, two prizes that I hoped to win yesterday eluded me," he said.

Joe opened the car door for the admiral, closed it, and returned to the driver's side. As he slipped in behind the wheel, he looked over at the admiral. "All set?"

"Yes. Let's go."

"What time is your plane?" Joe asked him.

"A little past two. How are we for time?"

"Okay. The airport is just an hour's drive from here."

"Good," said the admiral. "The sooner I get there and gone, the better."

He settled back in his seat as Joe pulled out of the parking lot. As they drove through the streets of Whitby, neither man spoke. Joe turned onto the ramp to the main highway and eased into the traffic.

They had not traveled far when the admiral noticed a peeling, sun-bleached sign atop a gray commercial building. The sign proclaimed SPEND TIME IN WHITBY, MAINE, AND YOU'LL HAVE MEMORIES TO LAST A LIFETIME!

The admiral grunted. "That's an understatement," he said.

The highway skirted the north end of the Whitby Ship Works. Although it was a Sunday afternoon the shipyard was as active as it was on weekdays. In the dock area the admiral could see people and equipment moving busily around a cruiser moored at the pier nearest to the highway. She was a new ship, obviously. Some of her fittings were not visible, but a big number 60 at her bow had been fully painted in. Steam was rising from her stacks, and the admiral guessed that the ship was being readied for a sea trial, probably that afternoon.

He and Joe continued past the ship works and entered the long ribbon of divided super highway that led to Brunswick and beyond. The admiral stared out his window at the occasional small lakes reflecting the fleecy clouds meandering above them, and the surrounding stands of firs and hemlocks. He realized that this was very likely the last time in his life he would see Maine. He had had many happy times here, years ago with Grace and through the last two weeks. But as of today, he had no reason or desire to return.

"Nice day, isn't it?" Joe asked to break the silence.

"What? Oh, yes, lovely," the admiral answered. "A perfect summer day."

"How was your evening last night?"

"Fine," the admiral said. "How was yours?"

"Fine."

"You know something, Joe," the admiral said, looking at the younger man. "I think both of us are liars. I know I am. My evening was awful. At least, that's how it ended."

"So was mine," Joe admitted.

"You mean, you and Miss Dodge . . . ?"

"I'm leaving for San Diego in a couple days. She's going back to college. I hope we can keep in touch."

"She's a lovely girl," the admiral said.

"The best." Joe lifted his hand from the steering wheel briefly. "We'll see what happens. . . . By the way, wasn't there some local lady you were seeing?"

"There was."

Joe looked at him a moment and decided he would change the subject. "It's too bad you're not staying one more day. It looks like a great day for a sail," he offered, trying to make a joke of it.

"Thank you, but I think I've had my fill of sailing for a while. Except I can think of someone who *will* probably be out there."

They drove on once again in silence, entering the town of Brunswick. Since it was the last weekend of July, the main road was crowded with the cars and vans of people just beginning their vacations, or concluding them and heading home.

As they slowed briefly, Joe said, "I hope it's okay with you if I don't stay at the airport to see you off. I'm due back at the shipyard at two."

"That'll be fine. I appreciate you taking me."

"There's another cruiser going out on a sea trial this afternoon," Joe explained. "And I've been asked to go along."

"Oh, yes," the admiral recalled. "That must have been the ship I saw at dockside as we passed by. Number sixty?"

"That's the one."

Leaving Brunswick, they rejoined the divided highway. Traffic had increased substantially, but the admiral did not appear to notice. He smiled to himself. "I remember a story," he began. "It concerns the captain of a PT boat during the battle of Midway. . . ."

More wartime reminiscences, thought Joe. Well, the old man has survived a lot of battles in his life. Why not let him reminisce? "The battle of Midway was a big one," Joe said. "At least, from what I've read."

"Big is not the word. It was one of the fiercest of the war. Hundreds of ships. And among them was this navy torpedo boat. During the heat of the battle her skipper zipped around firing everything he had. The battle went on for three days, and as darkness fell on the third day, the man found himself and his boat less than a mile from a Japanese battleship. He also discovered he was out of ammunition. All he had was one torpedo." The admiral held up a finger to emphasize the point. "One."

"What happened?"

"Ah, that's the best part of the story. The captain of the PT boat knew the wisest thing to do would be to turn around and run back to the safety of the U.S. fleet. Instead he faced that battleship and let go his last torpedo. It struck the ship directly in her powder magazine and she exploded. Later, when they acclaimed him as a hero, the skipper of the PT boat simply said, 'I did what any navy man would do. I had one shot left, and I took it.'"

"That's quite a story," Joe agreed.

"Turn the car around," the admiral requested.

"I beg your pardon?"

"Please turn the car around and take me back to Whitby. To the ship works."

Joe was dumbfounded. "Are you sure?"

"I'm sure." The admiral held onto the door handle as Joe slowed the car and turned in at a highway crossover.

"I have one shot left," the admiral announced, mostly to himself. "And I am going to take it."

At two thirty in the afternoon on the last day of July *Free Spirit* sailed out of Hasty Harbor and began to pass the Sawteeth. When the sailboat was clear of them, Peggy came about and set her heading southward in the direction of Big Momma. Her course, she realized, was much the same as it had been yesterday on the first leg of the race. Today as well there was an incoming tide and a breeze out of the west.

But unlike yesterday the sailboats and powerboats she saw today were scattered randomly across the estuary. Today there were no sounds of boat horns or cheering; only the keening cries of gulls, and the lapping of the waves against *Free Spirit*'s hull.

Peggy pushed her sailor hat down firmly on her head. She patted her shirt pocket for her sunglasses and discovered she'd forgotten them.

After some time Peggy tacked again. To her right, looming high above the river, Stiles Head appeared, and beyond it the twin turrets of Elysia-by-the-Sea. As she passed the stretch of shoreline filled with leisure condominiums she saw newly arrived groups of summer renters descending to the decks.

A mile further on the flagpole and the flags that flew in front of Peggy's house gradually emerged. Both flags were snapping briskly in the wind. But she recalled that when she'd raised the flags that morning the navy flag had seemed frayed and faded. She had ruefully admitted then that she felt a bit that way herself.

To her left, Big Momma was now visible. Today a dozen seagulls occupied the rock. Most slept; a few preened idly. The only boat in the vicinity was an unfamiliar scalloper at anchor.

Looking south past Lonely Point, Peggy saw the Kidds Rock Light. In the full brightness of the day it stood erect and white against the sky.

It was all familiar. The sea, the sky, the outline of the shore: they were exactly as they had always been. Since that day when she had had the confrontation with the navy ship a great deal had happened. But how much had changed? Nothing really. Not a thing. Today, as she had done for so many summers past, she'd set her course and trimmed her sails, and they were once more carrying her on the heading she had sought.

But when Peggy tried to make a small adjustment in the mainsail, she discovered that the line was slack. *Free Spirit* had begun to slow. Peggy looked up and realized that both the mainsail and jib were sagging and the telltale hung limp. She glanced around her at the water. A hundred yards ahead of her she could see waves scalloping the surface; small patches of spume rose and fell. But where she and *Free Spirit* drifted helplessly, the sea was smooth as glass.

Peggy was becalmed.

She went forward and found the small paddle she stowed near the bow. She knelt on the foredeck and leaned over the side to paddle out of the dead water. Peggy peered down at the surface of the sea—and with a start she saw her own reflection staring back at her. At that moment Peggy realized the truth: something *had* changed.

She had.

He had asked her last night if she was afraid, Peggy now knew she was. Afraid of time. Afraid of age. Afraid to change her life. Afraid to try.

Peggy thrust the paddle into the water and stroked rapidly. She could not sail any more today. All she wanted was to catch the wind again and return to Hasty Harbor as quickly as she could.

Slowly, the sailboat began to turn. Lying flat on the deck, Peggy paddled harder. The boat continued turning. Finally, her arms aching, Peggy paused to catch her breath. Unsure of which direction she was pointed, she raised her head—and could not believe the sight she saw.

Less than a mile from her was a large navy ship, a cruiser, moving slowly but relentlessly in her direction.

Her alarm grew as the ship came toward her, the noise of the engines growing louder, waves arcing upward at the prow. Peggy paddled furiously, but it did little good. When she looked up again the cruiser was a hundred yards away, the bow that bore the number 60 coming nearer, bearing down.

Then suddenly the cruiser slowed and turned away. Peggy could see several naval officers converging on the deck.

"Commander McCoy! Now hear this!" The words rang out over a loudspeaker.

In her shock Peggy grabbed *Free Spirit*'s mast and faced the navy ship.

"Commander McCoy," came the voice through the loudspeaker again.

Peggy realized it was the admiral standing at the cruiser's bow, bullhorn in his hand. Other naval officers surrounded him, including the young ensign who had become the admiral's sailing instructor and his friend.

Once more the bullhorn blared out across the water. "Commander McCoy! A few weeks ago in these same waters you and I met, so to speak. I suspected I would find you here again today. I hoped I would."

Peggy stood up. At the same time she felt a breeze begin to stir. Slowly, it was carrying *Free Spirit* in the direction of the navy ship.

"In a minute," the admiral went on, "the steps will be lowered on the starboard side. I will come down those steps."

He handed the bullhorn to the ensign and disappeared from view. A short time later a set of portable steps swung out from the cruiser and were lowered toward the water. As soon as they were in place, the admiral reappeared at the head of the steps and started down. When he reached the bottom step he stopped, held onto the railing, and looked out at Peggy's boat.

Free Spirit was now near enough the cruiser that the shadow of the large ship fell across the sailboat. Then, a gentle swell lifted her and eased her broadside toward the step on which the admiral stood.

"Commander McCoy," he called down to her. "I request permission to board."

Peggy reached out and caught hold of the bottom step. She said nothing, but continued to regard him with a look of incredulity.

"To repeat, Commander, I request—"

"Permission granted," Peggy said in a thin voice.

"Thank you," the admiral said. He stepped gingerly into the sailboat. "To begin with—"

"To begin with," Peggy said, "we'd better sit down, or your navy friends will have to rescue both of us."

"You're right." He sat at once opposite the mast while Peggy took her place astern beside the tiller.

Neither noticed as the steps were drawn up and the cruiser very gradually withdrew. Peggy and the admiral simply looked at one another silently as the wind began to fill *Free Spirit*'s sails.

It was Peggy who spoke first. "I didn't think I'd ever see you again."

"You almost didn't. Then I learned there was another ship scheduled for sea trials this afternoon. So I asked Captain Carnes if I could tag along." He smiled wryly. "You'll be glad to know I wasn't at the helm this time. Or I really might have caused a problem for 'that little woman in the sailboat.' As for asking the skipper of the cruiser to make a brief detour when I saw your boat, I felt that if we said good-bye, it should be under the same conditions as when we met. Also," he went on, "I believed that only a grand gesture—such as almost running you down in a navy cruiser for a second time—would get your attention."

"You certainly managed to do that," Peggy said.

"But the fact is, there were many things I hoped to say to you last night, and I never got the chance. I blame it on the fireworks. It's virtually impossible to propose to a woman with skyrockets bursting overhead. Therefore, I've decided to stay here in Maine for as long as it takes me to get those things said. Perhaps we can even sail together. I could help you with your book."

"What book?"

"*Peggy's Book of Sailing.* Wasn't that the title?"

"I think that's what you called it," Peggy told him.

"What *we* called it," he corrected her. "*We*—you and I. You're still not used to any other form except the singular."

"I guess that's true."

"There was also a chapter in the book entitled 'Changing Conditions—Be Aware.' Do you remember?"

"Yes."

He leaned back on the cockpit railing and spread both his hands outward on the deck. "Be aware, Peggy," he repeated. "The conditions are changing—*have* changed. Be aware."

Peggy realized she had such a tight grip on the tiller that her hand was numb. She relaxed her grasp.

"Charles," she said to him at last. "You are without a doubt the most persistent man I have ever known."

"And *you* are the most stubborn woman *I* have ever known," he told her. "Excuse me. 'Strong-minded' is a better term. And where in God's name were you going when the cruiser spotted you? You were paddling around in circles."

"I was becalmed."

"You looked it."

"I wanted to get back to Hasty Harbor."

"On that heading it would have taken you all day. By the way, there was another basic rule of sailing you pointed out to me the morning we had breakfast."

"Oh?"

"If you're going nowhere, you said, put some wind

behind you, reset your sails, and change course." He leaned toward her. "Do you think you can do that, Peggy? Change your course?"

For a few moments, Peggy held fast to the sail lines. Then she nodded. "Yes. I think I can. I'd like to try."

He took hold of the lines as well and helped to play them out. "Then let's try together, shall we? Ready about, Commander?"

"Ready about," Peggy said.

She eased the tiller over. The sails billowed forward, and *Free Spirit* began running with the wind toward home.